I THOUGHT MY NAME WAS SARAH

by

Jeanne L. Drouillard

Copyright © 2006 by Jeanne L. Drouillard

ISBN 0-7414-3205-6

Published by:

INFIN∞ITY
PUBLISHING.COM

1094 New DeHaven Street, Suite 100
West Conshohocken, PA 19428-2713
Info@buybooksontheweb.com
www.buybooksontheweb.com
Toll-free (877) BUY BOOK
Local Phone (610) 941-9999
Fax (610) 941-9959

Printed in the United States of America

Printed on Recycled Paper

Published February 2008

Dedicated to:

All the wonderful and brave children
Who allowed me inside their world
To share their Fears, Limitations,
Hopes and Realities

CHAPTER I

Amanda Peterson insisted on facing her past alone. She actually felt relieved when the plane finally took off from Scranton International airport as she left behind a crying mother, a slightly concerned brother, an extremely reluctant and unenthusiastic fiancé as well as a supporting father, who alone believed she could actually handle the situation. She reflected on the recent scene at the departure gate and realized it was another replay of the past two weeks.

Mom was crying. "Honey must you go on your own? For one last time…"

Dad said, "Amanda's right. It's her life, Jan, besides, for heaven's sake, we're at the airport. Her ticket's bought. Let it go."

Amanda gave him a grateful smile. "Mom I love you. I am forever grateful that you chose me to be your daughter. But I do have to find the people who gave me life. I need more information than you've got. And yes, I must do it by myself."

"I've done my best to give you all the facts we know," Mom added sadly, as Amanda realized her mom was now exhibiting the famous dejected look that used to intimidate her into giving in, but now merely challenged her to stand strong. That was the moment that Amanda finally realized that her mom probably wouldn't ever stop trying to get her to change her mind. And she did keep trying, even as she boarded the plane.

"Mom, we still don't know if my birth certificate is genuine. Honestly, I'll visit the orphanage, and if they can't help me, then, at least I'll know that nothing more can be done and I'll be satisfied, you know?"

Her brother Bryan simply smiled at her in agreement. His facial expression acknowledged that they had been through many similar scenes with their mother before and he didn't plan to add to the tension.

"If this is the way you want to leave, alone, I'll accept it," her fiancé added. "I know you need to do this and I'm glad that you're finally going to fill in some of the blanks in your life. I just wish you'd let me come with you. But, if you want to face this alone just remember, I'll only be a phone call away if you suddenly need me, okay?" Jeremy, was at last accepting her decision to go it alone with a sense of finality, and she saw him exhibit a slight display of pride as he looked at her with newfound respect.

She hugged each one separately, adding an individual message. For mom, "You taught me well, mom, I'll be fine. Thanks." For Jeremy, "I love you honey. Don't worry." For Bryan, "You were always my rock and now I can do it alone. Thanks." For her dad, "I'd love to know what you're thinking. Love you dad." Her relationship with her father had developed into a special silent communication most of her life wherein, under the guise of a game, they pushed each other intellectually and psychologically to their respective limit. She knew she wouldn't find out his thoughts at this moment, but she needed to try. And true to his personality, she saw a carefully disguised smile, purposely concealing his sentiments.

The month before had been difficult for her, as finding a way of telling her parents that she needed to search for her birth mom and birth father had given her many anxiety attacks, but she had managed to overcome that barrier without hurting them. Amanda's only drawback was a timidity about herself that she knew was conveyed to the world. She was a people pleaser, and she admitted it, knowing therefore that she must share part of the responsibility for others' reactions.

Making her own decisions and learning to stand alone, had been a goal of hers in the last few years. Amanda knew as she applied herself more she was having an easier time lessening the guilt she usually felt when going against others' opinions. She was proud how she handled her family at the last family meeting when she'd told them of her travel arrangements, since no one agreed with her, except her father.

"Amanda has made her decision; that's it for me," said Dave Peterson. Amanda appreciated her father's philosophy of letting his children to do their own growing.

Immediately, she saw the expected tears coming from her mother. "You shouldn't be alone at a time like this. What happens if you get information you don't want to hear, honey? I should come with you for support. I can't stand the fact that you'll be alone."

"Thanks mom. But I need to face this alone. I'll share everything with you later." Amanda stood strong and realized her inner strength had finally grown.

Bryan said, "I'm here if you need me, but it's your decision Amanda. If you want to go alone, then go alone. It's really up to you." She appreciated Bryan wanting her to spread her own wings.

"It's too much for you alone, don't you agree Dave?" repeated Janice, and as Amanda looked desperately at her father for help, he didn't disappoint her as he reminded his wife that it was Amanda's choice.

"Did you let Jeremy know? He'll have a fit if you go alone," added Janice.

As Amanda thought of Jeremy she figured that, if this was true, her fiancé, then, would simply have to have a fit. He had encouraged her to go and do what she had to do and she knew he wanted to be with her. But she wanted to do this alone.

The commotion continued well over a week until Amanda felt relieved when she finally left. The motion of the plane was actually soothing as it climbed into the cloud area and glided smoothly along. Taking a deep breath she realized that she could at last examine her own thoughts alone and in peace. Many fears existed inside that she attempted and succeeded in keeping under control and away from her doting family. Although families were great, they could be burdensome.

Now she realized in the tranquil atmosphere of the airplane flight that she was very fearful and worried at what she would find. Why had this return to the orphanage been so important to her? Possibly the information presented to her would only add to her nightmares and not lessen them. That could definitely happen, she thought, but she would surge forward anyway. She had to know. All of her life she'd wanted to know about her beginnings and with an impending marriage, some medical and psychological information would be valuable. She hoped her nightmares were behind her and not ahead. Anxiety traveled up her spine as she remembered her recurring dream of a little girl called Sarah who seemed frightened and alone, and another even more perplexing dream detailing the figure of a woman who was always annoyingly obscure in the background and never came forward where she could seen. Shifting slightly in her plane seat to relieve tension she admitted that the dreams caused her concern, but she wouldn't turn back. Never. She wanted to face her past and she wanted to face it alone.

Amanda sighed with relief as the plane made a smooth landing in Prescott, Arizona. She didn't fear flying although she had to concede that she was always happy when a safe landing was accomplished. After picking up her rental Jeep, she immediately drove to her motel, checked in, freshened up and headed promptly for the Friends of Little Children orphanage losing no more time than necessary.

As she stood waiting in the doorway of the children's ward watching the little ones interact, Amanda used all of the strength within her to wrestle away the rising urge of wanting to run away and just keep running and never look back. She felt like an impostor nervously attempting to avoid entrapment and wondered where these strange feelings came from. She thought that her reaction, although tense and uneasy, would be more pleasing and satisfactory.

"Would you like some tea or coffee while you wait, Miss Peterson?"

Startled out of her thoughts, Amanda returned immediately to the present as one of the staff members suggested the waiting room would be more relaxing for her.

"Yes thanks, that would be lovely," answered Amanda trying to hide her embarrassment of the moment.

"Okay, let me show you the way. We have magazines and a TV as well as coffee and tea to make you comfortable while you wait."

While waiting she looked out of the window and realized that the city of Prescott was very lovely especially at the end of October. Being situated slightly north in the state, its comfortable weather at this time of the year showed the seasonal colors still in full bloom. Today was particularly beautiful with the sky having a baby blue background with hints of darker blue in a most unusual pattern. Totally interspersed with clouds of silvery white they complimented the entire horizon just as if a painter had made a special effort to place them all in his own exact design to create awe and splendor.

"Mrs. Mallik will be in shortly to speak with you," said the same staff member as Amanda barely noticed her head lean into the room.

"Okay, thanks," answered Amanda automatically, yet hesitantly, as she suddenly felt a strange suspicion that disappointment was in the forecast. Why would Mrs. Mallik want to speak with her?

Looking around the waiting room diffidently yet thoughtfully, she tried to pull something from deep inside, possibly some memories of herself as a child but realized it wasn't happening. She thought maybe coming back here where it all began would drag up some experiences and bring them closer to the surface where they could be analyzed and dispersed. Yet, just being here conveyed a rather surreal experience. As she looked down, staring at her feet, she realized that these same two feet, although much smaller twenty-five years ago, stood in the same exact place she stood now. She tried so hard to picture herself here as a small child, hoping to recall anything and possibly collect a memory. Amanda hoped to remember feelings most of all, but she felt rather numb instead.

"Ms. Peterson?" came another voice that again startled her, as it was natural to slip back into distant memories in this place.

"Yes, I'm Amanda Peterson," she replied.

"It seems that Mrs. Benson has been delayed, through no fault of her own of course, but it may be tomorrow before she can get here. I am so sorry. I know she is the one with whom you had made the appointment, but it was an emergency."

She was looking at Stephanie Mallik, the director of the orphanage, a very somber person whose staunch, tall and rather slim body held a serious yet kind face which appeared to have been ordained to this type of position. The smile that occasionally crossed her middle-aged face seemed forced but kind intentions covered a very disciplined heart.

"I would be glad to spend some time with you, Ms. Peterson," she added.

Amanda noted quickly that Stephanie had only worked at the orphanage for five years, while Mrs. Benson had been there the day that Amanda arrived and most likely would have some of the answers that she needed.

"Oh dear," was all Amanda could manage as her expression displayed anxiety and her blank mind scrambled for something to say as the time lapse extended.

Amanda attempted hesitantly to rectify the quiet situation, feeling slightly uncomfortable at the awkward silence she had caused, but Stephanie began speaking before she could do so.

"I'm so sorry, Amanda but we had no control…"

Interrupting in a soft tone, Amanda said apologetically, "I am sorry too, but I know emergencies happen." She was trying, in the midst of devastating disappointment, to exhibit some manners and regain her composure. She had waited so long, so very, very long to talk to someone who knew what had happened to her.

"I'm just so disappointed," she continued. "Of course I would appreciate talking to you but I must still have a chance to talk with Mrs. Benson."

Amanda held her breath, nervously waiting for the reply.

"Well, of course. Then let me get us some tea and we'll talk today and you can be the first one on Mrs. Benson's agenda tomorrow, if you can stay until then. I'm sure she will give you all the time you need."

Amanda thought, "*If I can stay?*" Of course she would stay. She would probably have done anything she had to, just to stay. This meeting could be of the utmost importance to her and she would definitely stay another day or two to get answers and talk to Mrs. Benson, the most important person in the world to her and probably the only one who had answers to her questions. One more day. She had waited this long, partly because it took many years to mature and then a few more years to get up the nerve and courage to make this appointment. It hadn't been easy to get to this point, yet she had made it today and tomorrow would come soon enough.

Appreciating Stephanie's generosity she soon realized that she was receiving more information from the director than she thought she would.

"I still have a copy of your birth certificate in our files. Your parents have the original."

"I wanted to know if my birth date is true or only estimated. I would understand an estimate; I simply would like to know."

Amanda was trying to keep her emotions under control yet her voice sometimes cracked. Believing Stephanie must have noticed her emotional state, she gave her credit for

8

ignoring the agitation and creating an atmosphere of composure.

"That is your true birth date. I realize why you would question that. It's true there are times we have to make a guess, but your birth mom did provide us with your true birth date and the fact that you weighed 7 lbs. and 3 oz. with a length of 19 inches."

"Really, I didn't know that," said Amanda excitedly. "I don't think my parents knew that was true either. Thanks."

"Many records are estimated or not entirely accurate, and that's sad. But in your case I know these facts are true because the notation in the file states, "given by the birth mom and stated as accurate."

Amanda couldn't contain her excitement. "Really, she stated that. My birth mom actually said that."

"Yes Amanda, there is a notation so marked in the file."

Amanda felt satisfied knowing that this information actually came from her birth mother. Although this situation unnerved her and she felt suddenly drained, it was just a passing feeling.

"I asked my mom and dad and they were never sure but only assumed that November 7 was my birth date. I was hoping to know for sure and I'm so happy."

"I understand, of course. Whenever possible we do speak to the birth mother and confirm her story if we possibly can." Amanda could hear a sudden enthusiasm in Stephanie's voice, and was happy to see shared pleasure on her face.

Amanda got understandably quiet for a few moments. Stephanie had read her facts that her birth mom had actually taken the time to confirm creating a new bond of closeness that impacted her heart. Trying to fend off approaching tears, Amanda quickly continued, "Then it would also be true that I was born at St. Joseph's Hospital?"

"All facts on this certificate have been verified as true which means you were born at St. Joseph's Hospital in Prescott, Arizona."

Stephanie could be very sensitive and comfortable in a one-to-one conversation. When she put aside her role as director of the orphanage, some warmth did come through her presence, much to Amanda's surprise. She did realize that Stephanie must remain rather aloof in her director's role, as the seriousness and tremendous burden of such a gigantic task as placing orphans with the best possible families for them would probably consume anyone's inner balance and offset your equilibrium unless you deliberately guarded yourself against it.

"I came to the orphanage at about one and a half years old and left at three years old. Is that correct?"

"Hummm, that might be a better question for Mrs. Benson. The file is vague here and although that seems to be the case, she has more files and could check that for you tomorrow and give you the exact details."

"Yes of course," said Amanda, "I'll ask her tomorrow."

Informed that her birth mother had terminated her rights when Amanda was one and one-half years old, she presumed this orphanage had been her only home until she was almost three. Her body and mind sometimes ached trying to understand and remember how her life began. In time she planned to visit the hospital. She didn't believe anybody would remember one baby born way back then, but she wanted to see the hospital and maybe visit the baby ward and walk the hospital corridor where her birth mom must have walked.

Amanda noticed that Stephanie had been quiet for a few moments, as she was engrossed about reading some passage in the dossier. Finally, she spoke.

"There is a rather curious notation here though," added Stephanie. Amanda noticed that she raised the paper closer to her eyes and adjusted her bifocals attempting to get a clearer understanding of what she was reading.

Amanda sat patiently, waiting for a few long moments, in suspense. She noticed some confused expressions on the director's face as she attempted to understand and clarify the situation for both of them.

"I can't really make out a few of the words, but what I can read says, 'does not react good to males;' I'm not sure what that is all about. That's all it says. I'm sure Mrs. Benson can tell you more."

"That sounds rather strange, don't you think?"

"Yes, but there's something further I'm having trouble reading," stated Stephanie as she continued, "something about the director of the orphanage, back then it would have been Mr. John Lyman, had a lot of trouble having contact with you, but later you warmed up to him. It's noted that it took quite a while. Also, says you always reacted better to women."

"I'm certainly curious about that. Hopefully Mrs. Benson can shed some light on that tomorrow."

"I'm sure she will, Amanda. This is her handwriting. Probably an obvious reason for this notation and it does say that later you were doing fine. I'm sure Mrs. Benson will know about that. That is about all that I have in my file about you."

Stephanie also shared some of her most serious cases and Amanda reconfirmed to herself that most people just didn't realize the extreme ramifications that adoption would have on all the parties involved. Many children would have separation and possibly anger problems, some more serious than others, and most adults faced either guilt and/or fears raising children who came along with a lot of baggage. It was truly one of the great challenges of life.

After a few well-spent hours with Stephanie, Amanda was ready to leave partly satisfied, yet trying to calm her excitement regarding tomorrow and her eventual meeting with Mrs. Benson. She wondered if people's memories of twenty-five years ago would be accurate enough to satisfy her. With all of the children that must have passed through this orphanage since then, would she be one of the many that would remain in the background of everyone's mind without any sharp remembrances or episodes? One other important item for her would be whether there had been any pictures of her as a baby. Amanda so very much hoped that there would be at least one picture to help create the missing links in her mind.

"I do thank you very much for your time and assistance. I realize this was rather impromptu for you today so I really appreciate it."

"You are more than welcome. I understand you wanting to find out about your beginnings. We have quite a few who come back later for either medical or psychological records, or they just want to know about their early life. That is why we try to keep as complete records as possible."

"I found it very impressive," answered Amanda wanting to compliment Stephanie in a subtle way with praise she felt justified.

"Thank you, I truly appreciate your comments. We have really tried to improve our system." Stephanie looked justifiably proud of enhancements that had occurred during her tenure.

"I'm sure I'll see you tomorrow and I again thank you for your time and help."

Leaving the orphanage, she headed for the Pine Lawn Court motel that she had chosen because of its close proximity. She didn't usually like traveling by car alone in unfamiliar places, but the ride back to the motel was rather astonishing. She realized now that on the way to the orphanage her mind had been in total anticipation and expectancy so that she'd barely noticed the scenery. Now her mind and eyes opened up and she marveled at the beauty around her. The beautiful state of Arizona needed no special introduction to her. As a young child, she had spent a few investigative camping vacations with her adopted family in some of the many state parks. Driving near the Yarnell Hills awakened a kinship in her that made her realize how much she could be a part of everything.

The beauty of the earth which began exhibiting a little redness actually emphasized the fools' gold that glittered in nearby trails. Amanda pulled her rental car over to the side of the road and sat there for a few minutes, looking over her hot steering wheel into the hills that climbed higher and higher and seemed to go on continuously. Each surpassed the other in size, ruggedness and majesty. It certainly made her feel small sitting in her silver-colored jeep next to these magnificent signs of century-old civilizations. Amanda knew there were rattlesnakes, diamond heads, gila monsters and many other creeping creatures all merged into these areas so she thought better of leaving her jeep in high heels, yet she thought that sometime in the future she would like to come back here and take a hike into these hills. Something solid about the earth and scenery teased her memory and it felt especially good sitting here for a few minutes, becoming a part of it while old vacation memories overtook her.

She remembered one of her first family vacations in Arizona when she was still quite little and could almost hear brother Jonathon saying, "Amanda, I hope you didn't forget the insect repellent. We'll get eaten to death out here if you forgot." Her older brother Jonathon usually managed to find a way to lord it over her even when her mom and dad were there to stabilize the situation.

"I didn't forget it; it's right here in my bag—See!"

Amanda pulled out the item and put it within two feet of Jonathon's face. She truly never liked to get too close to him, so she made her point from a distance.

"Good girl, you always remember and do your part," said Bryan.

"Thanks Bryan. Mom and dad think so too, right dad? "

"I think our Amanda will make an excellent camper and has proven herself time and again. Let's all give her a cheer. All together—Yeah Amanda," demanded her father.

Although Amanda only heard three voices, her mom, dad and Bryan, she was satisfied. At six years old it was only her second camping trip and she was prepared to have fun despite her older brother, who had an entire regimen of bad moods to show. She remembered having a lot of fun on that trip and even alerted the family to a nearby rattlesnake, which her father had handled. Amanda felt very proud although she was a little bit timid about the snake.

"We're going to have some lessons on what to do about rattlesnakes?" said her father.

"Is that really necessary dad?" said Amanda. "Maybe

there are some other places that they don't visit."

"If we are out in the hills anywhere in Arizona, we could see different kinds of snakes. Doesn't everyone think that a study of snakes and what to do if you see one would be a good idea?"

"I'm sure Amanda and Bryan are just too scared," Jonathon added in his usual condescending tone.

"I'm with them," answered Mrs. Peterson. "Maybe staying in the state parks, but closer to the ranger station is a better idea."

"Gees mom, you too," said Jonathon disgustingly.

The loud sound of a car horn shocked Amanda out of her trance as she realized that she had rested her arm on the horn of her jeep. Laughing with herself at her clumsiness she slowly continued on her journey only to find herself in the vicinity of St. Joseph's Hospital where she'd been born. She hadn't consciously planned to visit the hospital today but just like a magnet finding its counterpart that couldn't be resisted, she turned into the parking lot and stared at the building where it had began for her. Even if the beginning of her life didn't play out exactly as she would have wanted, her life started in this hospital and at least now, she knew.

Getting out of her jeep slowly and looking around, Amanda's thoughts began to race again as she wondered what kind of a lasting impression she was opening up for herself. Slowly walking toward the entrance of the hospital she wondered what she could possibly say to get entrance to the baby ward. *Oh well, I guess I'll talk my way in*, she thought.

Inside the lobby Amanda strolled very slowly in the direction of the Information Desk and decided to pretend she was visiting someone since she felt the truth probably wouldn't gain her entrance, as her life seemed only important to her. Her racing thoughts were agonizing to come up with a reason and then it seemed that fate took over in the form of an older couple standing directly in front of her at the desk.

Smiling and excited the gentleman spoke first.

"We want to see Jackie Gater; she's our daughter and she just had our first grandchild. Can you tell us what room she is in?"

"Congratulations, your first grandchild. How nice for you. Mrs. Gater is on the third floor in Room 302. Take this front elevator to the right, up to the third floor."

"Thanks, thanks a lot," they both repeated as they moved quickly to the elevators.

Amanda purposely held back for a few moments and let a few other people in front of her before she confronted the receptionist, gave the name of Mrs. Gater and before she knew it she was given a visitor's pass to the third floor. Happy as she examined herself on the elevator, she felt good about herself dressed in her tapered black slacks and inexpensive yet stylish long-sleeved white blouse which, along with her small gold hoop earrings completed her ensemble and expressed good taste. At this moment she complimented herself on her attire as it was important, for a personal reason, to feel good about herself.

As the elevator stopped at the third floor, Amanda felt her heart start to beat faster and faster. As the doors opened, she slowly and cautiously walked out into the excited atmosphere of the baby ward. Something suddenly gripped her inside and was fiercely holding on. She felt like crying and screaming at the same moment and experienced dizziness as she walked on experiencing the scene as old movie. Was she really here? This was where her birth mom would have come to give birth to her? She knew it was but she didn't know how she felt inside. She felt shaky and scared but also amazed that it was such a heavy burden. Usually she could push all her disturbing thoughts to the back of her mind while she regained her peace and calm of the moment. She had learned to do that as a very young child. It was like different experiences in her life were filed away in different categories and therefore put in different places in her mind. If something hurt too much, Amanda could file it away and hide it, like closing a filing cabinet drawer. She sometimes hid things even from herself and that had always worked until now. In the present moment, she faced all of those hurtful feelings and emotions and it proved to be overpowering. Perhaps she shouldn't have come alone, yet she couldn't face it with anyone else. No, this was not yet to be shared.

A nurse walking by noticed her distress.

"Are you all right? Can I get you a glass of water or something?"

Amanda immediately made a special attempt to control her emotions and stop the tears from coming down her cheeks. Fearing she would be asked too many questions and possibly requested to leave she answered, "I'm okay, I just felt weak for a moment. I'm really okay now, thanks."

As she answered the concerned nurse, Amanda made sure that her visitor's pass could be seen. Accepting the staff's kindness with social grace, she accepted a chair and a glass of water and then luckily, she was left alone.

After a very few minutes Amanda regained control again and decided to implement her plan. She wanted to walk these same halls where her mom must have walked and just relish in the feeling it gave her. She met many smiling faces of those excited with new babies in their arms, heard many babies gurgling and some crying but all in all she walked and tried to picture her mom before she gave birth and after. Was her mom happy to have a baby girl? Maybe her mom and dad wanted a boy? Why did they keep her one and a half years and then give her up? What happened? Those questions were for Mrs. Benson tomorrow. For now she wanted to walk and feel and pretend. Her birth mom had been here physically on November 7, 1974. That was one true fact she knew and that made her feel good as she just repeated it over and over quietly in her mind. *My birth mom was actually here in this hospital giving birth to me on that date.* The feelings that welled up inside of her could only be felt as a dream. She knew she was here physically and mentally today on October 25, 2001 but in her imagination and childlike wishes, it was really November 7, 1974. Although the fact wasn't new to her anymore, it did feel like a completely new revelation.

As she stopped and leaned against the wall in the hallway for a moment, she paused to look into the nursery. No one could enter the nursery as that was off-limits, but you could look into the huge window and see most of the babies in the cradles. That is where she would have been. What a feeling of contentment that gave her. Amanda stood there for a moment while searching for a reason and hoping to keep a memory of this moment. Then, just as suddenly as could be, she felt a total calmness that started at the top of her head and ever so slowly yet lovingly inched itself all the way down to her feet comfortably nestled in her favorite black heels. Amanda reacted rather nervously to it at first because too much serenity inside of her didn't match her usual feelings when she thought of her early years. Yet at this moment, when she thought she would be the most upset, she felt happy and elated inside. Her feelings were telling her it was okay. Your beginning matched any other baby. Your mother was with you in this hospital and you got good care. Something just beyond words spoke to her silently and she felt like laughing and not crying; she felt more like singing and dancing for a moment. She didn't know how to explain it but she loved the feeling and relished in it for a while.

In time, a pleasant older gentleman, who had been strolling up and down the hall stopped next to her. It seemed that he had become a grandfather for the sixth time and pointed out his new grandson to Amanda. When he asked Amanda which baby she was related to she simply said that it hadn't been born yet. As he rambled on, Amanda enjoyed his conversation.

"Look at all those wonderful, innocent babies. Isn't that just great? It's a hard feeling to explain, isn't it?"

"Yes it is," replied Amanda happy to be talking to someone as the nurses wandered around—it made her look as if she belonged here.

"Sometimes I like to imagine what will happen to them in their lives, don't you? I mean this is my youngest son's first child and although he was a problem kid himself, he has straightened out and married a real nice girl. Now I look at his offspring and think, 'You've got a good chance in life.' You know what I mean? He has a mother and father that really care about him and of course a grandmother and grandfather that are just thrilled. That's a great start to life, don't you think? I think that certainly is what we all really need, just a great start in life."

This helped Amanda to focus somewhat as her philosophical friend continued.

"It's sad for some babies who aren't wanted and I think that makes life tough for them, but this little guy is wanted by everyone. That is great, isn't it?"

"Yes it is and congratulations."

"You're too young to be a grandmother so I'm assuming you have a sister or a friend here."

"Actually, a friend. What will they name your grandson?"

"It will be Michael Anthony. Anthony is after me. Michael is both my son's name and his father-in-law's name. So that worked out well. He will be one lucky baby."

"That's a nice name and it makes everyone happy."

"We used to call my son Mikey and he hated it—that's what he tells me now. So he made me promise that there would be no Mikey for his little one."

Amanda laughed. "Mike's a good name anyway."

"Well, he's the father so I will respect his wishes. But I thought Mikey was cute."

Amanda just smiled. Michael or Mike would be a lucky little baby. Philosophizing herself Amanda realized that having a good beginning seemed a very important step in a person's life. Then her friend continued.

"But you know, my son had a great beginning. We loved him and really wanted him, as did the rest of our family. But he went crazy and wild for several years. No one could seem to calm him down. Slowly, as he matured, he started to become sensible again but it took a while. He was searching for something like a direction for his life, you know, and then he met a real nice girl and together they've built a real nice life. But they wanted children and it took four years. We are so happy now he is living a good life and happy to be a husband and father. It makes a person think that probably a good beginning helps, but it isn't everything. It's also what a person develops inside and decides to do with his life, don't you think?"

"It would be hard not to agree with that. I guess each person makes a conscious decision as to what they want to do with their life." Amanda was very pensive as she thought about what her friend had just said.

"Yeah, sometimes I think of people like Helen Keller. She sure had a rough beginning. Couldn't speak or hear at a time when no one could help her communicate with other people. I just read her story. She was at least twelve I think before that other person, I forget her name, found a way to talk with her. She could have decided to live in her anger and forget everything else. But she didn't. She grew and learned and went on to college and she inspired many people. Oh dear, here I am rambling on."

Amanda's friend looked rather embarrassed for a quick moment and she wanted him to know that she was happy for his company.

"That's okay. I enjoy listening to you."

"Well, the bottom line to me is that it's great to have a good beginning but the rest of your life is still your choice. Besides, there are a lot of kids with bad beginnings who end up being role models. Oh oh, here comes my wife calling me so I gotta go. Nice talking to you."

"Same here."

As her friend left giving her a wonderful smile, Amanda thought that he probably never knew how much she needed to hear those words at this exact moment in her life. She had read a story once about angels in disguise who appear in your life sometimes just when you need them. Maybe this was one of those times.

She looked at the babies a little while longer knowing that someday she too would be a mother, and knowing that she planned to be nurturing and loving, while making sure the child felt wanted. When she was satisfied knowing she had created memories she could cherish, Amanda was ultimately willing to leave the baby ward. As she turned toward the elevator and walked down the hallway for the last time, she turned and looked at the busy scene of the baby ward and thought, *Thanks Mom, that's all, just thanks.* Amanda hoped that she would always remember this moment and how she felt because it was somewhat magical. Now she knew she was ready to face tomorrow.

As soon as she got back to her motel she grabbed the phone and called her mom. She needed to hear her voice.

"Hi Amanda, are you okay? We've all been very concerned."

"Yes, I'm fine. All is going well. There was a delay though and I'm going to have to stay another day. I'm going to talk to Mrs. Benson tomorrow," said Amanda knowing that her mother would have a slight problem with this.

"You didn't talk to her today? Amanda, your appointment was with her today?"

"I know mom, but there was a problem and she will be there tomorrow and, as for today, I talked to the director of the orphanage and she filled me in on other details. It's not really a problem."

"But that means you'll have to stay an extra day."

Amanda thought, *I better distract my mom.* "I forgot how much I loved Arizona and it's fun just to be back here. Remember those camping trips we took. We had so much fun."

"Do you remember them? You were very little when we went?"

"Yes mom I do remember them, and guess what? I drove near the Yarnell Hills today and I could see them in the distance. That sure brought back memories for me."

"So you won't be home for another day or so, right Amanda?"

"That's right mom but I'm enjoying being here and visiting the orphanage."

"You couldn't remember the orphanage—you were only three years old when we got you."

"That's true, I didn't remember it consciously of course, but somehow there are things in the back of your memory that sort of click in when you're in a place that has a memory for you, know what I mean?"

"Not really, but I'm glad you sound happy."

"I'm actually really excited to be here. It seems strange in one way but it's almost fun in another way."

"Well, okay. You seem to be doing okay by yourself, right?"

"Yeah, I'm fine mom. I needed some time to experience this alone." But Amanda had a question for her mom.

"Mom, when you first got me, I mean when you first took me home, how did I act with dad?"

"Huh, how did you act with your father? "

"Yes, how did I act with him? Did I cuddle up with him or hold his hand if we went somewhere. That's what I mean." Amanda bit her bottom lip, waiting for the answer.

"Well, that was such a long time ago, but I don't

remember anything out of the ordinary. However, Amanda, you weren't very cuddly with any of us for a little while. It took time for you to adjust to us but you were always nice and polite. Yet, you did keep your distance. Then all of a sudden, everything seemed okay."

"How long?"

"Well, I don't know," answered her mom, sounding a little frustrated, "You were cuddly with me in a few weeks I think. And you always seemed to be close to Bryan, you know. Not cuddly really but the two of you had a closeness. Nothing with Jonathon, but at that time, no one did. I think it was later with your dad. Why all these questions?"

Getting a caution signal, Amanda felt that she had better lighten up or her mom would think something was wrong and start worrying. And for her mom to begin worrying about her when she was so far away, would be a disaster for anyone in the house with her.

"No particular reason mom. I've been trying to get ideas and feelings of myself as a little girl and put them all together. That's all. Is dad home?"

"No, he's working late today and he'll be so sorry he missed your call."

"Then you just tell him that I love him, and I love you too mom. I'll talk to you tomorrow."

"Oh, I mustn't forget to tell you that Bryan called today and says 'hi' and wishes everything is going the way you want."

"Oh, that's nice. Tell him 'thanks' from me. Talk to you tomorrow mom. Okay? Bye for now."

As she put the phone down she paused for a few

moments before she called Jeremy. Mom didn't remember anything of her acting detached or unapproachable when they'd first adopted her. Smiling to herself she thought, *Dad would remember, if there was anything to remember.*

Jeremy wasn't home, which disappointed Amanda more than she thought it would. She left him a brief message regarding her circumstances and said that she would talk to him tomorrow.

About an hour later the telephone rang. Amanda expected it to be Jeremy, but it wasn't.

"Hi Jonathon, good to hear from you."

"How's is going? Mom says there was some delay?"

"Yes, an unexpected something delayed Mrs. Benson. So I'm going to meet with her tomorrow. It's okay. It gave me another day in Prescott. I really like this city."

"Yes, I remember we used to go camping there."

"Yeah," said Amanda, "with all the rattlesnakes, remember that?"

"Yeah, I do remember that," said Jonathon laughing. "Listen girl, whatever you find out is just fill-in information for you to decipher. You can learn from it, whatever it is, but it's open to your interpretation. How are you feeling with what you know so far?

"Most has been helpful and November 7 really is my birthday. Isn't it funny how important that is? Just one day in your life, but I was so happy to find out."

"Like you told me Amanda, it's the not knowing that's hard. So I imagine finding out, even little facts about yourself, will help you fill in the blanks. Like me, remember

25

all the anger and hate I had as a child. It was finally mended by discovery and understanding." Amanda continued to be impressed by Jonathon's change of behavior.

"Yes, it's always been the not knowing that was the hardest for me. There were a few peculiar comments made in my file that didn't make much sense, but I'll find out more tomorrow. Whatever I find out will be just one more thing for me to know. And everything helps me get a better picture. And what I don't know or can't find out won't bother me so much anymore because, at least, I tried. Know what I mean?"

"Yes I do. I know exactly what you mean. I was just thinking, Amanda, when I look back about fifteen or twenty years ago, I think I would probably be the least likely person you'd think would be calling you today and be real excited for you. But I am. Truly, I am. And even though you were adopted and I was born in this family, we have more in common than many would ever guess.

"Yes, it's funny how life turns out, isn't it?

Yes it is. Best of luck tomorrow. Love you and talk to you soon."

"Love you too Jonathon and I'll see you when I get home."

With Amanda's final comment the phone line went dead and she was left in a daze wondering about her life, but also about Jonathon. He had changed so much in the last ten years and because he'd shared his knowledge with her, she had made strides in the right direction.

Then the telephone rang again. This time it was Jeremy and they talked lovingly for about twenty minutes before calling it a night.

26

The next morning she awoke slowly and realized that she had slept rather comfortably considering she was so excited about today. She'd woken a few times during the night but managed to get back to sleep rather quickly guaranteeing that she would be refreshed and ready for her important day. She immediately arose, took a shower and was out the door to a restaurant in record time. She wanted to be on the road early and give herself plenty of time to arrive at her appointment.

As soon as she entered the highway, Amanda realized that the road seemed to be very busy for 7:30 in the morning. She'd hoped to get to the orphanage in record speed but soon realized that the traffic seemed to be slowing down and many brake lights were beginning to appear in the road ahead. Then, in a sudden moment, everything stopped. The traffic didn't move at all. Everything had completely halted. Checking her watch, she acknowledged that it was about 7:45 AM and she was happy that she had given herself plenty of time. Her appointment with Mrs. Benson had been scheduled for 8:30 AM. With the orphanage only another ten or fifteen minutes up the road, she still had plenty of time.

Five minutes later her car remained parked and no amount of praying or begging seemed to get the traffic moving again. Amanda had put on her radio to the local news and heard nothing to explain the situation. Now the time inched closer to 8:00 AM, but okay, she thought, she could still make her scheduled appointment. Just at that moment six police cars with sirens all flashing and alarms sounding loudly came speeding up the median of the road. Ten more minutes brought an announcement of a multiple tragic, fatal accident more than twenty miles up the road that would probably take an hour or more to clear.

With no other choice, she would have to wait like everyone else, but Amanda's heart just sank way down in her chest. She felt as numb again as she had yesterday and wondered what fate had in mind for her today.

"God, can't anyone get us out of here?" one man yelled.

"This is so stupid; When are they going to get us moving?" yelled another.

"Pipe down everyone, I'm sure they're doing what they can," offered another motorist.

At 8:30 AM Amanda placed a call to the orphanage from her car which had been in a parked position for the last forty-five minutes. It seemed that the staff at the orphanage had heard of the tragic crash and said that Mrs. Benson would be waiting for Amanda at whatever time she could get there, and she was not to worry. They understood her delay and her anxiety but she would get her meeting with Mrs. Benson and it would be today.

That phone call had somewhat calmed Amanda's nerves and she began to look around watching even more police cars heading in the direction of the crash. She chose to stay in her vehicle and let her mind wander. She often enjoyed moments like this, not usually in the face of tragedy, but just occasional moments where she could leisurely let her mind take her where it wanted to go. She began to think of her early life in vivid detail and started with the very first memory that crossed her mind, while trying to envision how her being adopted into this family had affected all of them.

CHAPTER II

"My name is Sarah, I know that. My name is Sarah."

Amanda insisted that her name was Sarah and she exhibited anxiety if anyone called her Amanda. She couldn't understand why her new mom wouldn't call her Sarah; she liked that name because it belonged to her. That was what she remembered and sadly, there wasn't much else that she could pluck from her memory. Amanda could still see the orphanage in her mind, especially her room and her bed, even the blanket that had a red and blue pattern that she liked. She could still see a few of the children's faces and it did upset her that she couldn't remember more. But she knew her name was Sarah.

"We can't call you Sarah because your name is Amanda. That is what it says on your birth certificate, honey. It says Amanda Lynn."

"I don't think so. My name is Sarah."

"Jonathon and Bryan are called by the name on their birth certificate. So is your dad and so am I. So I will call you Amanda."

"But my name is Sarah." And that's how Amanda finished that discussion.

Later on, Janice Peterson remembered that she had heard Amanda call herself Sarah during a few of their visits to the orphanage. She felt it was probably just a game the children were playing and thought nothing of it at the time. Her husband Dave, on the other hand, had told her that he wondered about a secret being kept from them as his logical mind questioned how a child of only three years old would insist that she had a different name than the one on her birth certificate. Usually children of that age had pride in their names since it set them apart and made them unique individuals. They both agreed that Sarah didn't seem to qualify as a nickname.

Dave and Janice had made five separate visits to the orphanage to get acquainted with Amanda. At scarcely three years old, taking her home immediately would have been entirely too frightening for her. The social worker felt five visits would be enough and during the last three occasions they were to bring their other two children Jonathon, eight years old and Bryan, five, to facilitate the changing of environments for Amanda. Janice could see the recognition in Amanda's eyes by their third and fourth visit and all agreed the next visit, they could bring her home.

On the fifth visit Amanda did leave the orphanage. She felt comfortable talking a lot in the car and became a chatter box at the local restaurant, which was a big deviation from her usual reserved demeanor. But she thought Dave and Janice were fun and hoped they had a lot of toys at home. She didn't like Jonathon very much because he yelled a lot and always looked angry, but Bryan seemed nicer and he talked softly to her.

Playing in the restaurant's child area worked very well and Amanda relaxed into her new life until the waitress came to their booth and asked Amanda if she liked hot dogs.

Amanda answered, "I'm Sarah and Sarah wants a hot

dog."

Her parents looked at each other very surprised wondering if Amanda was playing a game. Her mom asked her. "Is Sarah your imaginary friend, Amanda?"

"No, I'm Sarah. Not any friend. I'm Sarah," she said pointing to her chest with the index finger of her right hand and almost demanding that they acknowledge her name. "Me, I'm Sarah."

"Sweetie, your name is Amanda, Would Amanda like a hot dog?"

Amanda nodded up and down but felt confused. She knew she was pouting as she looked down at the floor, but kept very quiet. Her mom smiled nicely at her which alleviated her fear that her mom was mad and that she had done something wrong.

"Doesn't even know her own name. Gees, get real," added Jonathon as Amanda saw him glaring angrily at her. Getting a sister who didn't even show enough intelligence to know her own name seemed more than he could handle. Amanda felt that he didn't want her around.

"Hush up Jonathon. You must be kind to your younger sister. This has been a tough move for her." Her father smiled nicely at her.

"But she doesn't even know her own name. She's three years old, dad, and that's pretty bad you know."

"I know this must be hard for you Amanda," Bryan told her, "but we'll have lots of fun when we get home. I'm your brother now and I'm glad you're here."

"You would be glad Bryan, you don't have anything important in your life anyway."

"I do too and you're not the only one who is important Jonathon. It'll be nice to have someone to play with who doesn't pout if they don't get their own way all the time."

"Yeah, playing with a girl is just about your style."

"Hush up you two. Get some manners both of you. We don't want to scare Amanda with your usual bickering."

Arriving home, Amanda seemed happy as she looked around her new home but thought it was very big. How would she ever find everybody? Then she was shown her very own bedroom.

"Purple, lots of purple," she whispered out loud as her eyes grew very large and she slowly took in the entire bedroom meant only for her.

Janice had found out that Amanda's favorite color was purple, surprisingly, and not pink like a lot of little girls preferred. Her room had been decorated mainly in different shades of purple and the effect was not lost on Amanda. Her eyes widened as she looked from a dresser that was two-tone purple and lilac to carpeting that was deeper purple with plush design and mixtures of all shades of purple and some white for a contrasting effect.

"Big, big bed. Very big bed. And Raggedy Anne. I like Raggedy Anne."

Her new bed was a big double one that big people used, with three blankets all in different colors. It had a coverlet that matched the drapes in accenting shades of lilac that totally pulled you into its design. As she was given her Raggedy Anne doll, Amanda commented, "Doll is big like me. Has spots on face."

"Those are freckles Amanda."

"Oh, and huggy," remarked Amanda as she cuddled the doll and carried it with her around the room.

She could hardly believe that she would be sleeping alone in this big room. She thought there was too much space just for her and something else bothered her but she couldn't quite figure out what it was. Then, she knew.

"I'll be alone in here?"

"Our bedroom is right across the hall over there; see, right over there," said Janice pointing to their room, "so we'll be real close if you need us."

That calmed Amanda for the moment as she peeked out the door to see how close her parents would be. She was used to squeezing into one little bed with another girl at the orphanage and now she had this big bed all to herself. Slightly frightened but afraid to show it, she thought her mom and dad would think she didn't like her room and then they would be mad.

"Okay," answered Amanda.

Amanda thought that the house was very big. She didn't remember where the outside door was and she didn't even remember where the bathroom was. *Should I ask mom and dad now or wait until later?*

Janice added, "If you get nervous or afraid you can call us and one of us will come very quickly. Okay?" Amanda still felt nervous but didn't want to show it.

"Okay." She wasn't totally convinced as she looked again across the hall, but quickly her attention returned to her very own room.

"Do you like your room?" her mom asked.

"Yes, I like it."

Janice very proudly announced to her, "This is Amanda's room," and her mom leaned down close to her.

"I'm Sarah," she said as she skipped a short happy step into her big room.

"Sweetie, your name is Amanda and you'll have to get used to that, honey. Your new family will be calling you Amanda. We think it's a very pretty name and it is your name."

What is wrong with my new mom? thought Amanda. *I know my name is Sarah and she wants to call me Amanda. I think she was mad at me this time but I know my name. Yet, I saw her face and it was getting kind of red. Even though she called me honey, that doesn't matter—I know when people are getting mad.*

Although Amanda started to make a statement back to her new mom, she stopped herself and made an attempt at a smile instead. Amanda decided to say no more, but turning on the spot, she slowly and thoughtfully walked across the room that was now hers clapping her hands first in front of her and then behind her effortlessly as only children can do. She had seen a look of disappointment on this lady's face that had been introduced to her as "mom" and she didn't like to displease anyone, especially her new mom. So, she would let them call her Amanda and not say any more. She knew she needed to be a good girl or maybe they wouldn't want her. Okay, they could call her Amanda, but she knew her name was Sarah.

A few months later found Dave and Jan discussing their future prospects with contentment. Life was moving on nicely in a satisfactory direction.

"Aren't you glad that we decided on a five bedroom

home? We still have a spare room when some of the family come to visit." Jan was looking around their large family room as she commented.

"Sure and know what? For some reason, this house doesn't seem too big anymore. Remember when we first moved in, even with all the furniture, we had so much room. It's nice to see it getting filled up with life, you know."

"It's a good place to raise children," said Jan happily "which is our main purpose. Amanda is finally finding her way around and not having to ask how to get to her room. She looked very frustrated at first." Jan smiled as she remembered Amanda repeatedly asking how to get to her room.

"Yeah, I guess the stairs presented something in her mind that confused her at first. Probably because the orphanage was all on one floor. Now she smiles and states, 'I'm going to my room' and she is very proud of the fact that she knows where it is."

"And she's finally settled in about her name. She never mentions Sarah anymore. That was kind of weird in a way. The birth certificate did say Amanda Lynn and it had never been changed, at least not that anyone told us.

"Gees Jan, I'm sure they would have mentioned a name change, don't you? Probably she was just confused for a while, or maybe she was pretending with a name she liked."

"You know, they did tell us that we could have changed it. But I promised myself that I wouldn't change her name. It is a pretty name, I like it and it suits her, don't you think?"

"Yeah, she's Amanda to me."

"Right and besides, I sort of felt that I would always call her Amanda as a way of honoring her birth mother, you know. I felt that was the right thing to do."

"Jan, that's a nice thought. I like that," said Dave and then he added, "but she always acts so proper. You know what I mean?"

"Yes, she's well behaved." Jan was so proud of this fact. Other mothers often asked her what she did to have such a well-behaved daughter.

"Yeah, but you know what? She's acts like she shouldn't ever make a mistake. She's not even four years old and she's always so careful about what she says and does. Watch her eyes sometimes—she doesn't miss anything."

"I think she's very smart. Know what Dave? I don't think I told you but the other day she asked me if I liked her. Isn't that sweet? Of course, I told her that I liked her but I also loved her and she just stared at me trying to take it all in."

"Maybe she was trying to really believe it. It's only been six months and I don't think kids develop total trust that quickly. She probably still feels a little hesitant with us."

"You really think so? I think she trusts and loves us. I really do. I think we got the pick of the litter," said Jan as she gave Dave a quick wink.

"We'll see. Time will tell," answered Dave and Jan knew that he was in his usual thoughtful mode.

"I'm happy with our life in Scranton. We did make some good choices, didn't we? We've been lucky," added Jan feeling very smug and contented.

"Yeah, Compton Place is a good neighborhood, not rich but certainly not poor and friendly, lots of kids around, lots of activities. I think I know most people personally on this block, more than just waiving as you go by. I like that."

"That's what I mean Dave. We picked a great place and I love the people here. I know I'm more social than you but I like to have people around a lot. Yet you can be friendly here and still be yourself, sometimes a loner; sometimes not, and that works out good too."

"Yeah, you're right. I do like to be a loner sometimes. And that's okay. There's room for it all around here. I think we made a good choice." Dave nodded his head in agreement.

"All in all, I'm happy with everything, especially you," said Jan giving her favorite partner a very big smile. Happily he returned it as he shook his head at her playfulness.

"I'm glad you're here too. I usually need someone like you around to lift up my spirits occasionally."

"And I'm the one to do that for you, right?" added Jan, enjoying herself.

Dave countered with, "Yes, for sure, you and the three kids."

Amanda liked her new life. She was used to the name Amanda now and let her parents think she accepted it, but inside she still liked Sarah best. Occasionally when Amanda thought about the orphanage, she realized that most of her memories were gone and that made her sad. She couldn't even remember her bedroom anymore or the playroom where she'd had so much fun. It wasn't even a memory anymore but more like a dream. But she loved her new room and all the toys she had been given. She thought her parents must like her otherwise they wouldn't buy her all these nice toys and stuff. She would always have to remember to be a good girl so they would keep her. Bryan was fun and she liked him. Jonathon was the one who confused her. He didn't like her and she didn't know how to please him.

"Are you sure your name is Amanda now? No more Sarah right?" Jonathon still taunted her about her name and it was almost a year since she had even mentioned it. She vowed she would never mention that name to him again.

"What, now you can't talk either? Cat got your tongue?"

"Oh, oh, look at the little baby. Is she going to cry? Is she?"

Amanda knew Jonathon didn't like her and she felt he didn't even want her around. So she tried to stay away from him. She knew if there ever was a choice between Jonathon and Amanda, her parents would certainly pick Jonathon. It actually worked out quite well, she thought, since Jonathon didn't want to play or have much to do with her anyhow. He could be very mean at times and that sometimes scared her.

"That was really stupid, you know. Three years old and you didn't even know your own name. But then, you're a girl," taunted Jonathon always trying to get her to cry.

"Are you going to cry, Amanda or is it Sarah? Cry, why don't you?"

"You don't even know who you really are anyway. Somebody just gave you up and you don't even know your mother or father. Really pathetic Amanda."

Amanda never looked up or bothered to answer when Jonathon was in one of his mean moods. She just kept her head down and concentrated on doing whatever caught her interest. Bryan did the same thing. After Jonathon left they would usually look at each other and words weren't even necessary. They both just felt relieved.

What was wrong with Jonathon anyway? Amanda

wondered many, many times what his problem could possibly be. He had lots of toys and he lived with his birth parents. No one had given him away. Gees, he should be very happy. Amanda figured that some kids didn't know how to appreciate the important things in life. Sometimes when her mind wandered and she realized her birth mom didn't want her, she always felt something strange inside. She didn't know how to explain it, but it was very different from many of the other feelings she experienced.

Jonathon had walked away from his siblings in his rather smug demeanor knowing that he had won over Amanda again. He thought she was such a baby, although, he had to admit, that he couldn't get her to cry much anymore. He didn't like her at all but then, he didn't like Bryan either. Sometimes he wondered why and although he wouldn't admit it to a living soul, he wished he could like them, at least a little, and have fun playing with them. But he couldn't. He always felt so angry when they were around. Mostly, he didn't even know why.

His father got on his back a lot of times in the past and again just recently because he was mean to his siblings, or sometimes he wasn't even respectful to his mother, he'd been told. He remembered a recent lecture from his dad.

"Jonathon, I heard you speak to your mom with disrespect again. There is no reason for that and although she won't make you apologize, I will if I hear you again."

"I didn't say anything bad to her, What's the problem?" He thought life was getting tough for him in this household.

"Your tone with her is usually nasty and calling her "Heh you," won't work in this house anymore. One more time and you get grounded, understand?"

Looking at his father, Jonathon saw a lot of anger in his

face and the rest of his body was agitated. Sadly, he could relate to it. He could always relate to anger.

"Yeah, I get it." answered Jonathon grudgingly, although he didn't totally understand. He mostly found that his mom made him very angry, in spite of her efforts to the contrary. He had trouble being nice to her because he felt pain inside that no one would believe. He couldn't tell anybody because they would think he was stupid or crazy or a baby or something. He acknowledged that his mom did do some nice things for him, but strange as it seemed, right in the middle of some favor she was doing for him he would find himself wanting to do something nasty to hurt her. He didn't even know why. That confused him and it also scared him.

"I won't be giving you any more warnings about your mother. I'm not sure why you have to be so mean to her and to your brother and sister, but it has got to stop. I don't understand why you act this way," concluded his father.

No, you wouldn't know what I feel inside. You couldn't possibly know. I've had pain and tons of anger inside for years and it doesn't make sense to me either. Even with my friends I have to pretend I'm having a good time but usually I'm faking it. I don't know how to exist without this anger and pain. Should I tell you? You probably wouldn't care. And I don't trust you anymore. You only care about Amanda because she's an adopted kid. Well, if I'm your birth kid, why do I hurt so much? She seems to have a lot more fun than me. I try to hurt her all the time so she'll feel more the way I feel. Why should an adopted kid feel better than me? It's not fair.

"I keep asking you if there is anything bothering you Jonathon. Is there? Is there a problem that I can help you with?"

Jonathon looked at his father's face and he did see some concern but there was always more concern for Amanda he thought.

"No, dad, really. I just get mad sometimes." he answered as he tried to slough off the question. He didn't want anyone to get too close and figure it out.

"Well, why do you get so mad? There must be a reason?" Jonathon hated it when his father tried to play the shrink. They had taken him to counselors and psychologists before and nothing had worked. Why did his dad think he was better than them? There were no answers for him. He just had to be smarter in the future and keep his problems better hidden. His anger toward everyone wasn't worth getting grounded. He would have to be much more cautious in the future.

"I don't know dad. Sorry." He watched his dad walk away shaking his head in confusion and frustration and knew he was treading on thin ice. He would be very careful from now on.

Time moved on and Jan and Dave speculated about Amanda's progress. "It's been over two years and I think she has settled in beautifully with us, don't you think?" said Jan.

"Yeah it's been great," answered Dave carefully.

"When I found out that I couldn't have any more children I was so disappointed. I thought about adoption right away but wasn't sure how you would take it. I should have known you'd be with me. But then with the long wait for a baby I really didn't think you'd want an older child, although three isn't old, but you know what I mean."

"I know they come with more memories," added Dave, "and depending on what happened to them in their early years, you never know how they will behave. But things

41

happen with your birth children too. Look at Jonathon, he's changed a lot. Anyway, I remember when we first flew to Arizona to meet her, well that was just it for me. I felt she was meant for us."

"You can be sentimental for a guy, you know. I like that about you. Sometimes you keep a lot inside but at the most surprising moments you say it all in just a few words."

"Like what? What did I say?"

"You said, '"I felt she was meant for us.'

"Oh yeah, well I did feel that way." Dave felt slightly embarrassed.

"Well, she **was** meant for us."

"But I think maybe she is just too good to be true , you know what I mean?" Dave added.

"What do you mean? She seems to be happy, don't you agree that she's happy?"

"Yes but that's the problem Jan. She seems to be happy all the time. I've never seen a kid who doesn't get mad or do something wrong sometimes. It seems to me that Amanda still thinks she must please us or maybe we'll take her back. Just a thought, but think about the boys. When they were little they did naughty things and we corrected them and they learned. That is what little children do. How many times can you remember in more than two years that Amanda has done something that she knew was wrong? She doesn't. That's what I mean. She always does the right and proper thing."

This had been on Dave's mind for a while. He watched Amanda for any signs that she was unhappy or displeased, but he never saw any. That just wasn't normal. It was as if Amanda was playing a part in a play and Dave thought that she was a very good actress.

"I think she is so happy to be in a family again. She loves us, you know, she always says that and I think she means it. I think you worry too much. All is well, just enjoy it."

"I am enjoying it but remember we are her first family. She doesn't remember anything much before she came here," said Dave. "She doesn't seem to have many friends. She picks one or two friends only, other than that, she seems happy to a loner."

"Other kids only have a few friends too. I like to concentrate on the good things. She seems happy to me and I don't see any problems." Dave knew that he wanted to continue this conversation more than Jan. She probably would have been happy ending it now.

Dave continued. "I've seen her come out of her shell a few times and then Jonathon comes in with his nasty mood and back in she goes. She doesn't even fight back with him. She just gets very silent and doesn't seem to want to make any waves. It's like she puts up a barrier around herself and only opens it up occasionally and if anything is frightening to her, she goes back into her shell. I wonder sometimes if Jonathon keeps her from progressing."

"That's possible," said Jan. Even Bryan doesn't seem to fight too much with Jonathon anymore. But he's more sure of himself. Yet even he lets Jonathon take over and keeps out of his way. Or if they're together, they wait until Jonathon winds down and goes away, then they resume playing. I wish Jonathon would straighten out. I hate to say he's a bully, but he is. And Amanda get frightened at times. That certainly doesn't help."

"Yeah, Jonathon doesn't help matters," Dave agreed.

"But besides that, I think some of her words are just too mechanical like she thinks we expect her to say them. She really is very bright in knowing what we want of her. More so than the boys were. I'm not sure we have honest communication with her. I hope so, but we will just have to wait and see, I guess."

"But I sure enjoy her."

"Honey, I just want to see some normal feelings and behavior come out of her. We'll just watch her. That's all we can do," concluded Dave.

That seemed to end the conversation about Amanda but Dave wanted to open a conversation about Jonathon.

"You know, honey, I've got concerns about Jonathon. I know he was the first born and we had him for over two years before Bryan came along, so I did expect him to have some jealousy and fear about another sibling. Most first-borns do, but I feel that Jonathon never got over it. I've really tried to work with him, and I've asked him what's wrong and what he gets so mad about, but I can't anything out of him, I've heard him talking to the others when he didn't know I could hear and he isn't nice to his siblings. He can be so mean. I just don't get it."

"It concerns me too. But Jonathon really has a temper that he can barely keep under control at times. All kids are mean or angry at times but I'm almost surprised that he hasn't gotten into trouble yet. And he doesn't give the others a chance at all. "

"I've racked my brain trying to figure out what happened to that kid. I don't remember any temper tantrums in that first year—he was a happy little kid. Sometimes I think it was because he got sick so young. In those first few years I know we babied him, probably me even more than you, but he's been well for a long time now."

Dave remembered an incident. "Once a few months ago I had a talk with him when I was driving him over to the ice area. He says that he just can't help being nasty to Bryan and Amanda because he doesn't particularly like them. I was shocked to hear him say that and I told him that they were family and he backed off but didn't change his mind. Jonathon has always been more of a loner."

Janice continued. "He is different and some things he never seemed to be able to tolerate.

"I guess we'll see. But we have to watch him."

As time passed, Amanda continued in her same personality and demeanor, always being polite and always pleasing and not doing anything to disturb anyone. One time only, when she was sick with a flu bug, she ranted and raved for about five minutes but when she saw the surprised look on her parents' faces, she recoiled, totally upset and cried and cried. She had let her feelings out and she was even more careful in the future to keep her emotions under control.

When Amanda was in Grade 2, Dave and Janice had a chance to talk to her school counselor during a Parent/ Teachers' conference.

"How does Amanda behave at school? Does she ever misbehave or cause any trouble at all?" Dave and Janice, at this stage, almost hoped to hear about some slight or occasional misconduct.

Her counselor looked very surprised at the questions.

"No, no. Amanda is a very good student. She behaves perfectly and never causes any trouble. Why would you ask that?"

The Petersons related Amanda's almost perfect behavior at home and worried that she felt she had to act perfect all the time.

"She's very quiet and reserved here," said the counselor. "She never causes any trouble at all. She only has one close friend that I know of, Sachi Kumira, and talking to her about Amanda wouldn't be a good idea."

"We only wish that she could relax and trust us a little more. You know, like let go and even misbehave occasionally like most kids do. She's unusual in that way and we are concerned that she holds too much inside."

The counselor did have an idea. Get her something of her very own. Maybe get her a dog, but she would have to know it would be her dog and she would have to take care of it. The idea being that children always confided in animals and this seemed to work particularly well with adopted children.

Dave and Janice both loved the idea. Jonathon had had his gerbils and that was what he wanted at the time. Actually he had about ten gerbils at one time and his parents were happy when that part of his life was over and now it was hockey and skating. Bryan had fish and was still very excited about his large aquarium and he wouldn't be jealous anyway. A dog would be a nice addition to the household, just a small one, so they would approach Amanda to see if she liked the idea and of course, she could pick it out herself.

"I would love a dog. Could it sleep with me? It would be "my" dog? Wow. What kind would we get? I think I just want a little one."

"That's good Amanda because we thought we'd like it to be little," Janice added.

"Remember when we went to Aunt Shirley's house and

there was that little dog next door; I really liked it. Can I have one like that?" said Amanda waiting anxiously for a reaction.

She watched her mom and dad remember that little dog and nod in agreement. Amanda was getting very excited to own something of her very own.

"Yeah, I remember that dog, do you Dave? It's real cute and very friendly. Shirley always said that it was very playful and didn't seem to bark too much."

"That would be great. Getting a fairly quiet dog in the bargain would be a plus." Her dad winked at her and then she knew she had made a good choice.

"And you'll be responsible to take care of him because he will be your dog," he added.

"What about when I go to school? I can't take care of him when I'm in school."

"We'll take care of him when you are in school, but when you are home, you have to feed him and pick-up his toys and clean the yard. Do you think you want to handle that?"

Amanda gave them a very big smile that covered the entire bottom part of her face and nodded her head up and down very quickly.

"But you keep saying him. Can I have a girl dog?"

"Well I guess that would be okay. What do you think Dave?"

"It doesn't really matter, because we'll have it fixed anyway."

"What does that mean, getting it fixed?" asked Amanda with a total blank look on her face.

Dave had the task of explaining to Amanda what getting a dog fixed was all about. Later when he told Bryan and Jonathon about the addition to the family, they were fine with it. Bryan was excited too but Jonathon actually didn't care one way or the other as long as he never had to clean up the yard. After all, he reminded his parents that he was older now and had more important things to do than either of the younger children.

The next few weeks found Dave trying to find out what kind of dog Shirley's neighbor had. It seemed that the very liked animal was a Shih-Tzu and they also got a lead on a good breeder, which everyone visited, except of course, Jonathon.

"They are all so cute, I can pick out any one of them? Any one of these puppies could be mine?" asked Amanda.

"Yep, that's right. But remember, you said you wanted a female. Maybe you could ask Mrs. Brighton to point those out and that would help you narrow it down." Amanda thought her father had a good idea.

Noticing that her dad and mom were laughing and having fun as they looked at all of the cute puppies, Amanda thought that the puppy wasn't even home yet and everyone seemed happier. There was something about puppies, she thought, that just made you feel content.

"How about this one Amanda? It sure is friendly." Bryan had scooped up a little black and white puppy that Amanda found to be shy and cuddly at the same time. She liked it but continued looking.

Then there was a brown one that Amanda liked and while holding it, she discovered that she had made a mistake and picked up a male puppy. Although she admitted he was very cute, she wanted a female. Then, in a quick sudden moment, she spotted her lifelong friend. It was a little gray and white fur ball that was a little shy, yet a little playful; she was a little independent, but also very cuddly. She knew instantly.

"I found my puppy dad. It's that one that just went back to the corner," she said pointing at a puppy that needed to rest for a moment. "I held her for a few minutes and I think she's mine, okay dad?" Looking at her dad's face, she realized that he approved of her choice and his smile back to her made her realize that he shared in her excitement.

"I think that's a beautiful puppy. Jan, I think Amanda found her dog."

"Oh sweetie, she's just beautiful. Do you know what you will name her yet?"

"I think so but I'll tell you on the way home, okay?" Amanda wanted to be absolutely sure of the name before she shared it with anyone. Even Bryan tried to coax the name out of her, but he failed too.

"Okay, Amanda, tell me in my ear, no one else will hear? What will you name it?"

"Bryan, the dog is not an 'it,' it's a 'she;' she's a girl." With that comment, Amanda shared a special giggle that she reserved for Bryan alone.

After the business was concluded, the ride home began and Bryan immediately wanted to know the dog's name and Amanda let him persuade her, although she took her time about it.

"Amanda, I can't wait to hear her name. We are in the car and we are on the way home, so what's our new friend's name?" She noticed Bryan had such a lot of expectancy on his face that she thought he might burst in the next few moments. She decided she should tell him without delay.

"It's Muffin; my dog's name is Muffin. What do you think?"

"I love it," said Bryan ecstatically, "that a great name, don't you think so mom?"

"Yeah, and it does suit her. What do you think Dave?"

"I think we've just got a Muffin in our house."

Amanda was happy that everyone approved of the name she had picked. As Muffin moved on her lap, the bonding began.

"You are my little Muffin. Did you know that? You belong to me and I'm going to take good care of you. You and I will be best friends."

"She's really cute. Look how she just sits in the middle of your lap. She's not even moving. I think she's already asleep. Guess she feels real comfortable with you." Amanda liked the things that Bryan said.

"I'll bet the motion of the car is helping her to sleep Amanda. Just like a cradle for a baby," added Jan.

"Yep, she'll probably sleep all the way home. But that's okay. She's just a baby and babies need to sleep. You just go ahead and sleep Muffin, that's what you need to do." Amanda petted Muffin's head so she would feel secure.

And so it went all the way home. Everyone was happy with Muffin and Amanda was happy with everyone here and the world in general. Once home, she showed her dog to Jonathon who didn't make any fuss at all. But that was what

Amanda expected and everyone had to listen to his instructions.

"As long as I don't have to clean the yard, right dad? That's what you said. I don't hate dogs, but this is not my dog." Jonathon resented any attention paid to Amanda.

"No, this dog belongs to Amanda. It's her dog, and she will take care of it." His father confirmed what he wanted to hear.

"Well, that's good and I hope it doesn't whine all night. I need to sleep 'cause I've got lots of things to do." Sometimes Jonathon actually wondered why he couldn't share in the happiness of Amanda and Bryan, but he couldn't. At times, he thought they weren't too bad but chose not to show it. He wanted to keep his distance.

"Your gerbils caused me some sleepless nights, remember?" His dad still remembered that, "but I think after a few days, Muffin will get used to being here and she'll be just fine."

"Muffin, that's the dog's name. Muffin," added Jonathon with a disgusted look that he hoped Amanda could see.

"I think it's a nice name," added Bryan. Sure, thought Jonathon, *Bryan always sticks with her. They're two of the same kind. They both make me mad.*

"Muffin, it is. And I think the name suits that cute little puppy," said his dad which further angered Jonathon but lately, he chose to hide his feelings and forgo being grounded.

After the first night of having Muffin in the kitchen and hearing her cry, Amanda felt her pain and looked for another solution. She approached her father with an idea.

"Dad, can I put Muffin's crate in my room? I can take her outside from there as well as from anywhere else in the house."

"I think that would be okay. You've been acting very responsibly, if only for a day. But if that changes, I'll have to rethink my decision."

"Okay dad, can you help me? I can't get the crate in my room all by myself. Okay?"

"Sure, you take the food and water dish out of it and I'll bring up the crate for you.

"Thanks dad. I'm sure it will be much better and she won't cry as much when I'm right next to her, don't you think?"

"Yeah, you're probably right. Good idea."

Amanda loved to see Muffin run around the house and being happy and interested in everyone and everything. Amanda would go into hysterical giggles that she couldn't control even if she tried. She knew her parents were happy to hear her laugh so much and so loud; it wasn't what she usually did. But Muffin had made a difference. And it was her little five-pound puppy that had accomplished in two weeks' time what her parents hadn't been able to do in almost four years. For the first time that Amanda could remember, she felt satisfied, like she belonged.

"May I watch TV with you dad?" asked Amanda upon entering the family room.

"Yes of course, why would you ask?"

"Because Muffin will probably come too, Is that okay?"

"That will be fine, just take care of her, okay?" said

Dave smiling.

"Yep, Muffin's behavior and manners are my responsibility. I will make sure she behaves. Okay, dad?"

"That's a deal."

With Amanda home there just wasn't any other place in the entire household for Muffin to sleep except on her lap. She would make a few circles and then just snuggle in, let out a big sigh of contentment and fall immediately into a deep sleep. The bonding between these two, although very fast and immediate, would never change.

"You're my little girl, did you know that? You belong to me and I'm gonna take good care of you. You and I are always going to be best friends. I love you; did you know that? I trust you and I love you and I can't say that about anyone else in this whole entire world. I know you are a little sad right now because they took you away from your mother. They just don't know how that feels, but you and I know. And it hurts. But I can help you because I'm better now but I still think about my other mom. I can't say it to anyone here because they wouldn't like it. Do you know what Muffin? I really wanted to call you Sarah, but I thought everyone in this household would probably go nuts, especially my mom and dad. But I still think that's my real name. Anyway, I like the name Muffin. Don't you? Do you like your name?"

And on and on it went. Amanda realized that she talked more to her dog about her inner feelings than she talked to anyone in this house, ever. But that was because no one seemed to want to know what she felt inside. Her mom just wanted everything to be okay, and if it wasn't okay, she would just pretend it was. Her dad, Amanda suspected, really knew some of her inner thoughts, but somehow they had never talked about it. But now, she had Muffin. And that was enough.

"You know Muffin, I'm adopted too and I'm from another state far away. My mom and dad take good care of me, physically and all, but no one seems to know how much I hurt inside sometimes. I think you know. They don't seem to care that I lost a mother and father and they seem to pretend that it never happened because they never talk about it. Some people tell me that I should be very happy to have been adopted. And I am happy to have a mom and dad who care about me but no one seems to care that I lost a mother and father. So Muffin, I really have two moms and two dads. And that does seem strange to me."

Reflecting for a moment Amanda remembered hearing about a funeral when someone in the family had died. They said that she was too young to go at the time but everyone else went and they prayed and people actually acknowledged that someone had lost an important person in their life. No one did that for Amanda. She had lost her birthmother and her birthfather but no one even wanted her to talk about it. Why was that different?

"But I'm here for you Muffin. I'm your mom now and I'll take the best care of you that I can. It really helps to talk to you because you always listen to me. You make me feel so good inside."

One day Uncle Bill and his family had come over for dinner. They were all sitting around the table when Jonathon mentioned very proudly that Uncle Bill was his godfather and Aunt Emily was his godmother. Then he added that everyone said that he looked just like Uncle Bill. The conversation stayed on that topic for a while talking about Bryan and who he looked like, other than his mother and dad and who and where they thought the boys got their talents. In a sudden moment, Dave looked over at Amanda who just sat there in silent distress staring purposely at her dinner plate and realized this was probably very uncomfortable and hurtful for her and started changing the subject. But not before Jonathon had made his comments.

"Amanda doesn't have any godparents and couldn't possibly look like anyone in this family anyway."

"Jonathon, hush up, that isn't necessary and it's hurtful to Amanda," said Dave.

"What's the big deal? We all know that it's true. She's just a late addition to this family anyway." Jonathon stared directly at Amanda with this last point. She just sat there and wouldn't even look in his direction, which irritated him more.

"Jonathon, I don't want to hear another word out of your mouth except an apology to your sister."

"Sorry," was all Jonathon could manage in a very grumpy low tone of voice that had no sincerity behind it.

Jonathon never knew why they always seemed to side with Amanda. They always thought about Amanda's feelings getting hurt. Big deal. He had spoken the truth. This made him mad. They were having a fun conversation but had to change it because of Amanda. So, let her feelings get hurt once in a while. Everybody gets hurt, he thought. I get hurt a lot of times and I never heard them talk like that about me. And my mom just sat there and didn't even say anything. She certainly didn't come to the rescue. But then, she never did.

After the evening was over, Dave and Janice compared notes about Jonathon and they didn't like what they were seeing. Upon confronting him regarding his unkind remarks of the evening, he said that he was just telling the truth and didn't know why everyone was so stupid about it.

"She was adopted you know and everyone already knew that."

"Didn't you think how much that must have hurt her. She needs to feel she belongs as much as you do," Dave explained.

"She'll just have to get used to it. She is adopted and no one knows for sure where she comes from, or who she really is. That's just a fact of life."

"It seems I need to explain a few things to you about cooperating with the people in your life." And so his father began a rather lengthy lecture.

Jonathon didn't really listen to his explanation about manners and being kind to people and not hurting them on purpose. Oh, he pretended to listen so he didn't get grounded. But he would liked to have told them a thing or two. What about his feelings? What about his inside anger and pain that no one even knew about? He sometimes cried out inside for someone to figure out what was wrong with him. But no one ever did and now no one even seemed to try anymore. He was just labeled a bully and was expected to act better, regardless of his own hurt. He would have liked to yell out at his father so he would understand. But he didn't trust him anymore and he didn't want to get grounded.

Later that evening Amanda sat in her room with Muffin by her side. She just looked around her room and although it was pretty and she had lots of toys, she thought, sometimes I'm not very happy here. It's just too bad that other adults in this house never know what's on my mind. They never ask me. They just think I feel a certain way, but they never ask. Isn't that silly Muffin? She sat next to Amanda, tilting her head in empathy and listened as she usually did. She was very quiet and her tail hardly wagged at all. It seemed that Muffin knew.

As she amused herself in her room, there was a knock on her door. It was Bryan who looked sad and forlorn, while standing timidly at the door.

"Hi Amanda, can I come in?"

Bryan was looking dejected himself and rather nervous while waiting for Amanda's answer. Yet Amanda had always liked him and knew that he was the only other person who knew how mean Jonathon could be and so they had an instant connection.

Amanda didn't say anything in words but just nodded her head up and down and tried to hide the slight pout that was still visible on her bottom lip. She went back to sitting on the floor with her legs crossed in a yoga style position, with Muffin sitting next to her, now wagging her tail in double time.

"Don't you wonder sometimes how Muffin can do that? Wag her tail so fast. That is just amazing to me. Look at that tail, it just goes on and on so fast."

Bryan had to laugh as he joined her on the floor. He admitted that he'd never thought of it before. As for Amanda, she wondered about everything. She always wanted to know the reasons about everything, although she usually wondered privately in her own mind. But she knew Bryan understood a lot of things that he kept hidden. Sometimes, it was just the way he looked at her that made her realize he knew things, a lot of things for a kid.

"She is a cute little doggie. And she really loves you Amanda. I'm glad she makes you so happy because I think you deserve the best."

"Yeah," said Amanda as she looked at Bryan's sincere face, "I know you're my friend just like Muffin. I really love her too. Do you love her Bryan?"

"Yeah, I really do. I've always liked dogs but we never

had one before. We always had fish and gerbils and once we had a rabbit and a small snake, which mom hated, but never a dog. I'm surprised how much I love her, but she's a great little dog."

"I know that Jonathon doesn't like her at all. He has totally rejected Muffin just like me. I'm not sure I know why."

"Jonathon has always been different. Mom tells me that when they brought me home from the hospital he was very angry. He wanted to be an only child. Mom told me that it isn't very unusual at first when a second baby comes home, but he had a lot more trouble getting over it than most other kids. Dad said it was probably because he was sick for the first couple of years of his life. But I don't know. I don't think he ever really liked me either. He sometimes used to pretend to play with me when mom and dad were around, but it was just pretend."

"I think he's got real problems. But I decided a long time ago not to let what he said bother me too much. Otherwise, my feelings would get hurt all the time. I can put up barriers you know, when I need to."

"Really, you can do that. I'm sorry he's so mean to you. I feel bad when he says nasty things to you. And I know as much as anyone that he can be very nasty when he wants." Amanda noticed that Bryan got quiet for a moment.

"I remember once he told me that my birth parents probably wanted a boy and that's why they gave me away. I remember too that you told mom and dad, which is something you never usually do."

"He was too far beyond anything that was okay. Somebody had to tell on him and you never would."

"You're right there."

58

"I don't think at all like Jonathon, you know. I've never told you but I want you to know that I think you're just great and I like having you here. As far as I'm concerned, you're true family with me and you're my real sister. Besides, what's so great about looking like someone else in the family?"

"It's really hard to explain Bryan, sometimes I'm not sure I understand myself, but when you are given away you always wonder why. And when I look in the mirror I have a curiosity about where I came from. I can't explain it to you because I don't know myself but there is always that question of why and there's never an answer."

"Guess I don't understand what you mean. But I never thought it was so great or mattered that I looked like so and so or whoever; big deal. Who cares?"

"Maybe so, but maybe you might care if you didn't know," said Amanda reflectively.

"Yeah," said Bryan slowly and thoughtfully, "maybe I would. But to me you really are my true sister and I'm real glad that you are here. I wanted to make sure you knew that."

"Thanks, I like that. Anyway, it's kind of like you and me against Jonathon. I don't really mean against Jonathon, but ..." Amanda stopped abruptly. Had she said too much?

"No, No. I know exactly what you mean. That's probably one of the reasons I'm so glad you are here. I feel that I finally have one other kid in this house that I can talk to. It was no fun being with just Jonathon."

"I never thought about that. You must have had some rough times being with Jonathon alone."

"There were very few good times, that I can say

honestly. You never knew what to expect with him. He could be friendly for a few minutes and then something would set him off and usually I never knew what I did to make him mad."

"Yeah, I imagine being with Jonathon alone was tough. Do you want to hold Muffin for a minute?"

"Yeah, I like holding Muffin. She feels so good." Amanda could tell by the way Bryan held Muffin so carefully that he meant what he said.

"I love to hold her," said Amanda. "You know what, when I'm alone and I hurt about something, I just pick up Muffin and hold her. To me, that's like putting a bandage on a wound. She's magical to me."

Life had improved for Amanda and it continued on in an upward progression until she went into the 6th Grade at Wilson Middle School and ended up in Mrs. King's English class. That opened a new chapter that turned many settled things upside down again in Amanda's life.

CHAPTER III

Mrs. King fidgeted at her desk trying desperately to find her notes for today's class. Twenty-seven ten and eleven year olds were more children than she usually had but with the addition of a teacher's aid she mostly managed to keep the disturbances under control.

"Attention, Attention," she said as she slammed her hand down on her desk. "Remember you are all in a classroom. Jeffrey, take your seat in the usual place. You can talk to your friends after class. Nathan, that's enough for now. Sit up straight and face the front."

"Everyone, I want to introduce you to Debbie Sigmond. She will be my aide for this semester and she commands respect and attention at all times."

Realizing that Christine Biston had her hand up for a few minutes, she called on her since she could never be ignored.

"Yes, Christine, what is it?"

"I will probably need to leave early today for a monitor meeting."

"Okay, okay. I was given the schedule and you're on it so you can leave ten minutes before the end of class."

Christine's hand was still up.

"Yes, Christine, what is it now?"

"I just wanted to mention that the meeting will be every Monday for the next two months."

"Yes, Christine, I'm aware of that and it's okay."

"Nathan, again, I want you in your same seat and stay there. Thank you. I must remind you that I have two boys in middle school and one in high school so I've had a lot of practice and know most of the moves and excuses you can throw my way. If you need a reason for your behavior, try to be creative and think of something that I may not have heard of yet."

The laughter and giggles gave Nancy time to collect herself and her notes, which she had recently found. She wanted so much to teach these bright little minds more than just the basics of education and some years she couldn't seem to inspire her students as she planned. However, she planned to repeat an interesting project that had worked well in past years and while creating interest among the students it actually helped them to work in comradeship while learning more about each other.

Referring to her notes, Nancy called the class to attention and began roll call to get some sense of order. That being accomplished, she continued.

"Today we are going to begin a new project which will be creative, fun and educational for everyone. We are going to do a time line of your life. What that means is that you will follow your life from the time you were born until now. We'll do that by providing some pictures, essay writing and any other aids that you want to use. I will not detail everything out for you because this is where you have a chance to be creative. Everyone will present their project in front of the class and will be graded on your writing, art, (if you choose to use it), pictures and overall presentation. That's all I will say about it now but by next week I do want you to bring in a picture of yourself as a little baby."

Nancy gave the class a few minutes to talk about their new assignment and she heard the entire buzz of conversation intermingled with giggles of enthusiastic comments. She realized that this project always got rave reviews by students and parents alike. It was something they could all work on together and while the parents were supposed to support their child's efforts from a distance, she understood that many of them got into the middle of it reliving the early years of their offspring.

"Wow, this should be a lot of fun. I wonder who will be the ugliest baby," joked Nathan Jones, the class clown on most days.

"Not sure, but it won't be me. Believe it or not my mom tells me I was a real cute baby." That would be Tim Booth, trusted friend of Nathan and equally accomplished comic.

"You, a cute baby, my God, what happened?" asked Nathan.

"To you or to me," was the expected answer and then they giggled too loud and got reprimanded by Mrs. King.

Amanda couldn't help but smirk at Nathan and Tim. They always acted so silly.

Life was always a joke to them. Nathan didn't irritate her as much as Tim, but he made her nervous. She liked him at times but not when he was in his 'make a joke out of everything' mood, as he was today. Probably she thought that was how he hid his embarrassment.

"Heh Amanda, were you a cute baby? I'll bet you were,"

yelled Nathan.

"I don't remember Nathan; I was quite young at the time." Amanda had just said the words and regretted them immediately. Both Nathan and Tim went into hysterical laughter, which again caught Mrs. King's eye. They settled down quickly, however, and Amanda relaxed somewhat.

"Okay everyone, settle down, please. Here's the deal. I'm going to give you five minutes to discuss things and get all of the cute remarks and silliness out of your system, then we will seriously continue with class."

The buzz of conversation was deafening, and hysterical laughter was heard intermittently around the classroom. Everyone seemed to love this project. As the children around her exhibited excitement Amanda's exterior expression, that showed her smiling and agreeable, didn't match her inner person. She just couldn't show anyone her fears or how sad she felt. So she smiled like everyone else so they wouldn't guess her panic. Amanda still had lots of questions about her life and now this teacher wanted answers from her and she hadn't yet figured out all of the questions.

"Aren't you excited Amanda? This should be so much fun." That was her classmate Sachi, showing excitement of her own.

"Yes, I guess so," answered Amanda automatically but minus any enthusiasm.

"You don't sound very happy, but then I know you're such a private person. But it will be okay."

"Yes, it should be fun." Amanda readjusted her attitude quickly and tried to add some interest to her comment, unwilling to let anyone know of her fears.

"I know exactly what baby picture I'm gonna bring in. I

was such a cute baby," said Christine laughing and giggling with glee.

"I have a lot to choose from too, but I'm not sure which one I'll bring in. I'm going to get all the pictures out this weekend so I'll have enough time to look them over," said Linda Sims, a friend of Christine's.

"Isn't it great when your parents love you so much that they take a lot of pictures?" asked Christine.

"Yes, it is," answered two or three more in her clique as they huddled together and lowered their voices to whispers.

Amanda realized that no one would ever guess that Christine Biston was not one of her favorite people. Mainly it was because of her constant exhibition of self-centeredness and strong ego that needed so much attention. Being an agreeable person on the surface, although inwardly trusting very few, those Amanda disliked were only thought of when they were physically in front of her. It always amazed her that many of the little cliques around the school spent their time talking negatively about people they didn't like and who were not even present. Amanda didn't do that. She had too many important questions on her mind and also felt that you couldn't like everyone anyway. So when her few friends were around she had fun talking with them and other times Amanda kept trying to figure out in her mind the puzzle which was her life. That was almost a full-time job anyway.

After Christine walked away, Amanda felt a cloud of depression slowly descend upon her. She knew her life was different from other kids and unfortunately, she was the only adopted child in her 6th grade. It was the first time in quite a while that certain ideas came to the front of her mind. So many painful memories were hidden, even from herself, but now some were beginning to resurface slowly and the accompanying feelings were aggravating in their emptiness.

"*I don't have any baby pictures of myself*", she thought, "*not even one.*" *I've asked my mom and she said that the orphanage didn't have any. There must have been some pictures at the orphanage and I'll bet my mom never even bothered to ask. Sometimes she makes me so angry. There had to be some pictures of me as a baby. I'm sure my first mom probably took a lot of pictures of me,* she reflected. *She must have; any mother would.* The problem remained that she didn't have any baby pictures to bring to class next week. There were no pictures, no baby blankets, no booties, nothing. What would she do? How embarrassing that would be. Christine said she's got a real cute picture of herself with her first tooth and another when she took her first step. Sadly, Amanda knew that she didn't have anything from the first few years of her life and that realization created a huge dark void inside of her. It seemed like there was a big black hole within her that couldn't be understood or even approached. This not only scared her but it hurt a lot. Yet she knew it was her pain alone because no one else could understand.

In a sudden moment, the bell rang, and Amanda got up and pushed everything back in the different categories of her mind. She could always do this when things started upsetting her too much and this was definitely one of those times. She thought that she could get this all sorted out when she was home alone. She could even discuss it with Muffin, her best listener. Okay, that was enough of this until she got home. And with that Amanda turned and walked out with the other children holding a nice smile on her face so that no one would ever know the anguish going on inside of her.

The bus stop was only a few blocks from Amanda's house. But this day she walked the long way around which took her to a park and she sat on the bench for a few minutes thinking her unpleasant thoughts.

"Chirp, chirp; Chirp, chirp.," She noticed a little bird

had landed at the end of her park bench. A pretty little robin just sat there, perched and relaxed, apparently resting.

"It must be nice to a bird. And you're a pretty bird. But when you don't like something you can just fly away. You really are a free spirit, aren't you?"

And with that last comment the bird flew away, but suddenly came back for a brief moment, almost in acknowledgement of Amanda's comments.

"Yes, you are free and I acknowledge your freedom," said Amanda amused with the bird and herself and she watched it fly away quickly, never to return. Here she was almost twelve years old and circumstances from the first few years of her life still bothered her and she couldn't fly away. She didn't think of her difficulties most of the time anymore, at least not deliberately, but every now and again situations brought them up to a conscious level and then she had to use everything she had to keep good control. Why did life have to be this way? She did acknowledge that she had a good life and yet the unanswered questions inside of her pained her at times. *Why was I given away? Didn't my mother want me? What was wrong with me anyway?* Amanda never talked about her feelings to anyone because they would think she was a baby and yet these were not baby questions.

Looking up at the sky, she realized how far away the clouds were and how tall the trees at the park seemed to be. It made her feel so small as she recognized her stature in a big universe. Her teacher in Grade 5 had talked about planet earth and the universe while adding the perspective of other galaxies out there. She marveled about it at the time but now realized even earth was just one little blob in the whole entire universe. She liked to think of life that way as she could then feel her questions and problems were small too. Leisurely, she started on her way home in a shuffling manner, kicking every stone she could find with her new royal blue tennis shoes as getting home quickly wasn't a priority today. She wanted to talk to Muffin but no one else and she needed this time to get her mental state together and be able to present her agreeable face so no one would suspect her problem. She felt she needed a little more time to accomplish this as she walked unhurriedly home.

"Hi mom, how's it going?"

"Good, did you have a good day honey?"

"It was very interesting today," she offered, not wanting to lie, yet not ready to talk.

"Are you hungry, sweetie? I've got cookies and there's some milk. That should keep your stomach under control until dinner."

"That will do it, thanks mom. Got a lot of homework so I think I'll start now, if you don't need me."

"I'm all set honey. See ya later."

As luck would have it, Jonathon had already left for his hockey practice and she found Bryan playing with some friends. After nodding a welcome to him she went off to her room to be alone and talk to Muffin. As she closed the door to her bedroom, she let out a big sigh of relief, happy to have made it this far without crying, something she loathed to do in front of any person. Actually crying was not a familiar practice with her but she knew today that the tears would come and Muffin should be the only one to share them. Surprisingly enough, sitting on the edge of her bed with Muffin by her side, she couldn't cry no matter how much she tried. She actually tried to force crying hoping that the tears would follow, but they didn't. Why was life this way? She had a perfect opportunity to ease off her feelings with tears in the privacy of her own bedroom; it was her perfect plan from the moment she found out about the project in Mrs.

King's class. She knew her feelings of the past were rising and would be relieved somewhat mainly by tears, and now she couldn't even cry. How stupid.

The next thing Amanda remembered was Bryan waking her for dinner. She had fallen asleep on her bed and although she didn't feel much better about the project, she didn't feel like crying anymore. Yet the project was always on her mind and never left her. After dinner she tried sorting out her confused feelings by thinking of other pleasant things that would help her through this dilemma. She knew she would have to face the baby picture situation, but that was not until next week, and for now, she could take Muffin for a walk or after her chores, she could spend her free time doing anything she wanted. Amanda thought about that phrase, "free time." She knew what it meant but often wondered if she would ever truly feel free. She certainly hoped so. She knew that bad situations always seemed much worse at the time they were happening and looking back on her 6th grade project in five years or so, she would probably wonder about the big deal. Knowing she hated going to the doctor or to the dentist, Amanda would pretend as she walked in the office that everything was over and she was walking out. Sometimes she walked into the doctor's office backwards so in her mind she could pretend more effectively that she was finished and walking out. Her mom used to shake her head and laugh, but it worked for Amanda.

At school the next day, she knew the questions would eventually come in her direction so she wasn't surprised.

"Heh Amanda, what picture are you bringing in?" asked Christine.

"Don't know yet, still deciding." Amanda acted as nonchalant as she could, hoping Christine would go away. Others joined in on the conversation which was lucky for Amanda who escaped and walked away. She could still hear them from a distance. "I've got such a bunch of pictures to choose from that it's really difficult to choose. There are so many cute ones of me. Maybe I'll ask Mrs. King if I can bring in more than just one. One doesn't seem like enough," continued Christine.

Amanda didn't even raise her head for that comment. She knew it was Christine and although she recognized her voice it was mainly the content of the remark that assured her it could only be one person.

"We should start a group and just look at each other's baby pictures. That would be such fun."

Again Christine. Amanda walked into the classroom slowly from the hallway where the group had gathered to discuss the project. It was already Wednesday and time marched on with no decision in sight. What would she do? What could she possibly do?

By Thursday, she began to feel the pressure of no decision. Should she talk to her parents? That might be risky because then they would know the problems she felt inside. What if she talked to Mrs. King directly and just admitted she didn't have any baby pictures? Embarrassing, yet possibly she could do something else for the start of the project? However, everyone in her 6th grade class would know that she didn't have one baby picture of herself and no doubt that information would trickle down to her parents and be all over the school anyway. Some students would probably sympathize with her and some would laugh at her. Amanda wasn't sure which idea she hated more since both opinions took away some of her self worth. Why did Mrs. King have to pick this project? What bad luck.

Arriving home after school on Thursday Amanda found a note from her mom tacked onto the refrigerator.

Amanda,

I have to drive both Bryan and Jonathon for hockey practices today. Dad will be home by 5:00 and take you to dinner. Any problems, Mrs. Nordon is home next door.

Love you, Mom

While waiting for her dad Amanda walked around the house as if she were seeing it for the first time. She vaguely remembered the very first day that she'd entered this home but recalled that she'd liked it immediately, although it was very big and she was amazed that only five people lived here. She loved the smell of everything like the new rugs, the scent that mom always had going on somewhere which reminded her of lilacs or roses and other times it was like wooden smell as if you were in a forest. Always sawdust could be found on the floor of dad's woodwork shop but she always looked for a certain aroma that she had never found. Also, a certain texture escaped her that caused her to keep feeling fabrics in her search. She didn't even know what to look for but she knew that she had experienced both as a child and forever hunted for the sensation. She wished she knew where that memory came from. If she ever found that smell, or experienced that feeling, would it answer one of her questions? She wondered if it would make any difference.

Muffin walked around the house with her and in the middle of her reminiscence the telephone rang. It was her friend Sachi, and although Amanda usually liked to talk with her, she was now experiencing older memories and Sachi existed as part of her present. She chose to call her back later.

For some reason, Amanda was very aware of herself today. She realized at eleven years old she had only grown to 4'10" and many of the girls in her class were already considerably taller. She wanted to be at least 5'6" and felt that she probably wouldn't make it that tall. But she always pretended that she was tall, hoping she could put the thought into her brain and then her physical nature would accept the idea and give her a couple more inches. She didn't believe she had failed yet, so in this effort, she persisted. An incident of a few weeks ago crossed her mind.

"You know I'm going to be quite tall my mom says."

That of course was Christine, but Amanda realized, as she continued that she made some interesting points.

"Well, yes, you know," Christine continued, "my mom is only 5'3" tall but my father is 6'2" and both my grandparents on both sides are over 5'8". So we figured out that I have to be at least 5'8". I think that's a great height."

"I have the same thing in my family, so I should be tall too," added Linda, another gal in Christine's clique.

"Everyone tells me I take after my dad and my grandfather. But I don't want to be 6'2." Christine added giggles throughout most of her comments.

"I think I'm destined to be a little shorter, probably around 5'6". I think that is respectable too." That was Nancy, a tag-a-long part of the same group.

"What about you Amanda, how tall do you think you're going to be?"

Shocked at the question posed directly at her, Amanda fidgeted for a moment and as she was about to deliver a plausible answer, Mrs. King chose that instant to enter the door and begin class saving Amanda from embarrassment, at least for the moment. But it gave her more to wonder about. Being fairly attractive with her large blue/green eyes that showed expression easily while accenting her well-shaped nose with a slight upward tilt, Amanda knew she had an attractive profile. She actually stood out surprisingly well for her good taste in under applying her makeup rather than totally overdoing in that category which was more common for 6th grade girls. Satisfied with her appearance, she didn't spend much time admiring or criticizing her looks. But she did wonder who she looked like and whether she would be tall or short and many other things that wouldn't cross her mind at all if she lived with her birth family.

As she waited for her father, her mind constantly reverted to the project of next week. She just couldn't decide what to do. After all, she was eleven years old and should have some inner strength by now to handle this situation. Why couldn't she do it? She found herself getting somewhat upset and tears began to fill her eyes when she heard her father's car pull into the driveway. Immediately she shifted her thoughts into an agreeable realm so she could be pleasant.

"Hi dad," she said as Dave walked into the house. "How was your day?"

Amanda said the same thing every night when he came home. Although Dave liked the enthusiasm in her voice, it was again one of those episodes that set her apart from the boys. Many times Bryan and Jonathon, especially Jonathon, were busy and too much into what they were doing to even notice that he had come into the house. It was much more common to hear Bryan or Jonathon say something like, "Oh, is dad home?" And that was what normal kids did, at least some of the time. But not Amanda; she was always in the right place, saying the proper thing, at the right time. Dave seemed to remember only a few times that Amanda had missed being there when he came home and that occurred because of sickness.

"My day was great and how about your day?"

"It was okay too dad."

Somehow Dave did detect something in Amanda's demeanor. He had noticed expressions before as worrisome thoughts crossed her face but she always pretended that everything was just fine. When would she slip up? Would it ever happen? After all these years Dave felt that she had too much control of herself for that time to ever come. He knew there was a barrier that Amanda and her parents had never overcome. She still had to be the perfect child. Why did she feel that way? He didn't know.

"Hope you're not too hungry. I've got a few things to do but then I thought maybe we could go out to Subway. Do you still like them?"

"Oh yes, that would be nice," answered Amanda. "I'll be in the family room doing homework. Just let me know."

Dave sometimes wanted to scratch his head as he watched his daughter turn with her schoolbooks in hand and head for the family room. Everything was always just too perfect.

After his phone calls, he went looking for Amanda and realized the house had an unnerving air in its tranquility. As he approached the family room, he heard what he thought was someone crying ever so quietly. As he slowly entered the room, Amanda had her back toward him and when he spoke her name, she turned so quickly with a look of horror on her face that he could tell immediately she felt shame for not having the time to compose herself. Amanda had pretty long hair that she kept pulled back with barrettes but part of it had crossed her face and gotten damp in her tears.

"Amanda, are you ready?"

Having no time to hide her tears as she turned in immediate response to her father's voice, Amanda's face showed horrified fear. He saw tears coming down her cheeks and could tell these were not recent, but tears that had kept her company for a while. Shocked as Dave was at the moment, his immediate thought made him wonder whether he was experiencing the beginning of a chink in the armor.

"Oh, Oh dear."

Those were the only words that he heard come out of Amanda's mouth. She was at a loss and didn't know what to say or where to run. He knew that she would have liked to escape and totally disappear. The look of horror remained on her face for a few moments.

"What's wrong Amanda?"

Dave knew this was an opportunity and wanted to tread ever so softly so that Amanda didn't get frightened and clam up. He gave her a moment to recover from the first evidence of something being wrong that she had ever exhibited. Knowing her reserved demeanor and anxiety at closeness, he treaded slowly.

"Oh, Oh, I'm so sorry dad. I'm so sorry."

Amanda kept repeating those same words over and over. He knew she was shocked and stuck for words so he didn't push her. He realized she was acting like someone who got caught doing something very improper and was ashamed.

"It's okay Amanda. Everyone cries now and then. It's okay for you to cry. What's wrong, maybe I can help you?"

Using light and kind tones as he spoke very slowly and softly, Dave knew that Amanda was aware how much her parents cared for her. But this was the first chance at a breakthrough and he wanted to transmit caring and empathy in his voice as he quietly and almost magically took the several steps across the room to where she was lying on the couch. Caution was important here as he tried to take his cue from her.

"I'm so sorry dad; I'm being so bad. I'm so sorry."

Dave observed that Amanda couldn't seem to get herself in control. She was sobbing softly and taking deep interrupted breaths that continued on in spite of anything she tried. He saw her glance shyly at him to see his expression. and he hoped she saw caring and concern.

"You're not being bad at all Amanda. It's okay. Just cry if you need to. It's okay."

"I'm being so bad. You must be so disappointed in me. I'm so sorry."

Continuing in the same tone and theme, Dave realized how deep into Amanda's mind was the thought that she must always be good.

"Why do you think you're being bad, Amanda?"

"I'm sitting here crying and making a big fuss and you just got home from work and you must be tired and you still want to take me out for dinner and I don't even act like I appreciate it. I really do but I'm crying right now. Oh, Oh my gosh."

Amanda was still crying in deep sobs that came from the depths of her when Dave inched closer to her on the couch and managed to put his arm around her and stroke her hair gently. For the first time in eight years Amanda just grabbed on to her father and started crying and couldn't seem to stop. No more words were spoken but they weren't necessary. Years and years of held-in emotions began to surface and Dave knew that the armor had finally cracked. Amanda was reaching out to him and it was a happy moment for both of them, despite the tears. Even when the tears and sobs started to subside a little, Dave held on to Amanda and she didn't even try to pull away from her father but seemed to feel calm at being comforted by him. Amanda was the first to speak.

"You must be very mad at me, aren't you dad?"

"Why do you think I'd be mad at you?"

"I'm acting like a spoiled brat. I'm really sorry."

"Amanda, you have nothing to be sorry about. I see a very nice little girl who is upset about something and needed to cry. Why do you think that's wrong?"

"I don't know. I don't want to cause you any problems."

"You're not causing me any problems at all. But if you did cause problems once in a while, that'd be okay too. I want to help you. We're family, you know, and dads do help their children when they need help. Can you tell me why you are crying?"

Amanda was very slow to answer that question. Dave waited patiently giving her all the time she needed as he noticed her eyes were still mainly looking at the floor and took a few more moments before they raised up ready for more conversation.

"Um, Mrs. King umm wants us to do a um project."

The last word "project" drifted off so quickly that it was completely unintelligible to Dave. Understanding that this was a complete turnabout for Amanda's character, he waited a moment before he asked Amanda to repeat.

"Mrs. King wants us to do a project in class."

He noticed a pause as Amanda stopped for a moment, and took a long deep breath that covered the fact that she had been crying before she continued. "Mrs. King wants us to do a time line of our lives."

The statement, finally released, brought on more tears but finally Dave understood. In that one moment he knew what all of the tears were about and how hard this realization would be for Amanda. At first Dave thought it was bad luck that Mrs. King had picked that particular project for Amanda's class but then he realized that possibly it was a blessing in disguise. His daughter had to face many things in her life that she tried to hide. Someday she would have to face all of these hidden nightmares, if not now with her family around her, when?

"That must be real hard for you to face, right? Does Mrs. King want you to start when you were a baby right up until now or what?"

"Yes, we have to start when we were born and next week we have to bring in a picture of ourselves as a little baby. I don't have any. Are you sure that you and mom asked at the orphanage? My first mom must have taken some pictures of me, at least one. Why didn't we get any? And why did she give me away?"

Wow, Dave realized now, how deep these feelings went. The floodgates had definitely opened and his next few words could make a big difference in Amanda's life. He prayed for inspiration and realized that Amanda had carried all of this inside of her for years. She'd never once let on that all these memories bothered her or that she even wondered about the adoption. What a perfect little actress. Yet Dave was nervous too. Now was his long awaited moment and he hoped to handle it correctly.

"Now I know why you've been upset, Amanda. Why didn't you talk to your mother or me? When did you find out about the project?"

"Last week, but I didn't want you to be mad at me. I'm eleven and I should be able to handle this all by myself."

"Oh no, Amanda. That's not how human beings work. We all need someone to talk to and help us out sometime. We all get hurt and depressed and need help. I'm sure you've heard your mom crying once in a while. Tears are good."

"How come you never cry, dad? I don't think I've seen Jonathon or Bryan cry either."

"I have cried enough times in my life. Our world says men and boys aren't supposed to cry, but they need to cry too, same as women. Bryan sometimes cries and so has Jonathon."

Jonathon has cried? Really? I can't believe that. Why?"

"I'm not sure but everybody cries sometime. It's nothing to be ashamed of and it can give you a good feeling of relief. Don't you feel better now that you've cried?"

Yes, I do, and other times I cry but I just don't let anybody see me, except maybe Muffin. I'm ashamed."

"You never have to be ashamed to cry Amanda. It just shows that you have feelings inside. And it's okay. Nobody here is going to be mad if you cry."

"Jonathon would laugh at me, especially if he knew why."

"Yeah, I'd have to agree with you. But this isn't about Jonathon; it's about you. What can we do to help you get through this project? What other things do you have to do?"

"I don't know all of it yet, but we have to bring in a baby picture next week, *which I do not have*. Christine said she was a real cute baby and has several nice pictures of herself. I don't have anything. It's like part of my life is missing, at least at the beginning. That makes me so sad and sometimes it makes me mad."

"That is sad and even I can't do anything about that. Would you like me to talk to Mrs. King about what else you could do?" Dave watched Amanda and suddenly saw and heard a new strength coming from her.

"That's okay dad. I've pretty much decided that I'll talk to Mrs. King myself. I'll offer her a few alternatives as to what else I could do. And I do have lots of pictures after I'm three years old. It's just that everyone in the school will know that I don't have anything from before I came to live with you and I find that very embarrassing. Sometimes it hurts when I think of it alone but before I could keep in inside. But now everyone will know."

Maturity was revealing itself in his little girl and Dave marveled about it even as a feeling of pride emerged over his body. The last statement caused a few more tears but Amanda was in control.

"I think that we should share this with your mother and Bryan and see what we can come up with together. I'm sure all of us together can think of something."

"What about Jonathon?"

"Maybe this is something Jonathon doesn't have to know about, unless you want to tell him."

"No thanks, I'd rather not. But does mom have to know about all of our conversation today? I've always kind of felt that I could talk to you and you'd understand some things that I feel inside of me. I don't think you can understand all my feelings, but just some of them. I love my mom but somehow I don't think she would understand like you do."

"Even I can't understand all the feelings that you have inside. Only you can. Okay, how about this? I think your mom and Bryan would be a big help for the project. But we don't have to tell them about our total conversation today. I think we can keep some secrets between you and me."

"It's okay if you tell mom I cried a little but not a lot, okay?"

"That would be just fine. And then we could get the benefit of many different ideas."

"Yeah, I think I would like that. Do you think the other kids will laugh at me if they find out I have nothing from the first three years of my life?"

"That I don't know Amanda, but I do know this. Your mom and me and Bryan won't laugh. Your good friends won't laugh. And you can't worry about what other people think. As you grow older you'll learn not to worry about other people. And we'll all help you with that. Okay?"

Amanda didn't say anything more but he watched her as a thoughtful expression covered her face and she shrugged her head up and down in agreement.

"And now I'm really hungry. Do you still fell like a Subway?" asked Dave.

"Absolutely, Subway it is."

Dave liked the fact that he had finally, although casually had his arm around his daughter and she was comfortable with it. She would occasionally give him a very quick hug in special circumstances but then she always backed away fast. Closeness was not usually part of her demeanor, although she wasn't truly distant either. Dave felt that she was occasionally a little more cuddly with her mother, but not enough to merit special mention. He always felt that she was a more reserved child, and that was okay. But today, she had proven that she could be comforted and enjoy it; she could enjoy the closeness of a caring individual and relish in the relief it gave her.

Janice, as expected, was very concerned about Amanda when she heard about the project.

"What can we do about the project? That must be hard for her to realize that there is nothing from the first years of her life? A heartbreaking fact when you first think about it."

"Yes, but Jan, I realized a few things about Amanda today. She might be a little girl but within that small body is a very strong spirit of one who will survive. Imagine holding back tears and play acting all these years because she thought she had to. That takes a lot of strength and I can't tell you the proud feeling I had when she started talking with these well-thought-out words and feelings. I really was amazed."

"She really is something, isn't she? And she doesn't even know it yet," added Janice.

Dave continued. "I'm anxious for tomorrow to see what ideas she comes up with about the project. I have a notion that we are going to see tons of strength as an offshoot of these last few days. You remember when we decided to adopt her and realized that we didn't know her background, and still don't for that matter, but we wondered what kind of a little girl she would be. I thought we'd have to coddle her and help her along so she could step out in life. Instead, I feel that she is teaching me."

"You make me want to cry," Jan said, as she stopped for a moment overcome with emotion. "I feel as though there's something I just don't quite get. You always did feel things deeper than I could, I know that. Yet I do know that she is very strong and will certainly stand tall in her life. "

"We all experience life in different ways and you notice things that I don't but together we can watch a little person, who started out with a tough load to carry mentally and emotionally grow into something to be proud of. I know inside she still has a lot of issues to overcome and will have more tough days in the future but right now I have no doubt that she is a survivor and will teach most of us some valuable lessons."

When Bryan was told about the project, he felt a lot of sadness. He knew Amanda was given a picture of a local mountain view from the orphanage that had been hanging in her room, but that was all she had. She treasured it and kept moving it around her bedroom trying to find the perfect spot. It got to be a family joke as to when you walked into Amanda's room where that picture would be. Yet it was the only treasure she had of her young days and he knew it was very important to her.

"You don't have to feel sorry for me Bryan. I've got a nice family here and I like you as my brother." Bryan realized now that Amanda was growing stronger every day. Sometimes he wondered how she did it.

"At least we get along good," Bryan commented with a half-smile.

"Other kids I know at school hate their brothers and sisters and avoid them just like Jonathon does with us."

Bryan could only nod in agreement. "But wouldn't it be nice if you did have a few pictures? Maybe they were accidentally lost or something." Bryan still thought that was a hard fact to accept.

"Maybe or maybe there weren't any. Maybe there never were any baby pictures of me Bryan."

He saw Amanda look back at him with a look of acceptance, and that told him a lot about her strength.

On Friday Mrs. King reminded everyone that they had to bring in a baby picture on Monday. Walking out of the classroom, Amanda realized that she would worry about this all weekend so she decided to talk to Mrs. King now. Turning around just before she reached the door, she walked right up to her desk. "Mrs. King, I have a problem."

Surprised at how blunt and to the point she was able to express herself, Amanda detached herself from her problem and pretended that she was talking about someone else.

"And what is your problem Amanda?"

Amanda waited as Mrs. King pushed her glasses to the top of her head and relaxed from her workload for a moment. Amanda liked her. She was a caring teacher who knew how to be fair and treated the children with respect. Many other teachers, Amanda felt, never quite got to that point.

"Well," said Amanda, looking quickly down at the floor as if it was magically interesting all of a sudden. This allowed her a moment before her next remark.

"You know that I'm adopted, right?"

When she had spoken her line, Amanda looked up quickly and directly into Mrs. King's brown eyes searching for a reaction. There wasn't any.

"No, I didn't know. But okay, you're adopted. What's the problem?"

"I don't have any pictures of myself as a baby. Not even one baby picture. I was adopted when I was three years old and I guess my first mom forgot to give them any pictures, so the orphanage didn't have any. I can't bring in a baby picture next week because I don't have any. What else can I do?"

She had stated her problem very calmly, without emotion, just as a matter of fact. She looked into Mrs. King's large brown eyes, trying to control her emotions. Amanda's long blonde hair that was always held back with a barrette was escaping from its usual position and landing over one eye so that it made it difficult to see all of her expression. Amanda was happy about that.

"Well, okay Amanda. Why don't you bring in the first picture that you have of yourself? I'm sure your parents took a lot of pictures when they first brought you home, how about one of those pictures?"

"Would that be acceptable? I was already three years old. Will I get marked down on my project for starting with a picture of an older person?"

"Absolutely not. That is not under your control. It's okay that you don't have a baby picture, just bring in one that you have."

Not wanting to drag out this discussion more than necessary, she was happy to hear Mrs. King add, "You've done very well Amanda. Your record is one of the best in this class."

"Thank you Mrs. King. I appreciate that," but Amanda wasn't yet finished with the discussion. "I was just wondering. Everyone in this class will know that I don't have any baby pictures. That's kind of embarrassing. Maybe I could find a baby picture of some else in my family and bring it in. Would that be okay? You would know, but no one else would have to know?"

"If that's what you prefer, that would be okay too. But maybe you might want to think about this. Everyone's life is different and that's why I want to have this time line for you students. I feel I can talk to you because you are a very mature eleven year old, Amanda. Okay, you don't have any baby pictures. So what? You are who you are right now?"

What would you do Mrs. King?"

Amanda never lost eye contact with Mrs. King. It had taken a lot of effort for her to look into her teacher's eyes and wait for a response.

"Whoa, that's a tough question. Let me think for a second." She heard Mrs. King think out loud, *What would I do in this situation?* Amanda liked the fact that Mrs. King took her question seriously and was taking time to answer her question. As Mrs. King looked over at her, Amanda remarked, "It's not an easy question to answer, is it?"

"No, it's not and honestly Amanda. I'm not sure what I would do? I just don't know. Anyway, you're the only person who can decide what is right for you. I will accept either picture from you and it will be just fine. Why don't you think about it yourself and then maybe talk about it with your mom and dad? I'm sorry that I can't really give you an answer but I'm just being honest. I would have to give it a lot of thought before I made a decision."

"Thanks for your help and understanding."

Although answering in her usual proper manner, Amanda was thankful that this entire conversation had been much easier than she imagined. The beginning was the most difficult part. She had to admit out loud to her teacher about being adopted. Those were words that she didn't say or even think of very much as she liked to pretend that she was born into her present family. Pretending didn't change the facts but it did ease the pain.

Before she left the classroom, Amanda turned at the

door and took one final glance at Mrs. King. She would have liked to know what was going through her mind.

From Mrs. King's side, she was beginning to get a glimpse of what Amanda was about. She remembered knowing two adopted children when she was growing up and she suddenly realized that they'd acted a lot like Amanda. They always tried to please everyone and it was so important that everyone approved of them. Suddenly, Mrs. King had a slight understanding of this child's behavior that always had to be so perfect. That's why Amanda was so concerned about being marked down if she brought in a picture of what she considered an "older person." Most people probably wouldn't consider a three year old an "older person," thought Mrs. King, stifling a laugh. Yet starting off with a mark down might mean that Amanda wouldn't get a perfect grade on her project, and Amanda almost always got A's.

Amanda went home by way of the park and as she sat on her favorite park bench alone this particular Friday she realized she felt calm. She was lost for words as to what happened when she was out joining with nature because it never ceased to soothe her spirit. Mrs. King had given her a choice and now she had a decision to make. She knew the choice of the picture was entirely hers.

Arriving home she luckily discovered that Jonathon was gone for the weekend, allowing the household a more peaceful environment and giving each person their own chance in the spotlight, a scene that seldom happened with Jonathon home. There was laughter, fun and even silliness within the walls of this home. Bryan could make the funniest faces and he and his dad were quite juvenile today entertaining everyone. Even Jan got quite silly this particular evening, but not Amanda. She still maintained her control. Yet she liked being included in this fun time even as a spectator, and she was learning to laugh more often and more sincerely.

After dinner, a time had been set aside to help Amanda with her project. Dave had told Janice and Amanda had told Bryan. Bryan's ideas were what Amanda expected.

"Just be who you are and don't make any excuses. You don't have to."

"That's what you think?" said Amanda.

"That's exactly what I think. Just be you Amanda. You're okay just the way you are."

As they retreated to the family room Amanda realized that this was her most favorite room, second only to her bedroom. It had comfortable furniture, a large TV set with all of the latest gadgets, a sectional sofa of soft light brown fabric with pillows that were basically deep burnt orange, dark green and subtle yellow in a pattern that was always confusing to everyone. It was a pattern of design and yet it wasn't; the lines of soft yellow all went in one direction and yet they didn't. A large bookcase framed one of the walls and it was filled to capacity. This was one room where you could sit comfortably and enjoy alone or with friends and tonight it was the meeting room to discuss Amanda's project.

"Okay, Amanda said that she has something to say." announced Dave.

"Yes, well I talked to Mrs. King today. I hadn't actually planned on talking to her before we had our meeting tonight but as I was walking out of the classroom it just felt right and she was all alone and available, so I turned around and just walked right up to her desk and told her."

"What did she say? What did you tell her?" asked Janice, excitedly.

"I just told Mrs. King the basic facts about me and she said that she didn't know I was adopted. I mentioned that I

88

was already three years old at the time and that I didn't have any baby pictures at all."

"Wow, I thought maybe you would want your father or me to talk to her. But you just decided to talk to her yourself, huh?" Amanda couldn't tell if her mother was disappointed or just surprised.

"It was kind of a spur of the moment decision but sometimes I do things best that way. Anyway, she gave me a choice. She said I could pick out any baby picture of anyone in the family like we'd talked about or just bring in a picture of myself at three years old. The choice is up to me and it doesn't matter what I decide."

"Oh well, I could find you lots of baby pictures of your cousins that you'd like. Why don't I go and do that right now?" Amanda was quite sure that her mom would be ready to jump to the rescue.

"Thanks mom but I'm not sure yet what I want to do. I'm still thinking. If I do pick out a baby picture, no one would know it wasn't me. Mrs. King said she would keep my secret. On the other hand, I could bring in a picture of myself at three years old and it would be acceptable but then everyone in school would know I didn't have any baby pictures and I wouldn't like that. So I don't know yet what I want to do, but I do want to think about it and weigh all the sides."

Amanda looked at her father as he sat on the long brown sofa with his arms folded, wondering what he thought. He had a habit of camouflaging his expressions to fool everyone and never gave a hint as to what was going on inside his mind. She searched his face for a moment, thinking that a purposeful stare might force him to display some clue, but it didn't happen. Actually she was quite sure that she couldn't rattle him, she just needed to try.

"I'll get some pictures together for you in case you decide to look at some of them and they could help you make up your mind." She knew her mom was just being who she was, a loving and caring mom.

"Thanks mom. That would probably be helpful. What do you think dad? What would you do?"

Amanda decided to throw out the challenge to her dad in words, since looks didn't do it. Dave smiled at her and they held a very long glance. She knew that she wouldn't get a definite answer out of him, not in words either. Dave just grinned and shrugged his rather large shoulders for a moment and finally declared that he would probably have to think about it too. Amanda smiled back at her dad with her own look that let him know she realized he knew the game she was playing but she also knew his game too.

"What would you do Bryan? Tell me again." Amanda needed to feel more solid about his opinion and his reasons why, although she was quite sure he hadn't changed his mind.

"It's hard to say. I'm not in your position and I don't really know how you feel inside. But for me, I think I would probably go with the three-year old picture. But who knows?"

Yeah, Bryan was staying at the same choice—he hadn't wavered.

"I would definitely just grab any baby picture. You'll probably be the only one without one and you won't like that," answered Janice. "Why open yourself up to other kids making nasty comments? Maybe there wouldn't be many but there are always some kids that love to tease, you know that. I'd just grab a baby picture and forget it."

Amanda already knew her mother's perspective without

having to ask her. She'd always take the easy and social way out of a situation. Bryan wasn't really a surprise to her but she had pictured him on the fence post going either way. Her dad was the puzzle but she suspected she knew his thoughts this time.

"Of course I have to make the decision this weekend. I'll let you know later."

Just then Muffin jumped on Amanda's lap as she always did when she was home. *What would Muffin do?* Amanda wondered. Amanda would have loved to know Muffin's thoughts on this subject, but of course, she couldn't tell her. However, she couldn't believe that Muffin would really care one way or another what other people thought.

From the beginning, Amanda was quite sure what she would do. A lot like her father in this way, she considered every angle, got some opinions from people she respected, and then she would decide. Although she hadn't officially asked for her mom's opinion, she cared about it. But Amanda already knew with a big degree of certainty what it would be.

Many brief and rare memories rushed through her mind this weekend. Some took her completely by surprise. Trying occasionally to remember the life at the orphanage was an exercise that Amanda had practiced most of her life. Usually no useful memories came back to her and her routine left her slightly depressed and frustrated. But today, when she wasn't even trying, she remembered that she had learned to evaluate the character of a few of the caretakers and usually knew what their reaction would be in certain situations. She couldn't explain the feeling, even to herself but there was a clouded memory disturbing her mentally. The director of the school seemed blurry in her mind now but she remembered an uneasiness when he was around. Then the feeling left, just as quickly as it appeared. Amanda was tremendously disappointed with this short recollection but she wrote it down immediately in her diary. She had many recollections listed there; some were quite specific and almost detailed while others were discouraging in their vagueness and haziness, yet with the passing of time all of the memories were creating a picture for her that got clearer with each new addition.

This weekend having many heavy thoughts on her mind, Amanda still managed to get to the park on her favorite bench with Muffin at her side and just basked in the sunlight that came through the tall trees. She did her best thinking on this particular bench, but, surprisingly enough, she didn't really need to come today except for her own enjoyment. She had made up her mind about the project. Yet, time alone with Muffin at the park always felt like a gift to her. Her mom and dad worried that she spent a lot of time alone and had only a few friends, but she was comfortable with herself and required time alone in her thoughts. She enjoyed drawing, was good at it, and brought her sketch pad to the park most of the time.

Amanda chose early Sunday evening when everyone was relaxed to inform them of her decision. It was also about three hours before Jonathon was due to come home.

"I'd like to tell you my decision if you have time."

"Okay, what did you decide?" asked Janice. Her mouth was half open, her eyes fixed on her daughter.

Her father's face was almost blank on purpose but Amanda had a feeling that he knew what she would choose.

"I'm going to bring a picture of me as a three year old. I think I would like to bring the one of me at Christmas with the decorated tree in the background. Would that be okay?"

"Oh sweetie, are you sure? You have several cousins

that have adorable baby pictures and it would be so much easier for you," said her mother.

Amanda was quite sure that her mom would leap to her defense again. Although she didn't need it, as she would stand alone this time, she loved her mom for her concern.

"Thank you mom. But I am very sure this is what I want to do."

She quickly looked over at her dad who just had a hint of a smile on his face. He understood. He hadn't said one word but Amanda knew.

"I've thought it over very carefully and weighed everything that we talked about on Friday. I've decided that I'm not going to hide behind anything. I am who I am and I'm proud of it. I have a good family that cares about me and just because you didn't get me until I was three years old, so what? Why should that matter to anyone else? It doesn't matter to us. I don't want someone else's baby picture up there; it wouldn't be me. It would be a lie and why should I have to lie about my life?"

"Oh that's so sweet, honey" said Janice as she rushed up and gave Amanda a big hug.

"But if you change your mind it would be okay too." Amanda just smiled; this was just her helpful mom.

"I won't be changing my mind mom, but thanks anyway. "

Looking over at her dad, Amanda realized that he hadn't even moved yet and still sat there with the same half-smile on his face. When he eventually stirred he just nodded in agreement and then said rather softly. "It's your decision Amanda, but I'm proud of you."

That was all her father said, but it was enough.

On Monday morning Amanda was nervous, yet eager and ready to face whatever was destined for her. *Who knows*, she thought, *maybe no one will notice or say anything.* She didn't really believe that, yet she knew that she could handle whatever anyone said and that pleased her more than anyone's words.

Entering Mrs. King's class with her picture of herself as a three-year old, she proudly put it up on the bulletin board and took her seat. As Mrs. King entered the room, she looked over at the display and then looked over at Amanda. Was that a wink she had seen from her teacher? She thought it might have been and that pleased her. Even though some might choose to question and exhibit unpleasant behavior, many others would understand. Why had she been so tender about her past?

As Mrs. King talked about the project and opened the class for questions, other topics came out that needed explanations. But then, Christine had to ask the question.

"How come Amanda doesn't have a baby picture? I thought it had to be a baby picture."

Nancy King looked directly at Amanda and asked, "Amanda, would you like to answer?"

"Yes thank you. I don't have any baby pictures of myself. This is the youngest picture of myself that I could find."

Christine found this admission very amusing and entertaining.

"You don't even have one baby picture. Oh my." Amanda watched as Christine looked around the classroom quickly, smirking, giggling and almost laughing out loud to see how many other children were as much amused as she was at this surprising turn of events. And there were some, but mostly Christine's clique. She was really enjoying herself as one could tell by her condescending tone of voice. So Amanda just waited.

"I didn't hear any answer, Amanda."

"I didn't hear a question, Christine."

"Oh, oh, well, umm, why wouldn't you have any baby pictures?" she said with an additional giggle as she cupped her hand over her mouth.

"I really don't know."

That was all Amanda said and then she stopped. She felt that was all she needed to say.

"Well, I don't understand," continued Christine.

"You don't have to understand," answered Amanda and with that last comment she was finished with the conversation and sat down.

"But I don't..." said Christine as she tried to continue and prolong her entertainment.

"I think Amanda answered all of your questions nicely and let's move on now," ordered Mrs. King.

That did cause a small part of the class to whisper but Amanda didn't let it affect her. She thought sadly that if Jonathon had been there he definitely would have been on that side of the room. Yet, she comfortably opened her book to the next study session and put this episode out of her mind. She could always do that when necessary.

As she prepared to leave the classroom Mrs. King called

her over.

"I think you handled that situation very well Amanda."

"I really didn't handle it at all," she answered, surprised at Mrs. King's compliment.

"Exactly. Have a nice day."

The day of the presentation gave Amanda some jitters but she did keep her emotions under control. She felt she was prepared and when her turn came she walked up to the front of the class proudly. She began by answering, in advance, any of the blunt questions that anyone might ask stating that this was the youngest picture of herself that was available and followed up immediately by stating that she especially liked this particular picture and remembered that she was quite happy when it was taken. She also produced a few other pictures of herself as a very young child before she gradually moved on to her school years. Almost all of her pictures showed a smiling, happy child, especially the ones depicting her with her father.

When her five minutes were finished, Amanda had covered the years from three to eleven, speaking about her good relationship with her parents and family, most especially her brother Bryan. She talked about her beautiful home and her nice bedroom which she loved as well as some fun camping trips her family had taken in Arizona, adding a mention of her prize possession—her dog Muffin. Amanda presented excellent pictures to depict the adventures in her life as well as an impressive charcoal drawing that she had made of her dog, Muffin.

Amanda received an "A" on her project.

CHAPTER IV

Amanda suddenly sat up in the middle of her bed crying in fear and confusion. Her dream had not completely faded and she was aware of some people around her, talking, whispering while attempting to touch her. She sat very still trying to make sense of this morbid nightmare as her skin still crawled with fright and her eyes didn't focus as quickly as she wanted. She took some very purposeful deep breaths and let them out slowly. Her mind told her body that her breathing would awaken her completely and then everything would be okay. And very slowly, her breathing did the task. Amanda kept breathing consciously so she didn't have to think of anything else and then gradually she relaxed her body which was still hunched up in fright.

Taking a chance, she allowed herself to lie back down on her pillow, since her night light assured her that no one else was in her room. She kept her body very still for a few minutes, not wanting to disturb her bed position and then as logic took over her mind she began to recall her dream.

"Sarah, Sarah, where are you?" asked a young voice.

Sarah was little, about three years old and she kept very still in her secret spot.

"Sarah, Sarah, I can't find you. Tell me where you are?"

Sarah was hiding from someone, sort of like a game, yet she was very nervous. She was under a stairway and kept very still so as not to be noticed.

In a sudden moment, two other children came in trying to find her. They were much older and not nearly as patient as the first one.

"Sarah, you're going to get in a lot of trouble if you don't come out right now."

The boy's voice was rough and scared her. Then she started crying and they heard her and came over to get her.

The boy tried pulling her out from behind the stairway but Sarah recoiled from his touch. Then he swore at her. Another person pushed him back and talked roughly to him. The first kind voice of the young girl came back and coaxed her out from behind the staircase. Taking her by the hand, Sarah followed along scared and shaky but afraid to say anything.

"You shouldn't run away like that all by yourself. We could lose you, you know?"

The young girl talked to her kindly and held her hand gently as she persuaded her to walk down a long corridor that had a bright light at the end of it. She could make out a stairway up ahead, halfway down this dimly lit hallway.

"We're going back upstairs and then I'll put you to bed again. This time you'll stay in bed right? Tomorrow we can play games but not tonight. Okay?"

Sarah began to cry and stopped walking. The gentle girl reminded her.

"Don't cry Sarah. Everything is okay. We'll keep you and take care of you but you have to be good. You will be *good and behave, right?"*

Sarah nodded her head up and down.

"Then don't cry, cause you can stay."

Just about the time they reached the end of the corridor and were about to step into the beautifully lit stairway, Amanda woke up.

Amanda was definitely shaken by the dream. This was only the third time in fifteen years that she had a dream about Sarah. It had dazed her completely. What did that name mean to her? She knew that this dream would have faded quickly from her memory, except for the name of Sarah. Why was she haunted by that name? She recorded the dream in her diary. Maybe some day the name Sarah would make sense to her, maybe not.

This fantasy brought to memory another dream when she had gone somewhere for a sleepover and was never allowed to return home. On several occasions she dreamt about the orphanage and even got a glimpse of her bedroom. Occasionally her birth mother appeared as a shadowy figure always irritatingly in the background as a veiled shape, but leading her to believe the possibility that her birth mom was somewhere close at hand watching over her.

Amanda was jolted awake by her alarm clock that she thought rang louder than usual this morning as it roused her out of her dream state. She moved quickly to get ready for school as she was presently in her 12th year at Mumford High with a good attendance record and an impeccable behavioral reputation. Heading downstairs she found her mom in the kitchen.

"Hi mom, what time are you going to get home today?"

"Usual time, why? Do you need me for something?"

"Oh no, just wondered. You know me, mom, I just like to know what's going on and what everyone is doing."

As Amanda prepared eggs and toast for herself, they chatted.

"Oh, okay. I think your dad gets in earlier today, if you need someone or you can call me anytime."

"Thanks, I'll be okay. The teachers are really piling on the homework so I'll probably be here studying when you get home."

"Don't you have your extra art class today? It's today, right?"

"Yeah, but they're scheduling us earlier now, which makes me happy. I'll have more time after school to get my studying done. I might occasionally get some free time too."

Darn, Amanda thought as she burnt her toast again. When would she learn? This toaster needed to be watched and everyone knew it. And now she would have to scrape the toast. She grumbled loudly enough that her mother heard.

"We've got to get a new toaster. It needs a caretaker all the time. I know you keep up with your studies, honey, and that's good, but you've got to take time for fun too. What are you doing this weekend?"

"Nicole and I will probably get together, maybe Jason too. There is a dance but I'm not crazy about dances, you know."

"Really? I used to love them. Get to meet and mingle with all the kids at school," teased Janice. Amanda remembered her mom describing her young years at high school and how she made all the dances that she could manage.

"Mom, you are definitely more sociable than I am."

Amanda always marveled how her mom loved all the social parts of life. As she finished her last burnt toast she realized that the jelly helped make it palatable. Actually she was surprised that she liked it that way.

"Okay, you don't have to be like me, but just enjoy your life okay?"

"Thanks mom, I've got to go now to get to school on time. Love you."

"Love you too sweetie."

Walking slowly through the corridors of Mumford High to her locker, Amanda remembered that up until her 10th Grade, Bryan had attended the same school and that felt like someone was always there for her. In her daydreaming state of mind today, she pretended she could still see him in the hallways.

"Heh little one, what class is capturing you now?"

"On my way to history, Mr. Burns is my teacher."

"Oh yeah, I liked him. I'm on my way to geometry and I don't think any teacher could make me like that."

"How long before class?" asked Amanda.

"About 15 minutes. Want to get something to eat?" asked Bryan. "Imagine you in Grade 10. Like it?"

"I do. Time moves quickly. Only yesterday you and I were still in middle school."

"Yeah, that's true, Bryan answered. "Middle school was fun and we were more carefree." Now we have to work harder for everything and so much more homework. But I'm working hard this semester to make sure that I'm well prepared for college. Before I always studied just enough to pass. I wasn't like you. You always pushed hard to get the best possible grades."

"You do very well, Bryan. What's your GPA?"

"Right now its 3.1, up from 2.7, but that's because I really started working. You were the smart one."

"I always need to do my best Bryan, you know that? I hate to make too many mistakes that's why I study all the time. Besides, I want to get into a good college someday."

"Trying to do your best in education that's good. But don't connect it with your self-worth kid, because you're okay even if you make mistakes sometimes, you know that don't you?"

"Bryan, you know me too well. Yeah, I always feel that I have to do good or else. I don't know, it's just the way I am."

For some vague reason, Amanda suddenly remembered when, at five or six years of age, she finally accepted the fact that her birth mom probably wouldn't ever come back. She gave up on her dream then but got scared because she had lost a big part of herself and felt that she had to become very strong and always do her best so other people would like her.

"Heh you two, just sharing family secrets?"

"Heh Ben, how's it going?"

Ben Sadler was a good friend for Bryan and he left the scene as quickly as he had arrived after stealing one French fry from each of them. He said, laughingly, he needed to be fair, as he rushed out quickly joining his brother as they both headed to their class totally on the other side of the school.

"You couldn't miss them being brothers. They're not twins but they sure seem like it to me."

Amanda smiled to herself knowing that she always looked at people's faces wondering if she would ever see a resemblance. It could be strangers on the street, people in churches or in shopping malls. There was always a hope of finding a familiarity of either physical traits or features.

The clatter of her locker door snapped Amanda back to the present as she grabbed some notes out of her locker. Her friend Sachi walked up presently calling her name.

"Amanda, ready for the history test?"

"Yeah, hope I do well."

"Oh Amanda, you always do well. Aren't you carrying an A in this class?"

"Yeah but it can go down rather quickly with just one quiz, right?" answered Amanda who was always concerned about grades.

"I think it would take more than one quiz but you'll be alright. I really studied hard last weekend and during this week but I don't feel secure about Chapter II."

"We've got 10 minutes, let's review. Okay?"

"Sure, that would help. Thanks."

And help it did as Sachi and Amanda later walked out of history class feeling confident about their performance on the test, grinning with an awareness between each other that only seventeen year old girls have.

Upon arriving home, Amanda was informed by her mom that they were invited to a baby shower for a cousin the next Sunday. Her mom felt that they should both attend if Amanda could clear her schedule for about four hours in the afternoon.

"You think I should go? I don't know anybody in that part of the family at all."

"I haven't seen them for a while either. But that's what happens. People get so busy with their lives, that showers, weddings and funerals seem to be the only time we see them. I'd really like you to come with me."

"Okay, mom. I'll go with you."

Amanda didn't really want to go to a baby shower but her mother would never be aware of that fact. She had a difficult time seeing pregnant women, like neighbors and some of her parents' friends because they all seemed to keep their babies. It was nice to see people excited about having their first baby because that was an exciting time in their lives. But for Amanda, she didn't like the old memories that still caused her pain.

That Sunday morning found Amanda wandering aimlessly about the house nervous yet determined to make the best of this day. Her mom was very excited about seeing some of the family and from her point of view it was understandable. Being edgy was unusual for her so she worked hard to settle down and not ruin her mother's day. Some day she hoped to look forward to these events with happy anticipation.

Upon arrival she noticed that there was an air of jubilance about the party house and although Amanda got caught up in the excitement at the beginning, dark shadows brought unwanted reminders of her birth mother. She was able to separate the two situations logically and that did help her keep the happy exterior that she wanted to show everyone. She made the required complimentary comments about all the nice presents and was an agreeable guest. A solid hour of pretending had an affect on Amanda. Even her mother noticed something.

"Amanda, are you feeling okay? You look rather pale."

"I'm fine. Just a little warm. I think I'd like to go outside for a few moments, if that's okay?"

"Okay, but don't wander off. You don't know this area."

The look of concern on her mother's face at that moment registered with Amanda. Her mom probably knew that she was fine but most likely thought that she was just a little bored. Amanda would have been surprised if her mom had even the slightest clue of what was really bothering her. As she stepped out the side door a little voice called out to her.

"Heh want to play ball with us?"

There were two young children from the party house playing in the back yard. That appealed to Amanda and she played with them for a few minutes.

"You catch that ball very well. What your name?"

"I'm Beth. Who are you?"

"I'm Amanda."

"Well, Amanda, you catch a ball very well too."

"Thanks, I appreciate that."

Beth giggled all the five minutes that she played with

her in the back yard. Anything made her laugh and it was nice to see such a happy, carefree child.

"And who is your friend here?" Amanda asked.

"I'm Emily and I'm four."

Noticing quickly that Beth felt ignored, Amanda asked, "How old are you Beth?"

"I'm five, but I can't go out of the yard."

"I think that's a good idea, don't you?"

"Yeah my mom thinks that's a good idea."

And Beth giggled again. It was nice to get into the carefree attitude of the little ones. They really knew how to enjoy the happiness of any moment. Then, as if fate had demanded it, Emily began to cry.

"Why are you crying Emily?" Beth asked.

"I can't see my mom. Where is she Beth?"

"Your mom is inside the house at the party, remember?" Beth reminded Emily. That reassurance didn't seem to calm her down at all.

"Let's all go inside to find your mom, okay Emily?" offered Amanda.

Emily, still in tears, went into the house with the others and when her mom reappeared, there was a quick return of happiness for the little one.

Amanda began wondering how she had reacted when they'd first brought her to the orphanage. She was not yet two years old and she must have cried and cried when her mom never came back. Amanda shivered as she thought of the fear that must have gone through her little body and the feeling of despair as time stretched on and her mom never returned. She saw the difference that the connection with a trusted mom made on a little child. Emily stopped crying immediately when her mom appeared and started having fun again.

On the way home, Janice kept the conversation interesting and moving. She told Amanda about some of the family members that she had never met. The mood was light with some fun stories and some sad stories keeping Amanda interested and updating her about some of her kinfolk, if only by adoption. Then her mom mentioned how everyone had changed so much and seemed different than she remembered. Then she added, "Don't you think so Amanda?"

"Mom I don't even know them so I can't remember them. I can't know if they've changed or not."

"Oh, that's right," answered her mom and then looking at Amanda and realizing the silliness of her statement, she started to laugh and kept laughing and got Amanda laughing and soon they both had tears in their eyes. At one point her mom pulled off to the side of the road for a moment. That was one of the first good laughs they'd had together in a long time.

"I can't believe I can't stop laughing. It just wasn't that funny. What's the matter with me?" commented her mom.

"Nothing is the matter with you or else the same is the matter with me."

And with that they both started to laugh again and couldn't mention the party any more or they went into totally silly laughter. Arriving home they were met by Dave at the door who asked, "How was the party?"

Looking at each other they went into hysterical laughter again and when they tried to explain to Dave the simple statement that started it all he simply said, "I don't get it."

"We don't either."

And off they were laughing again until Dave just shook his head and said, "Women," and walked out of the room shaking his head.

That night at bedtime Amanda remembered an automobile accident that involved the entire family when she was only nine years old. It wasn't anyone's fault really; the roads were very icy in the cold February weather and two cars skidded equally into each other. Amanda's father and another man were talking.

"We were really lucky; no one was hurt. These roads are so bad tonight."

"I'm glad both of our families are okay. How many kids do you have?"

"Three," answered Amanda's father. "And everyone's safe. Thank God."

"We're okay too. Scared my two little ones and the baby cried. But we're okay."

Just then a little boy about three came running up to his dad, and grabbed onto his hand and just looked up at his protector.

"Yep this is my boy. He looks just like me, don't you think?"

"He sure does. You couldn't miss it."

Inwardly Amanda had a dreadful awakening. She thought that she possibly could have died that day without ever finding out who she was. She vowed at that moment that one day, she would search for her other identity. There were others out there who looked like her and who matched her genes and she had to find out who they were. That incident had happened several years ago, but Amanda always remembered the vow she made to herself.

Memories popped up frequently in Amanda's mind, sometimes at the most inopportune times. Although she would have liked to be able to turn them off at will, she realized that they were valuable in moving her forward.

The next week at school, she bumped into Christine Biston. Actually Christine had found out where Amanda's locker was and searched her out. She hadn't seen her very often in high school because of different classes but in Grade 12 they had two classes together. She always seemed to be with Linda Sims and Nancy Netlaw, which made Amanda realize that they hadn't truly left each other's side since middle school.

"Hi Amanda, what's new with you?" asked Christine.

"Not much. And you?" Amanda almost hated adding that last part because she knew that she would be in for a long dissertation of Christine's latest activities. But politeness didn't allow her to be rude.

"Well, I'm preparing for the senior prom, we all are," said Christine as Amanda noticed her including her friends in this discussion. Amanda only smiled for her response.

"Amanda, aren't you planning to go?" Linda asked.

Amanda noticed, rather uncomfortably, that all three of them were staring directly into her face for any hidden message that she may have. She didn't want to disappoint their need for gossip.

"I haven't decided yet. I'm thinking about it."

"Surely you've been asked, haven't you? We all have dates." added Christine smugly.

"Yes, I've been asked but I'm still deciding."

"Why? Everyone wants to go," said Linda. "I know a few girls who would do anything to go but haven't been asked yet. That is just the saddest thing, don't you think?"

Amanda again only smiled her reply. The prom wasn't the biggest thing on her mind. She could understand some of the excitement but she couldn't accept depression or a feeling of failure at not going, possibly only mild disappointment if you missed your objective. Just then another gal whose name she didn't even know came up and said "Hi Amanda, you're definitely going to the prom right?"

"Don't know yet," was all she answered.

The new face looked amazed as she turned to the famous trio and announced, "Amanda's been asked by Todd Jones. And I also heard that someone else asked you too but I'm not sure who that was." Todd Jones was a popular football player and considered quite a catch.

"I've heard the same rumor too; I'll have to look into it." Amanda's face was quite noncommittal and she chose that moment to shut her locker and excuse herself for her next class.

"Who else asked you Amanda?" asked Christine, not missing a beat.

Amanda tactfully avoided the question. "I simply haven't made up my mind yet about the prom." Amanda kept her answers short as she didn't like having her personal life thrown out there right in front of her locker. She recoiled inside somewhat, but outwardly she faced the challenge in a rather satisfied manner.

Although Christine and Linda, as well as Nancy walked along with her for a few moments, they didn't get another statement from her lips. Amanda usually had some serious thoughts on her mind but she had to admit that she enjoyed the games she played with this trio and their friends. They had to know everything about everybody all the time. Amanda knew that they had questioned other people about her but found out very little. And so, it was almost fun giving them little snippets and leave them begging for more.

"Heh Amanda, don't you miss us in your classes?" She turned to see Nathan Jones and Tim Booth, whom she felt was a good change of scenery from the trio and their friends. These guys were silly and rather comical most of the time, but they were real people. And Amanda realized that she did miss their humor.

"Yes, I do miss the both of you. How are you doing? I don't see you guys very much?"

"Nathan said, We're doing good and we'll graduate on time because we have been the core of good behavior here at high school."

"That is after we had a difficult start and were forced to learn the rules quickly," added Tim. Amanda had to laugh as she looked at two facial expressions that were almost angelic.

"You were always quiet, Amanda, but you were nice and not snobby like so many of these other girls here. We do miss you. Besides you were one of the few that always laughed at our jokes."

"Well, they were pretty funny, sometimes downright silly. But I think even Mrs. King had a soft spot for the both of you." Amanda added a slight wink with that last comment.

"Don't overdo it Amanda, or we won't think you're sincere."

Amanda did notice that the trio had left as soon as she began talking to Nathan and Tim. Apparently, these two were not considered good rumor material. She realized that she liked talking to these two friends because they said everything right to your face and looked at the funny side of life, which Amanda needed. Just then the blast of the bell sounded giving five minutes to get into your seats for class and everyone scattered, including Amanda.

During that same week at school Amanda was scheduled to have one of her extra meetings with her counselor, which was required in the 12th Grade.

"I'm not sure what I want to do with my life. I love to draw but I don't want to be an architect. What else can I do? I wish I knew exactly what I want to do. John Simons in my English class knows he is going to be an athletic director and Shelly Anderson wants to be a nurse. I wish I knew for sure."

"You could do a lot of things with your art. You really are quite good. How about portraits, or graphics or illustrations. Have you ever thought about that?"

Linda Tyson, her school counselor, completely startled Amanda as she hadn't realized she had drifted so totally inside her own world. She shifted in her chair to give herself a moment to get back to the present.

"I guess I haven't thought about anything but architecture and I don't think I would like to do that. I like nice buildings but they're so impersonal. Illustrations, maybe that would be better. And portraits, umm, I'll think about that."

"I'll give you some literature to read but I also want you to realize that during your first few years at college, you do have to take your basic classes. During that time you may realize other options. Have you decided for sure where you are going? I understand that you've been accepted by more than one college."

"I was thinking of Alma. It has a smaller campus that I like and it does have some good art programs. But then I like the community college near home and it also has a good curriculum in art. I'm not sure yet."

"You also need to consider if it would be a desire of yours to get out on your own more or if staying at home, at least for another two years would be preferable."

"Yeah, I know. That is something I must decide too. There are just so many decisions to make." Amanda felt her body tense with frustration.

"These decisions don't have to be made this week. You seem to have so much on your mind lately. Anything I can help with?"

Amanda's survival instincts seemed to jump into gear immediately. How did she know she had things on her mind? Did it show that much? She quickly put a smile on her face and sat up in a stronger position.

"Don't worry Amanda? All you seniors have a lot on your mind. Are you going to the prom?"

Oh, the prom. Here it came again. That subject was actually beginning to be slightly distasteful for her. She knew that most girls and boys were so excited about going to the prom they actually bored her on the subject. All the girls talked about was what they would wear, the color of their dress, where they would get their hair and nails done. And the boys were excited about their tuxedos and which girls they would take to show off. How boring.

"Most students really look forward to the prom. It is a celebration of all the work you've done and accomplished before you go on to the next phase of your life. Aren't you excited about going?" asked Linda.

Why did Ms. Tyson ask her about the prom? Did she know about her indecision? She really liked her counselor but lately felt that she was getting too close to some very personal subjects that Amanda didn't want to talk about.

"I probably should be excited but honestly, I don't think I have as much enthusiasm as I should have. I'm not sure why."

"You are always so serious about everything. You study hard and you focus very well and you've accomplished so much here at Mumford. Maybe you could just relax, let go and have some fun."

"I think I do have fun. At least I feel like I do."

"I think you do enjoy a lot of the activities here. But I'm talking about just forgetting about any little or big problems in your life and just have fun for one evening, the evening of the prom."

"I know. I'm still trying to decide. Maybe I will go."

"Think about it. You might really enjoy it."

"I will think about it."

As Amanda got up and left her office, Linda watched

her and wondered again what she was really all about. She began checking her dossier as she added her new notes and realized that she had never caused any problems during her entire time at high school. She was a very agreeable girl with a pleasing personality. That was what bothered her about Amanda. She was always pleasing everybody all the time and she had never slipped up as far as she knew. Even her sessions on the debate team which usually produced some very strained relationships for some, didn't create any enemies for her.

Linda knew Amanda had other concerns deep inside that never seemed to surface. Whenever she even hinted at something more private, Amanda's entire demeanor changed and the color of her face definitely paled as she changed the subject immediately. Linda always waited for an opening to discuss personal thoughts with Amanda, but that time never came. Linda could never get much conversation out of her. She felt that Amanda would be a very interesting person to know, if she ever let anyone on that journey.

At home that night, talking to Muffin, Amanda opened up her feelings.

"That counselor of mine is nice but she is always trying to find out things that she would probably just repeat to mom and dad. I know they are friends so I have to be very careful. You actually still know me the best, Muffin and that's okay with me. Maybe Bryan knows me a little but he's okay."

Muffin just sat there listening to her favorite human and tilting her head. With her dog by her side Amanda could be put ideas together that helped her. And when she was at home, Muffin was always by her side.

There was knock on her door. It was Bryan who came home on a few days' leave from college because of a teachers' seminar. Amanda was so happy to see him. Fate must just know when to bring him around.

"Heh little sister. I think you're getting taller."

"I am but so are you. How tall are you?"

"I think I'm 5'10" and so, at twenty-years old, I could get one or two more inches into this body. I hope so, 6' is my goal.

"Well, Bryan, I am now just a tad over 5' but I don't think I'll make my goal of 5'6" but I should get at least a couple more inches, don't you think? At least a few more."

"Oh yeah, you're only 17, you'll grow some more yet."

"You're too sensitive to mention about my genes because I don't know what my parents were but I guess I'll know when I stop growing," added Amanda thoughtfully.

"You're great at any height, little sister."

"I really need you around sometimes. I miss you at high school. Did you know Sachi moved a little while ago?

"No, when?"

"About two months ago, right in the middle of grade 12. But her father got transferred and that was it."

"She was your best friend."

"Yeah, but we write and sometimes we call. I want to keep in touch with her." Amanda felt a special connection with Sachi because she had moved here from Japan only five years ago. She missed her relatives back home and felt a void and emptiness in her life, that Amanda could relate to.

"You going to the prom?" asked Bryan bluntly. Amanda

searched his face quickly for a motive, but then she remembered; this was Bryan.

"Everybody asks that. Mom and dad, my counselor, other kids at school and now you.

"Just a question, honest."

"I know. I did get asked by two guys. Both are nice, but I just don't know if I want to go."

"Why not? The prom is lot of fun. I had a real good time." Amanda laughed because she knew that Bryan was almost as sociable as his mother but in a more subtle way.

Amanda liked to dance, but socializing with a lot people in the same large room at the same time was not appealing to an introvert like herself. And, of course, her only close friend, Sachi wouldn't be there. She wasn't totally negative about the prom but she felt that seventeen and eighteen year old girls and boys seemed very silly at times. They weren't concerned about the same things she was and finding a common ground was difficult.

"I'm not sure. I'm not that excited about it. I remember how much you looked forward to it but I don't feel like that. Maybe I'm just different."

"That's okay. Not everybody goes. Look at Muffin, she still sits right next to you no matter where you are. You two have a forever bond."

"Yes, she's great and very smart you know. She helped me figure out some math problems the other night. She's sort of taken your place."

Bryan laughed, "I guess it's okay to be replaced by a dog, since she's cute.

"Mom really wants me to go to the prom. She asks me every day."

"Well, you know mom. But she loves you and she means well."

"I know, I know," answered Amanda in an almost irritated way which was opposite to her true nature.

Bryan was looking at her caringly and she suspected he knew she had inner concerns. He was always sensitive to her feelings, too sensitive to ask her questions when he was sure she was not ready to talk. He was a nice brother and she knew he loved her. Amanda wished she could feel her family's love for her but mostly she couldn't. She also knew she loved them intellectually but she couldn't feel it in her heart. How she wished she could turn a key inside her soul and add in some information. She didn't think anyone suspected her disloyalty, except her dad. It was hard to fool him and although they played a game mentally with each other that Amanda enjoyed, it wasn't a game that she ever planned to lose. Whenever the game got a little dangerous, Amanda would back off and she knew by the look on her dad's face that he understood.

"You know what Amanda? I'm studying better these days and I learned that from my little sister. My GPA is now 3.4 and I'm working hard to hold it. Aren't you proud of me?"

"Absolutely. You're smart, you just have to apply yourself?"

"What about you? Do you still have a perfect GPA?"

"I'm not sure Bryan. I got a B+ on a math test so I might have brought it down a little. We'll see. How long are you home for?"

"I have to be back Monday but my friend Ben is having his birthday party on Saturday so I want to go to that."

"How's Ben doing?"

"About the same as me. We are from the same tree we think."

"You're so silly."

"I know. That's what makes life fun. Oh, Oh, did you hear that? That's mom calling us for dinner. I'll beat you down."

Life was great when Bryan was home but eventually he had to go back to school and so did Amanda. As she got closer to graduation all of the questions that remained somewhat dormant inside of her for years came closer to the surface again and more frequently. She wished she could erase them like chalk on a blackboard, but her mind didn't operate that way. The more she tried to ignore the questions the more they reminded her that they wanted answers.

Arriving home from school on the last Thursday before Easter Amanda went to do homework but realized she was just too tired. She lay across her bed with textbooks, notebooks and papers creating a pattern of their own as she again fell into her dream world. Another dream worth remembering crossed her mind.

"Do you want a donut and a glass of milk?"

Amanda looked at the woman and felt that they actually looked alike. She knew immediately that this was her birth mom.

"If you come and sit by me, I'll brush your beautiful hair. It's getting so long these days."

As she looked to her right she realized that there was another little girl sitting on the sofa next to her. She had very light blonde hair, unlike Amanda's dark blonde hair but she resembled this little girl and had a warm feeling when she thought about her. They actually held hands at one point and smiled at each other.

She awoke slowly with sadness and despair as she knew that she had finally found her birth family but upon awakening realized that it was only a dream. Being back in reality she realized that inside she thought so much about her beginnings that her unconscious mind was creating a picture for her early life, not necessarily a true picture but more like something helping her to adjust to a heavy load.

"Amanda, time for dinner! Are you awake Amanda?"

"Yes I'll be right down mom."

Getting control of herself she shook her head and headed to the bathroom to splash cool water on her face. She did have faith in a higher being and many times felt a strange kind of love settling around her. When she thought of this special love she could actually feel it and this always helped her when she was experiencing difficult moments. It was too bad she mused that you couldn't file away these warm and informative dreams and pull them back at full strength and awareness whenever she needed. But she couldn't. Finally, feeling refreshed and somehow pleasantly satisfied, she took a deep breath and headed downstairs for dinner.

CHAPTER V

"Some days the harder I try to concentrate, the more it escapes me," mused Dave Peterson as he slowly and very deliberately pushed his chair away from his computer. He had his chin in his hand as he usually did when he was considering an important option and wanted to make the best decision. His second gesture was to put his hand through his thick dark hair as that helped him concentrate. He was a thinker and considered all sides of a situation for days before coming to a conclusion.

It was almost eerie as he listened to the stillness of the house and realized there were natural sounds in his home. The tranquility itself seemed to have its own resonance. He couldn't seem to take advantage of the current serenity as it strangely had more irritation than having activity around him. Something was deep in his thoughts today and although it hadn't focused yet, it was making itself known. As he rolled his chair away from the computer he remembered that one of the wheels of the chair was rather lopsided and he'd always meant to fix it, but never did. To be honest, he rather liked it this way, as perfection sometimes bothered him more than the little reminders that life was just as it should be, sometimes very good and sometimes needing improvement.

"I really like what we did with this house. It suits all of us like part of our personality." They had converted this little room into a place where Dave could have some quiet

time necessary to do his work. It wasn't a big room but it was his very own and decorated in a masculine design which appealed to his sense of style. He was satisfied with his life but there were times he just needed to be alone. Today was a special treat with no one at home and he could walk around and openly express his thoughts.

"Dave, Dave, where are you?"

Jan appeared just as Dave was thinking about their college days. They had made an immediate connection and no matter that most of their family and friends believed that they were too opposite for a long-term relationship, Dave and Janice proved them wrong. Yes, they were different, quite different. Dave was a thinker and needed to challenge himself from all sides while Janice was quite capable of making instant decisions and if they proved wrong at the beginning, she would adjust and readjust until everything worked. Dave was social enough and liked people yet he never worried much what they thought about his life. He could go an entire weekend being around his own house, not seeing friends or extended family and be content.

Janice, on the other hand, was always very concerned about other people's opinions and spent many hours worrying about how neighbors and family would react to her. Dave would usually watch Janice worry and wonder why she cared so much and Janice would watch Dave being carefree and wonder how he could be that way. Yet their relationship worked. It seemed they kept each other within imaginary boundaries. Janice was a 5'7" blonde whose sweet demeanor appealed to Dave's protective instinct; Dave was 6'2," muscular, strong and gave Janice the secure feeling she desired.

"I'm in "the room," he answered, as that was the name he affectionately called his place. As she came in "the room," he knew immediately that she needed help but didn't want to ask. "You need help, right?"

"Yeah, especially with the heavy bags, okay?" Her smile told him that she appreciated not having to ask.

"Are they still in the car?" Dave knew they were but was trying to continue the conversation. "Okay, be right back."

He put the groceries on the counter and together they put them away as they chatted about the children.

"I don't think Amanda will go to her prom. I wish she would," said Janice.

"Maybe that's not her thing. She knows she could go if she wanted. We've got to realize that she is different in certain ways. Not different really, but her own person."

"Yeah, I know you're right. I just hope later on she's not sorry that she didn't go." Dave felt Jan's anxiety and wondered how he could ease her concerns.

"Jan, if she is sorry later, that will only be too bad. She'll handle it. Don't worry so much."

Dave smiled as he looked at Jan because he always teased her about worrying so much. It was written all over her face. She smiled at him and added. "You're right. I do worry too much about the children."

"It's hard not to worry a little but I think we did a good job raising them and that's all we can do. Now it's up to them to learn, right?" Dave felt strongly that it was now time for the children to take charge of their own lives, within boundaries.

After dinner, and with the children out for the evening, Jan and Dave settled in the family room, relaxing and enjoying the comfort of their home. Dave watched as Jan walked over and looked at the pictures that they had set up of the children. They had a section for each child at different ages, in different activities and occasional reminiscing was fun and pleasurable. Dave walked up behind her and together they relived a few years.

"Dave, look at this one. It was the first year that Bryan played hockey. He loved it but I don't think we have one picture of him without a bruise that doesn't show. He looks so damaged it's hard to believe he was having fun, but he did."

"Yeah, even when he was in a lot of pain, he would smile and say, 'I'm having so much fun.' I'm not sure whom he was trying to convince." Dave had to let out a loud laugh remembering this little kid with blood oozing out of his forehead, tears running down his cheeks claiming he was having a wonderful time.

"Oh, and look here at Amanda," said Jan, "she was so proud that her father went with her to the art show at school. Look at that smile. She was in the top ten and the youngest one in the art show. Remember how proud we were. And she was so pleased with herself."

"I especially remember that particular time because she held my hand all the time we walked around the displays. She didn't always do that, but she wanted to be close that night. How old was she there?"

"I think she was around seven, right? She was in Grade 2," added Jan and Dave saw her turn to him for confirmation.

"I think so, she was young." Dave truly enjoyed being at the school program with Amanda. For that particular night they had to ask one parent only and she had asked him, her father. He had trouble containing his happiness, which he usually kept inside very well.

"I remember how happy you were, hon. She was usually more affectionate with me in those days, but she chose you and admit it, you were thrilled about it."

"Yeah, I was. I admit it. It was like a breakthrough for the two of us. You know, I'm glad we created this wall in here. I love looking at these pictures."

As they walked further along, they came upon Jonathon's area and both were very quiet for a few moments. Jan spoke first.

"You know when I look at Jonathon's pictures, there is such a difference between the first year and later on. Look at those happy smiles before the age of one. It's amazing. He was a very happy and contented baby at first."

This moment began a discussion on Jonathon and a forever mind searching puzzle about their first child.

"How do you think Jonathon is doing? Have you seen any positive changes in him?" Dave was really talking to himself out loud.

"That is hard to say right now, isn't it?" Jan commented. "I mean, he's gone away to college and seldom comes home. He does call occasionally and usually is considerably more pleasant on the phone than he is at home. Remember how happy we were when we first had Jonathon? He was such a happy and carefree baby and normal on all of the scales. He didn't seem to get angry or pout very much—he was just pure joy."

"He was. He definitely was and he stayed that way until he got sick just after one and then his personality really changed."

"Yeah but he was such a pleasure before then."

Dave recalled the past. Those were very tough days. I know you remember, that malady that was never diagnosed. I still believe that if we could only have found out what it was, maybe that would have made a difference."

"Sure, at first they thought it was an extreme allergic reaction to food or clothing but then that was rejected for a possible virus that kept recurring. And then that was proved wrong. Those were difficult days." Dave saw Jan shake her head slowly in frustration.

"Yeah, Jan, rushing him to the hospital for breathing problems and fevers that wouldn't stop. Then they actually quarantined him,. remember that, and we couldn't even see him. Sure you would remember, what am I thinking? He was so scared and so were we. I still think his anger problems started there because he never again was the happy, carefree and trusting child we knew."

Just then the doorbell rang and surprised them both. "Are you expecting anyone Jan?"

"No, I can't imagine. I'll go see who it is."

Dave was still lost in his world about Jonathon as he heard familiar voices and laughter coming from the kitchen area. Then, as he turned around, he was face to face with his brother Bill.

"Hi there Dave. We were in the area and we had to stop in. Ha, Ha. That sounds like a line I've heard before. Hope this isn't inconvenient?"

"God, no, I'm glad to see you. What are you up to tonight?"

"Emily wanted to get over here to Target for some stuff and we were so close that we decided to swing over here and say Hi. How are you doing?"

"I'm good. Trying to finish up a few projects but got sidetracked."

Just then, Emily and Jan appeared with coffee and snacks and they all settled down to visit for a while. Dave was the first to speak, "We're getting real reminiscent here a few minutes ago and took a trip back into the young lives of our children. Did you ever finish your wall of pictures Bill? I know you started one."

"Don't say that too loud. Emily's sitting right here."

"Ha, that's my fault too," Emily added. "Of course we only have two kids but we did ours a lot like yours. I liked the style, so I copied it. But every time I walk by, my eye catches one of the pictures and I daydream. Don't always have the time to do it. But I like it, I really do."

"Is Bryan around? I wanted to task him about the prom. That kid of yours gets around and just knows all the information worth telling." Dave saw Emily get excited for little tidbits of information which soon turned to disappointment as she learned Bryan was out for the evening.

"Your Harry went too." said Dave. "Did they go together or not? I know they talked about it. But those kids change their minds so often."

"I'm not sure," Emily thought, "except that Harry took Cindy—she's a real nice girl that he's been dating for a while. It's quite dramatic for them right now since they aren't going to the same college." Dave enjoyed the enthusiasm that Emily brought into conversations. "Where is Bryan going to college?"

"He's going to Michigan State? Yeah, I was surprised too," joked Jan, "but he can list a lot of the reasons why that's the best choice for him. Imagine I'll have two kids in college this fall." Dave laughed as he heard Jan say that. They used to talk about when the children were grown and that had seemed like such a long time ago. But the time had now arrived.

"How's Jonathon these days? Bryan we know is doing good, but then, he always did. Amanda is fine; she's always been such a sweetie. But you guys, always worried so much about Jonathon? How is he doing?"

Dave saw Jan was about to speak so he just sat back. "He seems to be doing quite well. He's got good grades, has some friends at college. But he's Jonathon, you know. We're never sure what's going on inside of him. That hasn't changed. But he seems happy enough."

"Does he come home often?" Bill asked, "I know you've gone up to the college to visit him a few times."

"Yeah, but not as often as we'd like. Although," Dave added, "he calls a lot more lately than he used to."

"I really hope that Harry is like that. I can see that kid coming home every weekend. Mine needs to get more on his own, you know. Maybe he could take some lessons from Jonathon."

"Amanda's got two more years of high school. I don't know where she wants to go to college. But she will probably study some form of art. And your little Amy, she's in grade eight now. Won't be long for her either," added Jan.

"Don't remind me," Emily added. "All she talks about is that she can't wait to get into college far away and be able to do what she wants without parents around. But then she's fourteen. What can I say.?

"She's a lot of fun, isn't she?" Jan added.

"She's had a few problems with authority both at home and at school in the past year," Emily said, "but all in all, she's no worse than the rest of them I hope."

Bill looked a little more concerned as he added, "I guess the kids were more fun when they were little. But they all have their traits developing. She's quite demanding and now with Harry going off to college, she believes that she will call all of the shots. I think we have a fun year ahead of us."

"Her counselor has called us a few times. We have some concern but she is within the boundaries we've been told. But she is more difficult than Harry was. She seems to get very angry at times, mostly in the last few years."

"Fourteen is a tough age, especially nowadays. And of course, boys and girls are not to be compared." Dave saw Bill wink at him with that last remark hoping to lighten up the situation.

"I don't remember Amanda being any problem for you at fourteen or ever," said Emily. "She was such a nice, agreeable child."

"Yes, but she keeps a lot inside," mentioned Dave. "Sometimes I think she could stand with causing a little trouble here and there to know what it's like. Seriously though all kids are so different. We just have to give the situation our best guess."

"If you don't mind…" Emily paused for a moment before she continued. Dave could see she was a little upset. "I remember when Jonathon used to get angry. Did you ever find a way to handle it?"

True concern was revealed to Dave in Emily's face and possibly exposed the real reason for their visit. Very understandable and something he could sympathize with. Dave offered a few cautionary remarks. "I'm not sure that

Jonathon's anger has disappeared—I believe that as he got older he just kept it inside. Jan and I hope that he will someday discover the cause and work it out. You know how long we searched for help, but the answer didn't come. But it sounds that Amy is getting into the rebellious teenager age. It's difficult but with teacher and counselors keeping tabs on her, she'll be okay. Tell me, how are her grades? And does she get along okay with the two of you?

"Her grades are good and she's a fairly smart kid, right Bill? That helps. She has a few friends that I like but some others that I don't like at all. But you can't tell her no about anything right now. I think they're trouble for her. Not a new story for parents, is it? That's when we have some fights. But they're a lot of times that she acts okay. Other times, she's a terror. I just thought I'd ask because you raised a girl."

"Sure," Jan said, "I understand. We certainly talked to a lot of people about Jonathon. You two included. Remember, our story wore very thin at times. Is she in a lot of activities? That did seem to help Jonathon get a good focus. And he did seem to do better outside our home. Sad, isn't it?"

"I guess all parents have to figure out certain things." Bill continued in a slightly different mood. Dave noticed that he got more jovial. "Sometimes when I take her out with me, she laughs a lot and relaxes some. But you know, Jan, you brought up a real good point. She had tried out for basketball last year and didn't make it. She was pretty upset about that. She does have a few activities, but maybe not enough. Heh Emily, we should try to get her into more stuff. Not let her have too much spare time. Keep her really busy. I like that idea."

"Me too." Emily added. "She does cheerleading but not much else. She loves sports but isn't that good at it. Maybe that's part of it."

"You know," Bill said, "I think we get better ideas from the two of you than from some shrinks. Sometimes they can help, but sometimes they can make matters worse."

Dave added with humor, "I think this is called 'brainstorming.' It can work. But I would get that kid into a lot of physical stuff because I always suspected that all of the exercise and physical activities that Jonathon got into actually had helped him to keep his anger under control. Just a thought. What about roller skating? That's a good activity and they can even take lessons and do competition. Amanda loves it and still goes whenever she can. She usually comes home feeling she had a good workout. "

"Yeah, I like that and certain worth a try."

Dave asked, "Can we do some brainstorming on this engineering project I've got going in the other room? It might help. No, no, just kidding." And the rest of the evening turned to a more jovial mood but the atmosphere never left the four parents out of their responsibility realm. After his brother left, Dave and Jan returned to their previous conversation. Dave began with, "Jonathon's anger started so much younger than Emily's. I remember she was a sweet little girl even two years ago at that summer picnic we had. She was about twelve then, right?"

"Yeah, and she always seemed to get along well with the kids. You know," Jan continued, "it's so important to be popular and when she didn't make that basketball team I remember Emily telling me how devastated she was at the time. But maybe it affected her more than they thought. And now, who knows how she feels inside. Oh, the more I talk the more I don't know. Life is so complicated for these kids. But I do hope they try and get her into something. There are so many things and maybe she just needs to feel better about herself."

"Isn't it funny Jan, but with all those therapists and psychiatrists we took Jonathon to see, I didn't remember anything relevant that could help my brother. But then, Jonathon was a different situation. I think Amy is just showing the teenage years, at least I hope so. With Jonathon, well ..."

"I know, I know" Jan continued, "you and I always believed that those hospital stays must have had something to do with the change in his personality, but no one would even listen to us. I think Emily was okay as a little one and didn't have anything similar experiences happen, at least not that I can remember. Harry is more like Bryan. Funny, isn't it? Those two just breezed through life's disappointments. But then, children are all different, just like adults. "

"I always worried about Jonathon's physical health, but I was also worried about how these isolating hospital stays were affecting him. Honestly, Jan, the nurses said that he kept crying and crying for his mommy and daddy. Why wouldn't they let us see him?"

"Everyone said it would just take time and he would be back to normal. But that didn't happen. They were wrong Dave, they were wrong. And he was already three years old at that time. I have another thought that sometimes crosses my path. I wonder how Bryan would have handled all that. Maybe the same, maybe different. I just can't help but wonder."

"And when we brought Bryan home, well that wasn't much fun. Poor Bryan, he got put in the background too much for a new baby. But we had our hands full with Jonathon. So much jealousy and worry that he would hurt his little brother. I went out of my way to spend more time with Jonathon, but it didn't work. He was still very mad at me."

"Jan, do you remember that motel fire that they had in

Toronto when Jonathon was about eight years old? He and I and Bryan were together watching the report on TV and it was so tragic and sad. They showed the gory details, as they usually do and I remember that Bryan had tears in his eyes. He was only six at the time and he kept saying, 'So sad dad, so sad.' And it was very sad. I had tears too. But Jonathon said, 'Gees dad, why should I care? I don't even know those people. There nothing to me.' He wasn't kidding. He had absolutely no empathy within himself."

"Bryan learned to be the smart one, wasn't he Dave? He just stayed out of Jonathon's his way. After all, he had tried everything to be friends with his big brother and just kept getting rejected. Finally he gave up. But he was a happy little boy when Amanda came, wasn't he?"

"Yeah, he sure was. He had finally found a friend in this house."

The telephone rang and it was one of Jan's friends. She started a fairly long conversation leaving Dave to his own thoughts. Then she came back with a question.

"Dave, do you want to go out to dinner with Jack and Adrian Saturday night. They are celebrating something and thought the Vader's Lounge would be fun. I'd like to go, how about you?"

"Sure, I'd like that but I work until 6:00 PM this Saturday. We could meet them about 7:30 or 8:00.

"Yeah, they talked about a late dinner. Okay, I'll confirm with them. She's holding so I'll be a few minutes."

Dave laughed as he realized that as far as Jan was concerned, there was no such thing as a short phone call. But the Filmers were good people who lived a block away. They had met many years ago at a neighborhood watch meeting and connected ever since. Their children had gone to the same schools and while the women loved to talk and be social, Bill was more like himself, short on words but long on patience.

Left alone, Dave went into his own thoughts for a while and remembered a few occasions several years ago, when none of the children had realized that he was around. He heard first-hand some of Jonathon's bullying behavior and was secretly shocked and saddened that his son couldn't even find sympathy for a little orphan girl who was now his sister. Dave knew back then that Jonathon was becoming a master manipulator and needed to be watched.

"You know, I'm the first child here, so I have all of the rights. You're just living here because my mom and dad felt sorry for you."

"I've been here two years and they are my mom and dad now too, isn't that right Bryan?"

"Bryan doesn't know anything; I'm the smart one. They aren't really your mom and dad. You're just lucky they felt sorry for you."

"She really is my sister and she belongs here, so knock it off Jonathon. I don't know why you like to try and make Amanda cry."

"She's such a baby. She knows our parents aren't really her mom and dad. Are you too stupid to know it too?"

"I believe that she is really my sister and I'm glad. Mom and dad wouldn't agree with you."

"You better not tell them what I said or I can make it really miserable for both of you."

Finally, Jonathon realized that Amanda hadn't said anything for a while. So he started on her again.

"Just remember what I said. You're not really my sister and you'll never be. I would have been happier if you never came here. What do you think of that?"

Dave could see from his hidden spot that Amanda was coloring in her book and didn't even bother to look up or answer Jonathon. Although she'd answered him at the beginning of his attack, she apparently realized that if she didn't answer him, he finally got bored and found something else to do. Even when the remarks got extremely hurtful and nasty, Amanda just kept coloring which Dave thought was a clever way to attack the problem. It seemed to work because soon Jonathon got bored and moved on.

As Dave watched Jonathon walk away in his smug and bold manner, he couldn't imagine why he had to be so mean most of the time. Bryan and Amanda didn't threaten him and they were never mean to him. Dave didn't understand. He felt the answer had to lie somewhere inside Jonathon's head and heart, and hoped someday a clue would surface.

Dave remembered after witnessing that particular example of unbelievable meanness for no apparent reason, he'd been totally frustrated. He wanted to run in and pick up Amanda and give her a big hug and tell her he was her forever dad. But he couldn't. He had unintentionally walked into the hallway and overheard a conversation that he wasn't mean to hear. So he kept quiet and wondered anew what possessed Jonathon to be so mean.

"I'm sorry Jonathon is so mean to you. I don't know what wrong with him," said Bryan.

"He's mean to you a lot too. And you're nice to him."

"Listen Amanda, I'm real glad you're here and I'm glad that I have a nice sister that I can talk to and play with."

"I know that Bryan. The only time Jonathon is nice to

me is when mom and dad are around. And I don't care what he says, they are my mom and dad too."

"They sure are and they really love you. We're lucky we have each other."

"Yeah Bryan. Do you want to color with me? I have some more blank pages here."

"Sure and you really do good coloring with the lines. I saw a little thing you did the other day. Remember when you said you were going to draw Donald Duck? It looked really good to me."

"You really think so? I didn't think it was that good, but I'm going to practice a lot because I like to draw. Okay, here are your crayons and I'm going to finish my picture."

With that, Dave decided to walk into the room and make his presence known. Both Bryan and Amanda smiled and looked up saying, "Hi Dad." With that line, Amanda looked over at Bryan with an unexpressed thought that they both understood. It said, "He's my dad too."

Dave remembered that scene like it had happened yesterday and unfortunately he had witnessed plenty more as Jonathon grew older. Not wanting to upset Janice, he kept some of this information to himself and luckily, Jonathon presently got very busy with outside activities and he was gone a lot of the time. It was always determined with Jonathon's unpredictable behavior that he would never baby-sit his two younger siblings. Possibly he could find in his world of outside activities something to soften his heart and repair whatever had happened to him inside.

Dave snapped his mind back to the present as Jan entered the room. Apparently the Vader's Lounge had completely redecorated because of a new owner and Adrian felt that they would all love it.

"What are they celebrating anyway? I don't think its their wedding anniversary."

"No," said Jan as she looked down shyly for a moment, "they are celebrating the fact that all of their kids are now officially out of the house."

"Oh my God," Dave laughed, "really that has to be Adrian's idea."

"I think she said they both thought of it. And then Adrian added, that they just needed something to celebrate occasionally."

"That's something I can agree with Jan. We should celebrate when all of our kids are on their own and leading good lives. That I'd love to celebrate. I think Bill and Emily could enjoy something like that. What do you think?"

"I thought so too so I mentioned it to Adrian and she said sure, to bring them along. She remembered them from the picnic we had last summer."

"I guess you and I still think alike," said Dave as he settled back into his comfortable spot on the couch.

As Bryan and Amanda grew older, Dave realized they avoided Jonathon as best they could and that seemed to be the best solution for all involved. Although basically an introvert, Amanda was slowly becoming more self assured. It wasn't always easy knowing what was on her mind, but she freely shared what she felt was important. Jonathon got more introspective as the years continued and although his parents suspected the anger was still there, he kept it well under control. Bryan was the only child who was an open book. He had a kind heart and an approachable personality and it seemed everyone wanted to have him around. But it was obvious that he kept his soft spot for Amanda. Dave like to see the solid bond they had created continue.

With Amanda starting at the same high school, many of the junior and senior girls tried to get friendly with her because of Bryan. Sometimes Bryan would seek out Amanda for lunch and their conversations were sometimes revealing.

"Don't you sometimes wish that Jonathon wanted to be friends with us?" asked Amanda looking in the distance as if she was actually seeing something visible.

"Yeah, I think possibly we missed out by not having a relationship with him, but he just didn't want one. We tried even now but he still doesn't. You know Amanda, he missed out a lot by not being friends with us too."

"I know, in a perfect world we would have all been friends and lived happily ever after, right?"

"Do you think that you've had a good life with us? I often wonder."

"Yes, I do. I love mom and dad and you. I've had a good life here. It's too bad about Jonathon but you never know. He could change in the future and maybe we'll all have a better relationship someday."

"Amanda, Amanda. You are the eternal optimist. Just like mom. I wish that were true but I still wonder what bothered him. Why was he always so angry with us?"

"I wonder too. It's hard to understand. Guess you and I have a lot to learn about people. I've got to run now. Got my math class and after your help last night I should do well on my test. Thanks Big Brother."

"Good luck," said Bryan laughing. He always laughed when she called him Big Brother. He liked it.

The next few years saw more maturing in Amanda and the graduating prom came and went without Amanda attending. Bryan needed to understand why.

"Why did you decide not to go? You never said. I know you got asked."

"That was a tough one for me. I had to keep asking myself what I really wanted to do, know what I mean? I wasn't going just because everyone else was going or because I "should" go. I thought about it quietly to myself."

"I know you never liked big parties. Was that it?"

"Partly, but remember in Grade 6 when I had to make that time line in Mrs. King's class, well you and dad and mom as well as Mrs. King gave me some good advice. I remember you telling me that I should never make an excuse for myself. I took that to mean my decisions too. If I am not hurting anyone else then it is okay to be me, does that make sense?"

"Yes, of course it does. You do what's best for you."

"A few girls tried to make me believe that there was something wrong with me if I didn't want to go. I decided that there wasn't anything wrong with me at all, I just didn't care much for going to the prom."

"Not everyone wants the same things. It would be a boring world if we did. If you didn't want to go, then I'm glad you didn't go. It is a good feeling to be who you are in spite of contrary opinions, isn't it?"

"Yes it is Bryan. And my decision felt right back then and it feels right today. I'm not sorry I didn't go Actually I still had a date with Todd Jones, you know that football player. He and I and another couple went out to dinner at Carmen's Restaurant. It's the one in the Lackawanna Station Hotel and we danced to a band they had in the lounge. We'd been friends for a while and realized we had a lot in common."

"Oh yeah, I remember him. He's a nice guy."

"Well, because he was a football player, everyone said that he had to go to the prom and as time got closer, he did ask me if I wanted to go. I was surprised because he always has a lot of girls around him—gees, he was so popular. But he told me that kind of popularity was phony. Everyone liked him because he was good at football. By Grade 12, he was getting tired of it. So when I told him I didn't want to go to the prom he admitted that he didn't really want to go either. We talked a few more times and he asked me if I would consider going out to dinner with him and a few friends and we all decided that felt better for us. I had a real good time. I'm glad I celebrated in my own way.

"That's sounds good. I'm glad you had fun. Mom was afraid you'd be disappointed later if you didn't go, but that's mom."

"Actually I think mom finally understood and since I was going out to dinner with some friends, she felt that was a celebration too and she relaxed a little." Amanda smiled at that remark as they both always wanted to pacify mom, who they felt was just doing her job.

"I've learned an important fact too Amanda. It is amazing to me how many people care what I do. I usually don't care that much what other people are doing. It is good to discover this early, don't you think?"

"Yeah, good to be able to be who you are."

"I've like our conversations over the years. They've been good for me."

"Me too." said Amanda

Early Wednesday evening, Janice surprised Dave with the news that Jonathon had called and wanted to come home for a visit this weekend. Dave felt his nerves slightly tense up.

"Did he say why?"

"Nope, just said he wanted to come home this weekend. I asked him if school was okay and he said yes. He emphasized that there was nothing wrong but he just wanted to come home this weekend. He sounded different."

"How different?"

"Not sure if I can put this into words, but his tone of voice was changed and somehow he didn't seem as sure of himself, know what I mean? You know how Jonathon usually talks fast and somewhat pushy because he always knows exactly what he wants?"

"Oh yeah, that's one thing Jonathon has never lost. He mellowed a little but ..."

"Well, Dave, that was kind of missing today. And I did talk to him for about five minutes."

"He didn't say why he wanted to come home?"

"Nope, just that he would be here for a visit this weekend. Strange, huh?"

"Yeah, Jonathon was always the kind that would let you know if something was wrong. Probably everything is okay. Yet we were the ones always begging him to come and visit. We always had to go up there and have dinner with him just to see him. This is interesting."

"Yeah. Our Jonathon actually wants to visit us for an entire weekend. It isn't exams or anything, so he does have time. Still, it's not the norm. Honey, did you get your project done?"

"Not all of it—I'll finish it later."

That was when Amanda chose to turn up with her usual "Hi Mom, Hi Dad" routine. She still showed a happy face to the world even when her inside feelings weren't in agreement. Since Bryan was home this week they decided to tell the children at dinner about Jonathon's visit.

"You're kidding right?" said Bryan. "Jonathon never comes for a visit and never for the entire weekend. Did he say what's wrong?"

"He said nothing was wrong," answered Janice. "He just wants to come home for the weekend."

"Hmm, I wonder why," was all that Amanda could manage. Her thoughtful demeanor mirrored what her father was thinking.

"I know it does seem unusual," said Dave, "and maybe he has something on his mind or maybe not. He might just need to be away from college life for a weekend."

"I doubt that, since he loves to be away at school and we know he loves the social and athletic life there," Bryan added. "I do think it's strange," added Bryan.

Most of Jonathon's friends only came home for holiday weekends or family gatherings, so without even his friends here there was no real reason for him to want to come home.

"He does still live here, at least technically," Dave offered mischievously.

"Oh yes, of course," replied Bryan laughing, "but you have to admit a visit suddenly is rather unusual."

"I can't go as far to say that he misses all of us so tremendously that he just had to come home," Janice added, "but maybe a time away..." as her voice trailed off and no words came to finish the sentence.

"It will be good to see him and I sure hope he is happy to see me." That was Amanda, who had hope.

Bryan offered, "We'll just take our cues from him when he arrives, give him some space and see what he has to say. There probably is a reason and I for one would like to know what it is, if Jonathon is talking me."

And with that final comment from Bryan, the conversation turned to other topics and family business such as grades in school, extra school activities, and dad's presentation.

When Friday arrived, Jonathon made it home in time for dinner. Pulling into the driveway he thought the house looked different to him for some reason and although he hadn't been home for over three months there was another explanation. Jonathon felt different inside lately, although he couldn't yet put a definition to his newfound sensitivity. He knew he had changed inside and he knew partly why, but he had a long road yet to go. He wasn't ready to talk to his family about the modifications to his behavior and personality, because to be truthful, he didn't know totally what was happening to him. He was at the beginning of a major makeover that was completely unforeseen yet welcomed and his inside feelings were constantly demanding answers that were just beginning to appear.

Jonathon's changed demeanor was immediately noticed from the moment he walked in the door. From his mom's first glance, he knew she observed that he was dressed nicer. He used to dress the same as his attitude, which showed that he didn't care about anyone and his natural sloppiness was inviting anyone to question his choice of clothes. Now, he took pride in his appearance, and although he wouldn't be considered well dressed, there was a certain attempt at neatness that wasn't there before. At six feet he knew he had a basically rugged appearance, but his new attire made him more approachable. Walking in by the side door gave him entrance from the kitchen area and allowed him a partial view of the family room. His mom was in her usual apron just finishing up the meal when he arrived, and the rest of the house was vacant.

"Hi mom, how are you doing?" he asked in a rather friendly manner which he noticed was not lost on her.

Janice turned to look at Jonathon to see if he was being smart or not, which would have been his usual entrance. Met with a curious glance, Jonathon did his best to keep a pleasant look on his face, contradicting his usual sneer, as he waited for her reply.

"Hi Jonathon," answered Janice slowly, "hope you had a good drive here. Traffic can be tough about this time."

"Yeah, it was okay; it wasn't bad at all."

He knew he was known for his rather disagreeable encounters with his mother that usually preempted an argument. That was when he talked to her at all. When he first left for college he still had a lot of anger and rage and although it was mostly under control in his later teen years, his unpleasant personality traits that he exhibited mainly for his family and most especially for his mom, were always expected.

He realized suddenly that his mom was probably a little nervous without his dad around to remind him to show respect. He trod carefully until she could realize that there was a change in his attitude as the entrance with a pleasant smile showed. He decided to sit down at the kitchen table for a few moments and show some pleasantries which were long overdue.

"What are we having for dinner?"

"Pork chops, mashed potatoes and corn. What are you used to eating?"

"Anything available," said Jonathon with an attempt at humor. "But your menu sounds good to me. I'm kind of hungry."

"It will be a little while yet, I'm afraid. Your father doesn't get home from work until after 5:00 so we don't usually eat until 5:30." He noticed his mother watching his face curiously.

"That'll be just fine. How are things with you?" With his last question he noticed a look of total confusion coming from his mom as he knew she'd be surprised if he showed any concern for her at all.

"I'm okay. I hope everything is good with you. We were surprised that you came home this weekend," added Janice carefully.

"Yeah, it's been a while since I've been home. Maybe too long."

"Well, we're always happy to see you." said his mom as she smiled kindly at him. Jonathon thought to himself, *"I can't imagine why, but I guess that was spoken like a true mom."*

Just about this time Amanda came in the side door and stopped in her tracks when she saw Jonathon. He knew that she always had to guess what his attitude would be toward her, and because it was usually nasty, she cleverly just stayed out of his way. This time there was a rather uncomfortable pause before anyone spoke. He saw Amanda attempt a small smile so finally he spoke.

"Hi," was all he could manage but he did use a friendly tone of voice.

"Hi," was all Amanda answered but her smile got wider.

"I see you cut your hair."

"Yeah, I like it shorter right now," answered Amanda suspiciously.

"Looks nice," he said and with that he told his mom that he would like to take a shower before dinner and slowly left the room.

Amanda looked at her mom in shock and noticed that she was surprised too. First of all, Jonathon never noticed anything about her, yet he had given her a compliment. And he was actually sitting in the kitchen talking nicely to this mother. Amanda was quite slow to respond. Peeking around the corner to be absolutely sure that Jonathon couldn't hear them, Amanda commented.

"Mom, is he okay?"

"Yeah I think so, honey."

"He actually gave me a compliment about my hair. First, I can't even believe that he actually noticed anything about me, but then he gave me a compliment. Did you hear it?"

"Yes, wasn't that nice?"

"Yes, but really strange, huh? He seems different. I wonder what's going on with him? Something is definitely different about him."

"I don't know Amanda. "I Just hope everything is okay. What are you doing tonight?"

"I might go roller skating with Betty. Her parents said they would drive us and pick us up. Actually, they will probably go skating themselves. Okay, with you?"

"Skating isn't over until midnight, right? Sure, as long as you are with Betty and her parents. That should be fun."

"Think I'll start my homework before dinner. I have tons this weekend."

"Dinner will be a little late but I'll call you."

"Yes, call me. I wouldn't want to miss dinner," added Amanda with a slight giggle. She always had a good appetite.

Getting back to her own thoughts while finishing up dinner, Janice had to admit to a big change in Jonathon. She knew at that moment that there was a definite reason he had come home for the weekend. Then when Janice's worrisome heart started to bother her because she felt catastrophic thoughts from every direction and she imagined the very worst scenarios. The Jonathon she had just witnessed was a Jonathon that she'd loved to have known. More importantly, this was not her Jonathon whose constant anger and lack of empathy hadn't made anyone's life in this household pleasant or peaceful for a very long time. She almost broke into a sweat with chaos-like ideas crossing her mind as Dave entered the door.

"Hi honey, I see that Jonathon already made it home."

"Yeah," replied Janice and then made a sign for Dave to be quiet for a moment while she checked to see if the shower was still running. It was.

"And he really seems different. He was nice to me and actually complimented Amanda on her hair."

"Really?"

"Yeah, and his smug and smart attitude was missing too. Of course I just talked to him for a few minutes but he actually sat down at the kitchen table and talked before he went to take a shower."

Janice was talking rather low but the expression on her face left no doubt to Dave that she was absolutely shocked at what she had seen and heard.

"That would seem like a normal kid, but not usually the way Jonathon acts."

"That's right. It not normal for Jonathon. But I sure liked it."

"Maybe he is maturing some. He had mellowed a little before he left but was basically the same. Who knows? Maybe he had a course in family psychology and picked up a few good pointers."

As Jan watched Dave, she knew that he was trying to keep the situation light but she knew him well. He would make his own decision after he talked to Jonathon himself and had time to study the situation.

"Don't know if it will last or not," added Jan "but he was very nice."

Just then the bathroom door opened and Janice and Dave quickly changed their conversation as to what was happening on the weekend. Dave retreated to clean up before dinner when he saw Jonathon in the hallway.

"Hi dad, bet everyone is surprised I came home for the

weekend?"

"Yeah, somewhat. You don't do it very often. Everything okay?"

"Yep everything's okay. Just needed some time to myself. That can be kind of hard at college, you know. Think I'll grab a quick nap before dinner. That drive home was rather hectic. See ya later."

"Okay," answered Dave as he watched Jonathon walk away to his bedroom.

There was no doubt that Jonathon's attitude was different. His personality was definitely warmer and his tone was pleasant. Dave had never been able to say that before. What had happened to him? It didn't seem like he was very open to talking about things, but something had happened. As usual, he would have to wait and take his cue from his son, but Dave was good at waiting.

Dinner was probably one of the most pleasant experiences this family had together in a very long time.

"Mom I love your pork chops. Guess I picked a good weekend to come home."

"Yeah you did but then mom's cooking is always good," said Bryan with a grin winking at his mom.

"I don't think I can handle all these compliments. Amanda fixed the mashed potatoes. Aren't they good? She has a special something she does but won't tell anyone."

Amanda grinned and she looked around the table.

"The mashed potatoes are very good. What do you do Amanda?" asked Jonathon.

"It's my secret. Remember I used to try all kinds of different things because I always thought mashed potatoes could be boring. Sometimes everyone hated them. But I found this certain something that I do now and everyone likes them. Maybe someday I'll tell, but not tonight."

"I hope it's not something too weird," teased Bryan. "You've gotten very inventive since you took that science class."

"No," laughed Amanda, "it's just something normal from the kitchen."

"Where's your picture these days?" teased Bryan.

Amanda did get very red in the face on this one as she answered. "Bryan, I've had my picture in the same place for six months. I think I finally found the right spot."

"I'm only teasing. It's your room; it's your little locale away from the rest of the world. You can do what you want." But Bryan used a teasing tone of voice.

"I know. I know." Amanda answered, recovering slightly from her embarrassment of always moving that picture around her room.

"How's the food at college?" asked Amada.

"Not nearly this good so my roommate and I eat a lot of pizza and subs. We really like subs."

"Amanda and I love subs, right honey?" said Dave. "We try to get there as often as we can."

"What's your favorite?" Jonathon asked both of them.

"I like the sizzling steak and I always get that one. You do too sometimes don't you Amanda?"

"Yes, I think I like them all but I my favorite is the veggie with honey mustard dressing. That is soooo good."

And on the dinner conversation went with everyone talking and adding details. At one point, Jonathon actually encouraged Bryan to finish a story and asked a few questions so he would tell more. Janice also caught Jonathon watching her very carefully a few times, enough to make her feel uncomfortable. She wondered if she might have imagined it. Amanda told one joke and Jonathon really laughed at it and told her how great it was.

Then Janice offered dessert, to which Jonathon quickly replied. "I have to pass on that until later. This was one of the best meals I've had in a long time."

At that point almost everyone paused for a moment and unintentionally looked directly at Jonathon who suddenly looked down in nervous shyness. Janice was the first to recover and said there would be dessert later for anyone who wanted some.

Later, after dinner, everybody left to do their thing. Amanda went skating and Bryan went to a friend's house. Janice and Dave would be home for the evening and Jonathon chose to stay with them in the family room and after an ordinary conversation about school, work, family business, weddings, funerals, politics, etc. a very quiet few moments spread over the three minds relaxing in this room. After a long silence elapsed, Jonathon spoke. "I know you wonder why I came home this weekend, don't you?"

"Well," answered Dave, "It is a bit unusual for you but this is your home and so…"

"First of all, nothing is wrong. My school is fine. I'm doing well, no problems, nothing is wrong."

"That's good." added Janice. Jonathon felt that it was

good sitting here with his mom and dad having a conversation. He didn't remember that ever happening before.

"I'm sure you have probably noticed a change in me. Maybe not a big one, but you have noticed something different about me, right?"

Jonathon sat and waited looking first at his mom and then at his dad, anxiously listening for some reaction. He felt his mom would be the first to speak as long periods of silence usually made her uncomfortable. And he was right.

"Well, you are dressing nicer, like you have more pride in yourself. You look good."

"Thanks. Yeah, I actually try to dress better; it makes me feel good. What about you dad? Have you noticed a change in me?"

"I think that we've had one of the nicest evenings here in a long time. I'm sure Amanda and Bryan enjoyed you too. You don't seem to have as much anger toward them or us and, you seem more peaceful. I'm not sure if that is what you are asking, but that is what I've noticed."

Jonathon paused for quite a while before he continued. His parents just sat there in silence, giving him a chance to collect his thoughts. This had been a very hard conversation for him. A few times, he had a lump in his throat, but after a moment or two, he gathered new strength to continue.

"I'm not trying to be mysterious here, but I'm not ready to talk about a lot of things because I don't know a lot of things at this time. But I did accidentally run into some information that has helped me a lot. I've been seeing a counselor for a while now and I'm beginning to understand a few reaons for my anger. I just wanted you to know what I was doing. Again, I'm not being secretive but right now my mind is still trying to understand certain areas of my life that need improving. I wanted to tell you first because I know how hard you both tried to get me some help. And no one seemed to be able to help me. I appreciate what you both tried to do and I don't blame either one of you. I wanted to make sure you knew that. All that anger that I was showing wasn't only on the outside. I was angry on the inside and most of the time and I didn't even know why. Medicine, science, psychology doesn't know everything and being in college for a few years now I realize more and more that we have to help ourselves too."

"What can you tell us and is there anything we can do?" asked Dave.

"No, but thanks. I knew you would be supportive as I start this journey and when I can put these complicated thoughts and ideas into a logical focus, I'll tell you more. I'm thinking I might possibly change my major, dad or at least add another minor to my degree. I'm thinking of studying psychology. I've already taken two extra course last semester. And I wanted to tell you."

That surprised both his parents, yet Jonathon realized they were so happy about the positive change in him they didn't mind.

"I hope you're not disappointed dad. I haven't yet made up my mind for sure. Psychology might just be a minor and I may still make engineering my major."

"Jonathon, you do what you want. You are the one who will be working the rest of your life and it should be in a career that you really love and will satisfy you."

"We want you to be happy in your career, whatever it is," added Jan.

"I'm kind of at a crossroad and have to find out more

about who I am and what I want before I can make that decision. But I've learned a lot about my anger and where I think it came from and we'll discuss it more in the future, okay?"

"Absolutely," said Dave. "I'm glad you're feeling better about yourself. Whenever you're ready to talk, we'll be here to listen."

"Thanks mom and dad. I'm kind of tired now and I'm going to turn in early. See you in the morning."

After Jonathon left, Janice and Dave just sat there looking at each other for a while. Whatever was happening was a positive and welcomed change. It seemed that Jonathon had found a clue that had escaped Dave and Janice in all their years of searching. Both had their own thoughts and feelings that they were trying to digest and Janice had only one question for Dave.

"Was I imagining it or was Jonathon staring at me during dinner? It felt to me that he was seeing me for the first time or something. Was it just me?"

"No, I noticed it too and that faraway look on his face, well, it caught my attention."

Neither talked anymore. It wasn't necessary. All of the anguish, pain and fear that they had spent worry about Jonathon's behavior was lessened considerably. The solution would now come from Jonathon himself, while he exhibited thoughtfulness, maturity and determination to solve the problem of his anger troubles.

Back in his room that night, Jonathon let out a sign of relief. When he'd first entered the house, it had hurt to see his mom uncomfortable around him. But he had caused it with his anger over the years. And his sister was extremely timid with him for no small reason. Bryan was still easygoing and could go along with any situation. But his dad was more reflective and that was probably good. He realized that he had a lot of bridges to repair, yet his worry about whether anyone would even want to have him around was solved in a positive way. Everyone had been congenial to him. He could tell by the tone of both his mom and dad during their conversation tonight, that he didn't even have to ask for their forgiveness. They still loved him. He felt he owed Amanda, the biggest apology, yet she had acted quite friendly with him. That showed she had a good heart. But he had a long way to go; his road to travel had just begun.

The weekend passed quickly and the new Jonathon, although introspective at times, was pleasant to be around. When it was time for him to leave, even Bryan and Amanda were sad to see him go.

"How is Lindsey Holloway? Do you still see her?" asked his mom.

A strange and satisfying look came across Jonathon's face. He had met Lindsey the first day of college in English class and they became instant friends. His mom always hoped something might develop between them after they had met her on a visit to the college. She was levelheaded with a good sense or humor, often seeing the light side of life while adding in some dry wit. She was good for Jonathon.

"Yes, I see her all the time. But we're just good friends ma," added Jonathon with a wink before he continued.

"That's all it is but we'll always be good friends. Her family lives about forty miles from the university and sometimes we get a group and get over there for Friday evening dinner. Her family is very nice."

"That's lovely. Have a safe trip and call when you can."

"Yes I will, Thanks."

As all four of them stood by watching and waving to Jonathon as he left, a pleasant atmosphere settled on them and for the first time ever, all four knew they would miss him and wished he could have stayed longer.

CHAPTER VI

"I sure made it back to school in record time," thought Jonathon. The highways had been very kind to him and luckily the traffic was either ahead or behind him but nevertheless, he got there in less than two hours. That was great for a Sunday evening, which usually added more and more traffic congestion the closer you got to the college town. He was doing better mentally and emotionally since his talk with his mom and dad. Many of his school decisions were in the future, but his more pressing need was a development that had happened so accidentally that looking back on his luck, he was amazed at his good fortune. Sometimes he laughed at the word accident or coincidence. Some people believed that there were no coincidences or accidents and he was beginning to agree more and more with that theory.

After unpacking he decided to rest before he finished his homework and his mind started thinking back to the amazing happenstance that occurred just three months ago. Startled at his own thoughts, he realized that it was less than three months ago that his new direction had occurred. In his healing heart, it seemed so much longer. Surprising him to awareness, his roommate entered the dorm room.

"Heh Jonathon, how's it going? Have a nice visit home?"

"Yeah I did, how was your weekend Bill?"

His roommate Bill Eaton was a good guy who liked to tease in a light-hearted way and have fun on weekends, but he was very serious about his college work, excelling in several subjects. They got along quite well and conferred often being in the same engineering program.

"Great. We played cards last night and I won thirty dollars. Had a big fire here too."

"What? Fire? Where was the fire?"

"Two dorms down. One of the crazy ones got drunk and fell asleep smoking. I'm glad we've got better kids in this dorm. I mean, I know we are all a little crazy at times but we don't have too many drunks here and no one I know of takes heavy drugs."

"Anybody get hurt? How much damage?"

"No one got hurt permanently but that one dorm room is almost gutted. That kid is in one big amount of trouble. Did you know George Madison? I don't know him myself."

Jonathon thought he had heard his name mentioned before but he didn't know him either.

"No, I don't know him. Probably get expelled right?"

"Yes, I don't think there's any doubt. No one is supposed to smoke in these dorms anymore. If you want a smoke you're supposed to go outside. I know that some do but they have to pay fines if they get caught. But getting drunk, which is also against the rules and then smoking and starting a fire. I'm sure they'll expel him."

"What a waste, don't you think?" Jonathon just shook his head at the thought of changing your life by having one stupid night.

"I know it's a terri○○○e. I know that you and I and most of us for that matter do stupid things occasionally, but not dangerous and stupid things. And now his life is changed forever."

Jonathon asked, "How much did he get burnt?"

"They said one of his arms is messed up enough to give him trouble for a while and I think he got some burns on his face. In a way, I kind of feel sorry for him."

"Me too Bill, but like you said, we all do stupid things but most of the kids I know want to get a degree and get a good career in something. We don't party all night all the time; we usually study. I'm just glad no one else got hurt."

"The guy that lives with him lost all of his school notes and even his computer got all messed up. I did hear that his professors are going to work with him and not penalize him for someone's else mistake. That's pretty decent of them."

"Yeah, it is. Yeah it is."

Then Bill Eaton decided to nod off for a while giving Jonathon some time to himself. Funny how one incident can change a life forever. And Jonathon remembered back to his Friday nights and some weekends at the Holloway house. Usually there were a group of students that went as Linda was a very social girl. Three or four extra friends were always welcomed and usually expected. Many times Jonathon took advantage of being away from the college and also to get a chance of studying in a quiet place. But one particular Sunday, he was the only one invited.

Jonathon had made a good friendship with Bill Holloway. Many occasions found them in a corner talking for several hours. Having reared three daughters, Bill liked to

159

talk to another male and Jonathon liked Bill's reserved ways and was comfortable in his company. This particular Sunday evening at dinner, the house was void of the usual company and Jonathon sensed immediately that something out of the ordinary was taking place. Bill, usually so casual, friendly and nonchalant, seemed a little uptight and nervous. He was up and down several times during dinner and just couldn't seem to relax at all. Everyone noticed it but no one said anything at first. Then just as dinner was coming to an end, Bill spoke out.

"I think we can take Jonathon into our confidence. What do you think Lilly?"

"That's your decision but Jonathon is like an extended member of our family," answered his wife who thought of Jonathon as a son. He thought she looked at him in a very motherly way.

"Okay, then I will." And with that and an added wink at Lindsey, Bill began to tell a story.

"You know, Jonathon, I was adopted when I was five years old. I don't suppose you knew that."

Jonathon shrugged his shoulders and shook his head in the negative.

"Well, no one from the orphanage knew anything much about me, at least that is what they said when I went to live with a real nice family who took me in as their own. Now here I am, 52 years old and later tomorrow night, I'm going to meet my birth mother for the very first time and I can't tell you how nervous I am."

Bill paused for a moment before he continued. Jonathon was happy at that moment that he had never told Lindsey or her family that his sister Amanda was adopted. Somehow he never cared that much about her story. But all of a sudden, he was interested in what Bill had to say. He unknowingly leaned forward and was more intense in his listening. Some feeling inside him was nudging him to pay close attention along with the foreboding thought that something important to his own future was about to take place that couldn't be overlooked. Bill continued almost shyly with a nervousness that was evident to Jonathon.

"I just found out about a month ago that she'd been looking for me for a long time. The adoption agencies don't like to give out a lot of information so it has taken quite a while. I'm not sure what happened or why I was put up for adoption but I'm just interested in seeing somebody else that I might look like. Probably sounds funny but it's hard to put into words."

"Doesn't sound funny at all. I would probably be very nervous too," answered Jonathon who was beginning to think about Amanda in another light. She must have wondered about her birth mom and dad too. She apparently kept a lot of feelings inside her. Just at that moment, Jonathon remembered how mean he used to be to her and tell her that she was not really a part of the family. How awful he felt now. A new realization was beginning to rise up inside of him. If this grown man of 52 years still had such strong emotions about meeting his birth mother, especially when he had a nice wife and family and a good life, Amanda must have felt those feelings too.

"I've always wondered, you know. That's something that never goes away. Even if you luck out and get adopted by a nice family and marry well, like I did, and have nice kids. You still wonder about why you were given away and what your parents look like and you just wonder many things that can never be answered. Just a big void in your life."

Lindsey and her mother offered to clear the table and give the men a chance to go into the library and talk. Bill very obviously connected well with Jonathon and wanted to be able to sit and talk and Jonathon wanted nothing less. So off they went into the library.

"I don't want to bore you with all the details but I like talking with you."

Jonathon was surprised to see a shy look on Bill's face. He realized that telling this kind of story couldn't be easy so he opted to show his interest. Besides, it certainly would have surprised Bill to know that Jonathon wanted to hear his story just as much as he wanted to tell it.

"You will never bore me and I'm very interested in your story. Please start at the beginning. Tell me, when you were first adopted, did you try to please everyone in your family?"

Of course Jonathon was thinking of Amanda. That little girl from the very beginning had tried desperately to please everyone and was very successful, except with him. Hoping to learn more about Amanda's thoughts and feelings, Jonathon put all his attention on Bill as they sat comfortably in brown leather chairs with Espresso coffee at their sides. Relaxed and seemingly sitting even deeper in his chair, Bill paused for a few moment before he began. Searching Bill's face for clues as to how he was feeling about his story, Jonathon realized that there was so much more to him than the happy and friendly person he had come to know as Lindsey's father.

"No, no, I was not a pleasant little kid at all. Hopefully I had some good moments but what I can remember most about those first few years was a lot of anger and confusion that I had inside and I'm very lucky my adopted parents didn't return me for bad behavior." Jonathon noticed that as Bill chuckled at that last comment, but he also let out a big sigh.

Looking over at him, Jonathon noticed for the first time that his hair already had a lot of gray in it that gave him a distinguished yet approachable demeanor. He was a handsome man and his friendliness and pleasant personality made him socially popular. Despite entering into middle age, Bill was actively playing tennis and some occasional basketball so that his physique and energy related more to a forty-year old.

"Like I said before, I was adopted from an orphanage at the age of five. Apparently I had been there for a little more than a year. It seems that another family adopted me but I was returned in six months because my anger was too difficult for them to handle. Of course, that caused more anger, I was told. Other than that, not much information came with me because in those days everything about adoption was very quiet and kept secret. It was hard to find out anything. I was told my adopted parents, whom I consider my real parents by the way, tried to find out some data that they felt I might want to know later on, but nothing was given. No pictures, no information, nothing. Sometimes I wish that I had some early pictures. I'd have liked to see me as a baby, you know. When I had kids I could have compared them to my pictures just like my wife did."

"They really didn't give you anything?"

"No, they said they didn't have anything. And maybe they didn't. I did have a Teddy Bear, which I still have to this day. Silly, isn't it? But it's the only thing I have. And I think that is why I was always so interested in President Teddy Roosevelt. That is even crazier, except I studied a lot of the presidents; I just like history."

Sure, thought Jonathon, Amanda must have felt exactly the same way. She had no pictures of herself as a baby. That is why she treasured that picture she took from the orphanage and used to move it around her room all the time, hoping to find her perfect spot.

"What about your birth certificate? Did that have some information on it?"

"Yes, it did have some names on it but I'm not sure if they were real. When I was a young man in my early twenties, I made some inquiries, but nothing came of it—all dead ends. It is hard to explain about someone like me but I wanted so much to know something of where I came from, and what my parents were like, who I resembled and maybe from where I got my talents."

Jonathon had to guard himself from being too reflective or Bill might wonder why.

"Also, I would really have liked to know why I was abandoned. That's really hard to take. I like to think that there was a good reason, but you never know. At least I should find out something tomorrow night."

How was your life growing up? You were five years old. That must have been difficult but you must have felt lucky too?"

"Looking back I think I should have felt lucky. But like you said, I was only five years old. I was confused, scared and very, very angry most of the time for the first few years. Sometimes I used to go into total rages and I just hated everyone and everything. Whatever happened to me before, I'll probably never totally know but I felt abandoned and didn't trust anyone and when they took me from the orphanage that was tough for me again. I guess I had gotten used to the people who took care of me there. I think kids are lucky if they are in good families and their birth parents can keep them. That would be the most stable beginning for a life. But of course, that can't always be."

"But you always seem so happy and social, people like

you and I know you like people. I've never detected any anger in you. Do you still get angry inside?"

Jonathon hoped that Bill wouldn't guess why he asked that question. He was hoping to find a connection.

"Not any more, at least not any more than any other person. But it did last for quite a while. My parents took me around to doctors and psychologists for a long time and nothing seemed to help. Then, someone told them about a particular type of psychologist who dealt with children who had special problems because they were adopted or abandoned and he really helped me. I was almost nine years old and had spent most of my life being angry with my parents, especially my mom, and the whole world. That was the type of problem I had, just tons of anger inside and most of the time I didn't know why I was angry."

"That does seem to be strange, although a lot of people feel that way at times, for a while at least."

There was a comparison here and Jonathon was trying so hard to find it. He felt he was on the verge of a discovery that was still escaping him.

"Anyway, I went to see this therapist and slowly my anger started to go away. He was the first one who seemed to understand me and he could validate my feelings. Funny about your first question though, as to whether I was someone who tried to please everybody. That is another type of problem some adopted kids have because they feel if they aren't nice to everyone all the time, they may get sent back. Yet they have anger too, they just keep it inside. So you see there are two types, the one who emits anger all over the place like I did and the others who keep everything inside. I think, subconsciously of course, the child chooses which role they will play. Tough on little kids you know."

"You seem to know a lot about these problems. Where did you learn?"

"After I understood my own anger problems, I settled down a lot inside. I wasn't very old then, just over nine or maybe ten, yet just understanding the causes of my anger seemed to help me. Of course the psychologist worked with me on this for quite a while. Yet, as I grew older I wanted to understand and learn more, so I took a few classes in psychology. That's when I realized that not every area of psychology even deals with these special anger problem of adopted children. So I kept searching on my own until I found more information."

"You just looked up special problems adopted kids have?" asked Jonathon, and as yet for an unknown reason to him, he was extremely interested in what Bill was saying.

"There a little more to it than that. Have you ever heard about RAD (Reactive Attachment Disorder)?"

"No, I can't say that I have."

"It is a basic heading for different problems that some adoptive children or adults have. Not everyone adopted has these problems but quite a few have some degree of emotional or psychological difficulty due to abandonment and neglect among other things. Once I knew what name was associated with my anger and my inside confusion, I became very interested. I also realized that the more I learned about my condition, the more I could logically handle it. Understanding some of the connections between my angry behavior and what had happened to me as a child seemed to help a lot. Also, for many years I've worked as a volunteer with some children who benefited from the information I had learned."

"You've worked with other adopted children?"

"Oh yes, as an adult who'd gone through it myself, whenever I saw some of these little ones hurting and their parents desperately searching for answers, I had to step in and point them in the right direction. You can waste a lot of years going to the wrong people for help."

"That is quite a story Bill. So, besides your work and all the social and athletic things you do, you seem to have gotten your hand into another very worthwhile commitment."

Jonathon was trying to set to memory much of the dialogue that had gone on between them. Many loose ends were beginning to come together for him, although he didn't seem to know why. He had been such an angry child and still suffered from the unresolved residue. Never had he been able to find an answer and, of course, he didn't fall into this category since he wasn't adopted. Then the conversation took another turn.

"Even though my life has been good and turned out well for me, I still want to meet my birth mom and get some of the answers to the questions I've always had over the years. And you know Jonathon, I just want to look into her face and see what she looks like. And if I'm really lucky, maybe she will have a picture of my father. That is so important to me. I'd just like to know what they were like, their personalities, their interests and what they could tell me about my grandparents. These missing links probably seem insignificant to you, but if they were a missing piece of the puzzle in your life, you would wonder too."

"I'm sure you're right. I've never thought about any of this before. I mean, looking at life from the point of view of someone who was adopted; it never occurred to me before."

"No reason why it should."

Jonathon thought, *"If he only knew, I wonder what he would think of me."*

"My children were only interested because of me. When you are close to someone, then you can begin to understand how much it hurts to have part of your life missing. I don't mean to make all this so serious and depressing, it's not anymore. But I'm still curious about my beginnings and most especially why I was abandoned. Those questions never go away. Therefore when my birth mother contacted me, I was very excited and I'm looking forward to meeting her, but I'm very nervous."

Jonathon sat there taking in all of this information and realized that it was affecting him deeply. Partly it was because of Amanda. Looking back on his relationship with her, or possibly lack of relationship to be more exact, he wondered why he had so much anger toward her and toward his brother Bryan too. He did have the anger problem in common with Bill. He would have loved to tell Bill about his problems as a young child, but his discomfort wouldn't let any words go in that direction. Yet he kept wondering about a possible connection. Then Bill said something that Jonathon would never forget. It was just one of those moments in time.

"You know, Jonathon, I've been talking about adopted children and adults only. You don't have to be adopted to have attachment disorder problems."

The look on Jonathon's face must have spoken volumes to Bill. Jonathon was worried that possibly his overly eager interest in that last comment had given him away but Bill was too classy of a guy to mention anything.

"How can that be?" asked Jonathon, totally perplexed.

"Any young child who has had a break in the

relationship with his parents could be seriously affected. If parents divorce and the father goes to live somewhere else and very seldom sees his child, that child could feel abandoned."

Jonathon didn't see where he could fit into that category. But there was more.

"Again, if a parent gets sick and has to go to the hospital, many times the children at home feel abandoned. If a young child gets sick and has to go in the hospital, that could trigger the beginning of distrust of the world around him and they could feel abandoned by their parents. Parents can visit the hospital and try to explain the situation, but a young child only remembers how he feels when he is alone and scared among strangers. A lot of situations can trigger these feelings. One little boy I worked with had lost both of his parents in a car accident when he was six years old. I met him at eight years old and he was still very angry and didn't trust anyone. His aunt had taken custody and tried to get him help, but to no avail. I suggested that she should make an appointment with a certain type of psychologist who understood these issues and slowly he came around. But it does take time."

Jonathon's mind was spinning taking everything in and realized that he couldn't wait to get back to his dorm and look up RAD on his computer. He presently had trouble making eye contact with Bill since he was afraid that he would give him too much information by his expression. Bill must have interpreted his edgy demeanor as possibly getting tired of this conversation and brought it to an end.

"So tomorrow night I should get some information. I hope I settle down a little, but then, she is probably nervous too."

"I'll be anxious to hear how this meeting goes. I sure

hope you find out everything that you want. Best of luck."

On the return drive back to college, Lindsey let Jonathon know that she was appreciative that he was so interested in her dad's story.

"Hope my dad didn't bore you too much this evening but he is so excited and nervous. I can't even imagine what he is going through."

"Yeah, must be tough not to know those things most of us take for granted," said Jonathon.

"He hardly ever talks about it anymore but then his birth mom contacted him and he's been talking about it for weeks. He likes you a lot and that's why I invited only you today, Jonathon. I knew you'd be a good listener for him."

"I liked listening to him and I learned a lot too."

Jonathon had to admit that he wasn't a very good conversationalist on the drive back to college. Lindsey talked for a little while but suddenly gave up and took a nap as Jonathon drove the rest of the way back in silence. He didn't even turn on the radio, but he could have since his thoughts were very erratic and flying in every direction making no sense at all. Too many ideas were trying to take center stage at the same time and resulted in nothing being accomplished. The sun had set a few hours before and the darkness of the night matched how he felt inside, mostly dark and confused with very little light being shed on his disconcerted feelings. An occasional light in the distance signaled that another car was approaching on this two-lane highway that took them back to college on back roads and avoided facing the heavily burdened expressway that would have been another choice.

"How far do we have to go yet?" Lindsey asked suddenly awakening from a deep sleep.

"Another thirty minutes at least. Even though the back roads take a little longer, I like avoiding lengthy traffic jams. Get some sleep while you can. I don't mind."

"Okay, thanks."

And that was enough for Lindsey to be back in her dream world.

Jonathon had taken to memory many things that Bill had said. Some words just screamed at him so loud that he thought he would go crazy. The fact that you didn't have to be adopted to have these attachment problems was a major discovery. This one line kept repeating itself over and over again in his teeming head. When Bill started telling about his anger problems as a child, Jonathon felt that he could have been telling his own story. With proper help, Bill had greatly improved in spite of the failures of other therapists who didn't help at all. This was good for Jonathon to know.

Jonathon still had anger at his mother. Bill had stressed that the largest percentage of his own anger was at his mother. And the other similar point was that Bill didn't know why he was mad. Jonathon knew he was perceived as a bully or a mean kid but inside he hated the way he felt. He loved his mom, yet he hated her much of the time. He was so tired of being angry all the time and just knowing that someone else felt the same way helped a lot.

"Are we there yet? I know I must sound like a nutty kid. How far yet?"

"About twenty minutes I think. The traffic has caught up to us."

"You don't even have the radio on. How come?"

"Lindsey, I think I'm entertaining myself."

"How? By driving funny."

"No silly but I was just thinking of a time when I got this bag of popcorn at the movies and when I got to the bottom of the bag, I found several kernels that hadn't popped."

"Okay, Jonathon, am I missing something here?"

"It's just that sometimes I feel that could be me. Did you ever feel like that?"

"Like what?"

"I sometimes think of myself as just one of the kernels of popcorn that didn't pop."

"You are really weird tonight."

"And you are tired, just go back to sleep. I'll wake you when we get there."

Jonathon felt that way, one of the kernels that didn't pop. Now he was finding out that there were many other kernels of corn that needed help to pop. When Bill mentioned the rages he had experienced, Jonathon felt right at home. During most of the conversation, he had wanted to say, "Me too," but he didn't dare. He still kept this part of his life to himself.

Lindsey woke again and talked but Jonathon couldn't quite make out what she was saying and believed she was really still asleep. That was okay. Jonathon still wanted to be alone with his thoughts before anything could be forgotten. He planned to write these ideas down in a secure part of his computer when he got home.

Jonathon finally had some hope. Most times he pushed things to the back of his mind but always knew something was not right. When he was out socially he laughed and carried on just like the other kids with one big difference. He was faking it. The dark clouds were always there. Okay, he had some investigating to do but at least he had a place to start.

Monday's class schedule was agonizingly long since Jonathon just wanted to get back to his dorm room and begin researching RAD. Yet he knew what he had to do and realized that he could work long into the night on Monday since his first class on Tuesday morning was at 10:00 AM. That would give him the cherished time that he needed to delve into the new assignment he had given himself. From his conversation with Bill, he was quite sure that at least some of the answers he was looking for would be found. In class his mind kept wandering.

"Amanda must have been a strong little girl, a real survivor. She overcame all my meanness and was going through the same thing that Bill experienced. But she was always agreeable; that must have been her chosen role. Probably distrustful and scared. I wonder if she ever got angry. Sure she did. Everyone gets angry. Inside anger is very tough too. I've got to put this in the back of my mind for now. I missed what my professor just said about that calculus equation. I've got to concentrate on this class for now. Tonight I'll have plenty of time."

Getting back to his dorm Jonathon was surprised to notice how different everything looked to him. He knew this was the same dorm and the same room that he had lived in for over two years but it was different today. The change, he realized, was that he was looking at everything from a sudden spark of hope that was settling in on him and creating a different attitude and a different sense of expectation. He had given up before of ever finding an answer to his problems and now there was hope. And that made him look at life from another point of view.

"First, I've got to learn what I'm dealing with. I've got to get a solid explanation of RAD that I can understand." As soon as he walked into his dorm he turned on his computer and plugged in RAD (Reactive Attachment Disorder) and began to read. There was a lot of information for him to decipher and some very interesting facts were coming his way at last. He got totally lost in the first article presented to him.

Causes of RAD:

1) unwanted pregnancy
2) neglect
3) inconsistent or inadequate day care
4) dramatic prenatal experience (exposure to drugs/alcohol)
5) sudden separation from the primary caretaker (illness, death, hospitalization, esp. in first few years of life)
6) on-going illness and pain such as colic, hernia, ear infection or chronic illness
7) moms with serious depression
8) abuse (physical, emotional mental, sexual)
9) frequent moves (foster care, failed adoptions)

"Wow, #5 and #6 apply to me. I was sick and in the hospital in the first few years of my life and I was always sick. Very interesting."

He remembered being told that he had spent many weeks in the hospital when he was between one and two and a half years old for some illness that kept recurring. None of the doctors were able to put a name to it but then it just stopped shortly before he was three years old. He didn't consciously remember being in the hospital anymore but he did remember at five, six and seven years old having an intense fear of hospitals, doctors, ambulances, nurses and any of their counterparts. It was so serious that many times when the family was on an outing, his father would take different routes in order to avoid passing a hospital since he would start crying and screaming and no amount of good parental intentions could convince him that there was nothing to fear. He remembered these episodes and wondered why hospitals had scared him so much. He didn't know. It was true that even today his adult logic had to consciously take control whenever he got too close to a doctor, ambulance or hospital so that he could avoid palpitations and sweating.

#2 - neglect
#3 - inconsistent or inadequate day care
#5 - sudden separation from primary caretaker
#9 - frequent moves

"Those apply to Amanda. Maybe more too, but those I know for sure. She must have had a rough road inside. Amanda and I actually have some of these things in common but we handled them differently. Interesting."

For a moment Jonathon just sat there staring at his computer, crossed his arms over his chest as he sat far back in his chair. His long blue pullover sweater that had been a present on his twentieth birthday kept him warm and cozy and he smiled as he remembered his mom saying that she had chosen the color because it would accentuate his blue eyes. This gave him a rather warm feeling about his mom and searching his mind he realized that he did have some good feelings about her too. He had always felt closer to his dad and many times hated and disliked his mom, but right now it was nice to have one pleasing memory.

"Heh Jonathon, you're working entirely too hard. Some of us are going to get a pizza just to get out of here for a while. Wanna come?" His roommate Bill almost shocked him back to the present.

"You know what Bill, any other time I'd love it. But I'm

on a project here that I have to finish."

"Understood good buddy. Want me to bring anything back for you?"

"How about the two biggest slices of pizza you can find. I would really appreciate that today. I don't want to break from what I'm doing."

"Not a problem. We take turns, right? See ya later," said Bill and then he added, "with pizza."

"I owe you," he answered and noticed that Bill just waved his arm as he left their room.

Back to his project he thought, *"Amanda, Amanda, how did you do it?"* She had chosen the pleasing personality role and kept everything inside. He realized he hardly knew her at all and regretted that he hadn't even given her a chance but instead had made her life much more difficult. Yet he was quite sure that Amanda didn't trust anybody, not completely at least. His anger came out all over the place and Amanda's anger stayed inside. *"Did Amanda realize that she had anger?"* That he would like to know. But first, he had enough to do in trying to get himself on the right road. It was time to read on. Next were the symptoms of RAD:

1) superficially engaging and charming
2) indiscriminately affectionate with strangers
3) not usually affectionate on parent's terms (not cuddly, esp. with mom)
3) lack of eye contact with parents
4) destructive with self, others and material things
5) accident prone
6) cruelty to animals
7) lying about the obvious (crazy lying)
8) stealing
9) no impulse controls (frequently acts hyperactive)

10) learning lags
11) lack of cause and effect thinking
12) lack of conscience
13) preoccupation with fire
14) poor peer relations (no close & lasting friendships)
15) inappropriately demanding and clingy
16) abnormal speech patterns
17) triangulation of adults (tries to divide adults)
18) abnormal eating patterns

"This is a long list and there are many more, they say. These are just the main ones. Wow."

The list was long and quite intensive and Jonathon read it slowly and then he read it again. It was true that not all of these symptoms were evident in his life. Some were totally missing. However, it stated strongly that not all symptoms were necessary to cause psychological and emotional problems for a child. There were many gradations of RAD and the more symptoms you had, the more serious. Most could be helped with the proper therapy. Then he read a very concise definition of RAD that had been developed by professionals.

"Attachment disorder is a condition where individuals do not bond and form lasting relationships. They do not allow people to be in control of them and as little children can go into total rages against their parents for this reason. They have not learned to trust and have not developed a conscience, at least not a full conscience. If they were physically or emotionally separated from the primary caregiver in their life sometime during the first three years of their life for an extended period of time, damage has been done. How much damage will depend on the circumstances and also on the personality and character of the child. Everyone is an individual and reacts to life's problems differently. If a child is not attached and does not form a loving bond with the mother, he will not develop good attachments later with his outer world. At their innermost being is deep-seated rage, far beyond normal anger. And this rage is suppressed in their psyche."

Jonathon read this paragraph several times, first quickly, then slowly and deliberately trying to inhale all of the words and definitions. He knew he had opened up a new direction for his life and discovered for himself what no counselor or therapist had been able to convey to his parents. *"I know mom and dad tried. How come no one figured this out for me years ago? This could make me mad, but I don't want to go there."* He was trying to apply all this knowledge, as in psychoanalyzing yourself, which he soon realized was totally impossible. First of all, he'd only been about one year old when his problems began. His parents would be more apt to remember his change in behavior than he would. He was too young at the time to remember anything definite, except possibly feelings that he had encountered. And the thought of discussing this information with his parents was repugnant to him.

As he read on he realized that we all have rage to some degree but some psychopathic rage is begun by unfulfilled needs as infants. Then, he ran across an unforgettable quote on RAD by (Magid & McKelvey, 1988), "There is an inability to love or feel guilty. There is no conscience. Their inability to enter into any relationship makes treatment or even education impossible." Then one more quote stayed with him. This was (Bowlby, 1955), "Some infamous people with Attachment Disorder that did not get help in time were: Adolph Hitler, Saddam Hussein, Edgar Allen Poe, Jeffrey Dahmer and Ted Bundy. One famous person with Attachment Disorder who did get help in time (in 1887) and became one of the greatest humanitarians of all time, is Helen Keller."

"I have so much to learn and I know I can't do it on my own. I'm no expert. I've got to find an RAD therapist. How?

Oh sure, I know Bill would help and he has a lot of experience but I just can't. I can't go to him. Am I being stupid? I have a perfectly knowledgeable and available understanding source very convenient to me, but I can't."

The next few weeks found Jonathon studying and researching RAD and related subjects and spending many hours delving into complicated explanations, reasons and theories. He needed to learn as much as he could. Learning some of the possible reasons for his anger, rage and distrust seemed to help but didn't alleviate his anger. However it did make it less frightening and he had hoped to learn to heal himself privately. Sadly, he slowly realized that that was not and would not be the case. He had taken some small steps but the rest of the road could only be traveled with an expert on RAD.

Jonathon remembered Lester Anderson, a school counselor he had come to know and admire. Other than his proficiency in counseling work at the college, Lester was also a psychologist with rather impressive credentials for a guy under thirty-five. Reluctantly Jonathon made a confidential appointment and he knew it felt right.

After the preliminaries were over, Lester took a long time to speak. Truly the time elapsed wasn't more than a few moments but it was long enough to make Jonathon uncomfortable, fidgety and somewhat fearsome. Noticing his newly acquired skepticism, Lester broke the silence.

"First of all, this seems like quite a burden you've been carrying around for a very long time. Knowing you as I have at college, I would never have suspected what was going on inside you and I can say confidently that most of the other students wouldn't guess either. Yet, you have to realize that many of the other students have their own problems and some may even share your anger and rage for the same or similar reasons. No one gets out of childhood totally unscathed. But, we need to talk about you. It must have taken a lot of thought and courage to finally decide to do something about this. What happened?"

Lester listened thoughtfully as Jonathon related his encounter with Bill Holloway. He also added some extra information about himself as a child and his parents' wide search for help. Lester encouraged him to share as much as he remembered and wrote notes as Jonathon revealed that he'd never liked the way he felt inside but also never understood his ugly feelings. His mom had been a target for years and although his relationship with his father was better, he didn't totally trust him either. He brought up his adopted sister Amanda and his meanness toward her and his brother Bryan. He had a sadness as to whether it would be too late to rectify some of the damage that he had caused in his relationship to his family. Now Lester had enough information to continue.

"Jonathon, you are feeling very guilty for some things that weren't your fault. You are asking me if I believe that you have this RAD and I think there is a very good chance that your anger stems from it. However, I only know about RAD. I'm not an expert in it. I want you to see a friend of mine who is an expert in attachment disorder. You told me that as a little child your parents took you to counselors and psychologists for several years but there was no improvement. I would guess that they were not fluent in RAD. It is a very specialized treatment and ordinary therapy usually doesn't work. Will you be willing to go to a real expert and follow through?"

"Yes I need to do that. It's what I want. But I want to keep it quiet at school."

"Of course, this is your private life. However, as I mentioned before, we have a lot of students here who see professionals for one reason or another and there is no shame attached to seeking help. It would be worse if you knew you could use help and didn't go. I'm going to set you up with Jeffrey Alexander. He has dealt with RAD for many years and truly is an expert. He can determine if you have it and at what gradation. Some who are only slightly affected with RAD can have emotional and psychological problems that irritate their lives and relationships. This is Step 1 for you. If you want, I would like to be kept informed. Being right here at college, I'm always available for you."

Jonathon realized as he left Lester's office that he had developed a bounce in his step. His expectancy was on the positive side and he felt he was going in the right direction. He would pursue RAD as if it were another class he was taking, since he would probably have homework just like he had in his psychology class. By the end of this semester he hoped that he would have alleviated some of his anger and learned the important "whys" he wanted to know.

Jeffrey Alexander was a comfortable man, maybe fifty years old, with some grey in his hair and a quick smile that instantly welcomed you. Jonathon couldn't explain how but Jeffrey related differently to him than other therapists and almost instantly he established a rapport. Jonathon didn't have to pretend, as he usually did with people, because he felt comfortable with some trust slowly surfacing. *"He really knows me and what I'm all about. Somehow that doesn't scare me."* And that fact was true. Jeffrey knew and suspected more in their first two-hour session than probably Jonathon's parents knew in more than twenty years. This was not to blame his parents in any way because he'd continuously lied, and manipulated them as he felt he had to do to feel safe. He didn't trust his parents, especially his mother, but he never knew why. But with the help of Jeffrey, the pieces were starting to fit together.

By the third and fourth session, the conversations were very informative.

"Do you now have a better understanding as to what happened to you when you were in the hospital?" Jeffrey asked appealing to his intellect as a mature, intelligent adult, although Jonathon's inner child was causing him pain and needed to be dealt with.

"I'm thinking that before I went to the hospital I was told by my parents that I was a normal child who loved and trusted his mom and dad and the world around me. Then I was left alone and I thought my parents had abandoned me. It didn't matter that they came once in a while to see me; I wanted to go home and they wouldn't take me home. I thought they didn't want me and didn't love me and I was scared so I didn't trust them anymore."

"That's right," continued Jeffrey, "and once you begin to lose that trust as a little child, it is very hard to retrieve. You have no abstract thinking yet, no logic to help you to reason things out; you are strictly in concrete thinking. No matter how many times your parents told you they loved you, you had to stay in the hospital to get better and what they said made no difference at all. You only knew how you felt and you're feelings said you were scared because mommy and daddy left you. All your mind could conceive was that they were gone and you were scared. In your mind they were not supposed to leave you, but they did."

"But I understand it now as an adult so how come the feelings are still there?"

"Jonathon, you told me that already you are having some feelings of love toward your mom. You mentioned the blue sweater that she gave you and other things. We will continue to go back, as much as we can, in your memory and change your reaction to events. It is like recreating the umbilical cord experience that still exists symbolically for little children for several years. I want you to understand that you will not, nor do you have to, remember everything and turn it around. That would be impossible and not necessary. But once you begin to get a new pattern of love and trust toward your parents in your mind, chunks of information will come back and you can re-evaluate it in light of your new information."

"Why my mom?" asked Jonathon. "I was always so mean to her. Looking back I know I must have hurt her so much, yet there were times when I was older, maybe six or seven when I remember thinking that I wasn't sure why I got so angry with her. She did many nice things for me."

"And as you remember these nice things and see them in a new light, the trust and love will be a new decision to make, not necessarily consciously, but inside you will automatically begin to see things differently."

"But why my mom? I don't think I was nearly as mean to my dad."

"With RAD children, unfortunately the mom is almost always the target. Until that inner pain is confronted, your mom wouldn't have a chance. Subconsciously we know that our moms carried us before we were born and we associate moms with being taken care of and that feeling of being safe and loved; that job we give to our mom. At least that job is given to the main caregiver and it is usually the mom, but can be the father or someone else in some cases. Usually, though it is the mom and in your case, your mom was the target."

"I was so awful to her. Sometimes when I look back…" as Jonathon's voice trailed off, Jeffrey gave him the few moments that he needed.

"You are looking through the eyes of a young adult, who is intelligent and logical and has developed some feelings of empathy already and you feel very guilty. Let's back track to the very little child who had to be put in the hospital because he was ill and didn't understand any of this but just wanted to know why his parents, mostly his mom, abandoned him. You most likely were asking yourself questions like, 'Why did my mom abandon me? Where are my parents? Was I a bad boy and she put me here? I don't remember being a bad boy and I really tried to be good. I want to go home."

Jeffrey let some of these sentences take their time to register with Jonathon and before he continued he could visibly see that the questions had triggered some very hurtful memories. Then he continued.

"You were not being a mean little kid. You were a baby and you were scared, upset and you wanted to go home and your mom didn't take you back home. So you learned not to trust her and you felt abandoned and you blamed your mom. The constant change of caregivers in the hospital only heightened your fear and confusion. This could have happened if you had been in the hospital for only one week and one time. But you had many hospital stays in the next year and a half. At the time, they were necessary for your physical health, but most likely the doctors were not taking into account your emotional and psychological well being. Sometimes these two areas of medicine don't connect very well, even to this day."

"I'm sure they were most concerned with my physical health because they have told me that they were worried I would die."

"Of course, that would have been their main concern and should have been, but I'm sure your parents noticed a difference in you and probably didn't know what to do about it. This type of inside pain in a very little child in not an easy fix. Besides, you were their birth child so probably some of the therapist didn't even connect the dots. Many people believe that you have to be adopted to have RAD and this is not true and also sad since some people are out there today living angry and frustrated lives because they are not getting the correct help."

The next few weeks found Jonathon thinking back on his life and realized the many years spent in pain and in anger. He also spent many frustrated years growing further apart from his family. He thought about his mom and dad, brother Bryan and sister Amanda, all of whom he felt must have a very negative opinion of him. He suspected his sister Amanda must have some dark shadows of her own in spite of her happy exterior. Bryan must have always wondered why his older brother didn't want to be friends with him. And although his mom and dad had never quit loving him and trying to get a good relationship with him, their connection was strained. Jonathon hoped it wasn't too late. He would do everything he had to do to heal himself and then he would work with his family, if they still wanted him. *"I really hope I'm not too late."*

Jonathon went through specialized RAD therapy which included a type of holding therapy, some regression and feeling exercises to rebuild his frame of mind as a child. Other methods were employed to help him realize his inner feelings as a child, relive them so as to be able to let them go and replace them with new understanding and forgiveness for himself and his parents. This occurrence expanded over the next year and half, although Jonathon was beginning to experience normal feelings of empathy and trust much sooner. He knew he had more years to discover himself and secretly he realized that it would be a lifelong process, but instead of being depressed he felt rather jubilant since the more he learned, the more he could pass on to others. This desire to help others alleviate their anger and pain was a new feeling to him.

As he finished his college degree, Jonathon felt he was

completing a degree in RAD, although there was no degree or diploma for this course. However, because of his intensive study with Jeffrey and in coordination with his counselor Lester, he did receive a minor in psychology. Furthering his study in RAD would lead Jonathon to other specialized schools and this new association could be pursued as he began a career in mechanical engineering. His life was now full and one of the best moments in recent times was when he was home alone one night, just relaxing after a very stressful day at work. He had his dinner on the stove and had turned on the television to a news report about a bombing in another country where over twenty-five people were killed. Jonathon got himself totally involved in the story and before he knew what happened, he realized that his eyes were watering and inside he felt such sadness for these people and their families. Then suddenly, he just stood there in a moment of total realization to find himself having genuine sympathy for people he didn't even know. This was the first moment that Jonathon knew for sure he was well on his way to recovery and beginning to experience the same feelings that other people felt. He could get out beyond himself and feel empathy for others.

CHAPTER VII

Amanda couldn't believe it was three o'clock already. For once she wanted to leave work on time since it was a very special day for her. It was her twenty-fifth birthday and she would celebrate it with her mom and dad and her two brothers. For a quick moment she paused as an old annoyance sprung up inside of her and cast its unpleasant dark shadow trying to upset her. She wasn't one hundred percent sure that November 7 was her birthday. That was what the orphanage personnel wrote down on her birth certificate but Amanda wondered if it was an educated guess made with the only data available at the time. No confirmation of the birth date was ever validated and that irritated her even at twenty-five years of age..

"And I'm bringing someone special home with me," Amanda mused. His name was Jeremy Sloane and they had been dating for most of the year, although she had known him much longer. It was important that she should leave work on time today, at exactly 4:30 PM since she needed time to look her best and Amanda wanted to relax and be ready for a good celebration. Jonathon, her now thirty years old older brother, was married with one little boy and Bryan, almost twenty-eight, was engaged since last year to a girl he'd dated for four years. Everyone who had helped Amanda flourish and grow would be at her party, most especially her mom and dad, the only mom and dad she had ever known.

Finishing up her illustration, she placed it on her boss's desk realizing she would probably have his approval or criticism by the end of the week. Amanda liked her job as an illustrator for a major book company and although she did mostly covers for books, there were times that she had done individual artwork and portraits that had been favorably noticed. She liked to think that her birth mom was an artist or maybe her dad had a talent in that direction, but she would probably never know. Those were her own private and personal thoughts that she shared with no one and at this precise moment she had to get herself in the now and finish her work so she could leave.

Driving home Amanda got caught in traffic but instead of being upset or agitated she spent the moment reflecting on her life. At least that's what she planned to do until her cell phone rang. It was Jeremy.

"Hi honey, where are you? I'm just leaving work and want to know what time to meet you?"

Jeremy was an architect so he could always appreciate Amanda's art and she could see value in his work. They sometimes tossed ideas back and forth which made their relationship insightful as well as meaningful.

"I've been stuck in traffic for the last twenty minutes and we are just inching along. Looks like it's starting to move now. I should be home in about fifteen minutes. What time are you coming over?"

"I planned to pick you up around 5:30 PM. Is that okay?"

"No, give me at least until 6:00."

"Right. Did you get your illustration done?"

"Yes and I think you'll like what I've done. I'll show

you my rough drafts later."

"Good. Since you don't like to talk on the phone when you drive hon, I'll let you go. See you around 6:00 PM."

"Okay. Bye Jeremy."

Amanda smiled because Jeremy was right. She didn't like talking on the phone while she was driving, and traffic was now going at the speed limit so she was glad the call was over. Today was a day for reflection and she skipped over the early years and remembered her high school graduation that placed her in the top ten percent of her class. She had joined the debate team which was a real stretch for her. She wanted to overcome her need to always be pleasing and nice to everyone. This brought on palpitations and sweats and many sleepless nights worrying about whether she should have joined this group at all. Yet, she stuck with it and realized she had grown up in her strength of character. She could handle other classmates not being happy with her because of her strong discussions, that she managed, at least intellectually. Emotionally was an entirely different matter but she was inching along in the right direction. She even considered joining the debate team in college to further her need to improve but backed off quickly after reading the syllabus which called for intensive and strong arguments that she didn't want to handle.

Her phone rang again, but she was on a comfortable stretch of road.

"Happy Birthday, little sister."

"Hi Bryan," she laughed "I thought you might call."

"How does twenty-five feel?"

"Pretty good, big brother, it really feels pretty good, even though it's a landmark. Quarter of a century. I've actually lived for a quarter of a century."

"I just talked to mom and she said that we are having steaks. Great, huh but she also made mashed potatoes and she will wait until you get there to add your special ingredient. What is it?"

"Ha," laughed Amanda, "maybe this will be the year I tell you and maybe not. You don't have to know."

"Actually I do. Because after I get married I'll have to tell Kathy so she can make them for me."

"Or you could make them for her."

"That's true too and Kathy would probably agree. You've got me there. Anyway, I just wanted to call you and I'll see you tonight. Love you little sister."

"I love you, Big Brother."

Amanda considered Bryan to have been her strong anchor for years. Yet Jonathon had once again become part of the clan and finally they had a happy family. It had taken a while after his specialized RAD therapy but he began by having some private meetings with his parents and clued them in to what caused his extreme change of behavior as a child. He touched on his angry behavior toward his siblings and the fear and anguish he'd felt inside. Bryan and Amanda were included in later discussions which was a process necessary to help Jonathon heal. Amanda saw Jonathon suffer tremendously, senselessly blaming himself for years of bad behavior that was not his fault or even remotely under his control. Yet she knew, until he could resolve the guilt and blame he felt inside, he couldn't move forward. He had told her that felt that he had to get his relationship with his parents straightened out first and then he could move on to his siblings.

Reminiscing at home while getting ready for her party, Amanda knew that mom and dad had forgiven Jonathon immediately. Together her parents had tried to help him erase the guilt and remorse that tortured him. Now, during this time, he kept his family up-to-date on what his therapist advised and being included in the process helped all of them connect again. It was reported that sorrow and regret were part of the healing process and an important part. Amanda had seen Jonathon go from an angry brother with very little conscience or empathy for others to an adult who was tormented by what he thought he had caused. Therapy helped him to realize somewhat that he was not in control of his behavior as a young child, but he was haunted by the way he had treated his mom and Bryan and most especially Amanda. In an effort to help him resolve some of these past issues, his therapist suggested that he write a letter to each member of his family. The letter to Amanda, received a few years ago, was priceless to her and today, as she waited for Jeremy, she read it again.

Dear Amanda,

This is a very difficult letter for me to write to you as I believe forgiveness for me will be difficult for you to develop in your heart. We have discussed the disorder I developed as a child which accounts for the anger that I always expressed toward you and Bryan, but particularly you. Now that I realize the confusion and anxiety that you were feeling as an adopted child in a new family, new surroundings and new life, I cannot feel there is any excuse for my behavior. In words, you told me that you forgave me. I remember your comment that I couldn't control my behavior with attachment disorder any more than I could help being sick if I got cancer. I truly appreciate your forgiving heart. I can only hope that I might have done likewise if I had been in your position. I don't know; I hope so.

Life is very strange when you think about it. All every one of us ever wanted was to be accepted and loved, to be able to trust and feel safe. You and I probably had the toughest time realizing that but I know you tried very hard. You tried so hard to get me to like you, and I'm so sorry that I wasn't able to return your kind acceptance. When I think back on the most horrible words that I inflicted on you, I am even more ashamed and contrite. In my logical mind, I know that I was sick but in my heart and emotional state I am having a difficult time forgiving myself. I don't want this to ruin any further relationship we will have so I'm working very hard at forgiving myself. Please have patience with me.

Again, I want to thank you for having such a kind and educated heart. I do appreciate you, now more than ever.

I hope you want me to remain,

Your brother—Jonathon

Reading the letter never failed to bring tears to Amanda's eyes. She knew the torment that was going on inside of Jonathon and she couldn't convince him that she understood now and that the past was over and she felt that they should all go on enjoying each other in the future. She remembered part of the letter she wrote back to him, which he said he would keep forever.

Dear Jonathon,

Forgiveness is a tough word to deal with. Somehow it is always easier for the injured party to accept a deep and true contrition as you have professed to me, than for you to forgive yourself or realize that I can put these circumstances behind me and look forward to a great relationship with you in the future. Earlier in our lives, you had the upper hand and I was the target, but now I believe the roles are reversed. You would do me a great favor if you put the past behind both of us and let us take what we both learned from our experiences and become better adults.

Know that I will always remain,

Jonathon and Amanda had talked over their younger years face to face on several occasions and although Jonathon was making progress, Amanda felt that he still gave himself a hard time as regret showed on his face. Sometimes the conversation turned to Amanda who hadn't faced all of her demons yet but she kept careful notes when he spoke to her of similar feelings. Amanda still didn't express her feelings outwardly and kept them in her private domain and no one was ever yet invited to trespass. Mostly she felt that she was doing okay, but occasionally she could admit to herself that therapy would probably help her too. She just didn't have it within her to share herself.

It was only about a month ago that Amanda had the courage to tell Jeremy she'd been adopted. For some reason she worried what he would think about it. Would it make a difference to him? After all, they had talked about children, mostly in general; and only casually discussed marriage. It was a little soon. Most people knew their genealogy and so could be reasonably sure what to expect in their children physically and mentally. But Amanda had no idea what her parents looked like, their emotional make up, or physical history nor anything in her family tree. She often wondered about her grandparents and whether or not she had brothers and sisters somewhere or even half-brothers and half-sisters. So one time when the discussion came up, Amanda just tossed out the statement to Jeremy very quickly and matter-of-factly.

"I'm adopted you know. I'm sure I never told you because I don't usually tell people unless there is a reason for them to know."

"Really, you're adopted." That's all she heard Jeremy say at first, but his expression was serious and slightly surprised.

Amanda sat there, fidgety and slightly nervous, hoping that her feelings were not showing themselves through her anxious behavior. Since Jeremy had made no further comment, Amanda continued, "Yes, I am. I've had very good adoptive parents. They've been good to me and I love them. And of course I've mentioned Bryan and Jonathon. That's my family."

At this point Amanda just waited. She was sure he was thinking over the situation. After all, she had known him for several years and never mentioned her adoption. Finally he began to speak. "How old were you?"

"I was almost three years old when I came to live with the Peterson family but I had been in an orphanage in Arizona for well over a year. I guess I was about one and a half when the orphanage took me in."

"Do you know anything about your parents?"

Amanda realized that Jeremy was asking his questions very calmly and with a considerate tonality of voice, while he looked at her in a caring manner. She was sure he wanted to make her admission of a delicate situation easier for her. He seemed to know her so well, she thought.

"No, I don't know anything at all. I don't even know my father's name. Everything was so closed and private. My mom said that they asked for information and pictures, you know, stuff like that, but the orphanage said there was nothing. I have one little picture of a scenery but even my mom said that it was hanging in my bedroom at the orphanage and she wasn't sure if it had just been there or if I brought it with me. You know sometimes…"

Amanda's voice trailed off for a second and she had to stop. She didn't feel like she was going to cry but it was more like she was holding in a lot of emotions and fighting not to lose her grip. She looked down at the floor with her hands in her lap and for a few moments she was unaware Jeremy was even there. She took a deep breath and continued.

"As you probably can tell, this is not a part of my life that I like to talk about. It's kind of hard to think about it."

"I would image that it would be very difficult. How do you feel about it?"

"I wish I had been born to the Petersons, but I wasn't. I used to pretend that I was, and my brother Bryan always pretended with me that I was his real sister. Then later on as we grew up, we decided we really were true brother and sister. The reason I was thinking about it now was because we were talking about later in our lives, getting married to someone someday and I worry a lot about that. If and when I do have children, I won't be sure about them until they are born. Maybe there are bad diseases in my family history. Maybe something mental or something physical could be wrong."

"Amanda, that could happen anyway. There aren't any guarantees that children will be born perfect. Even if there is nothing known in your family history, sometimes things develop and medicine has no answers why. You can't let that bother you. I know that I had a distant cousin who ended up in a mental hospital but that doesn't mean that my children will have those same problems. Every family has some problems in their background, I'm sure."

"That's probably true. But I suppose if you at least know your parents and your grandparents that must give you some reassurance. I'm afraid that I do spend time thinking about who my parents and grandparents were and what they accomplished in their lives. I also wonder from where I got my artistic talent. There are so many unanswered questions in my life."

"I've never thought about life from the point of view of someone adopted. I guess it's hard not to know certain things about yourself." Amanda watched as Jeremy got reflective for a moment or two.

"There are so many voids in my life. There weren't any pictures of my birth mother or me. I wonder if I look like her. I'd love to see one of my baby pictures. Another thing. When I first went to live with the Petersons, they tell me I called myself Sarah. I was sure that was my name and I wouldn't answer to Amanda and I would cry about it. After a few weeks, I didn't cry about it anymore because I was afraid they would get mad. Occasionally I have a dream about a little girl named Sarah."

"You probably have a lot of memories that seem mixed up because you were so young?"

"When I got older I still had a warm feeling about the name of Sarah and I still feel a relationship with that name. Isn't that strange? But my parents never changed my name and they showed me my birth certificate and it says Amanda Lynn. As far as I know, my name was never Sarah. I've always wondered where that came from. And one more thing, there is a certain feeling I've been looking for. It's not an internal feeling as much as the touch of some fabric or material, like a texture. It's kind of confusing in my mind but it's something I've never been able to discover."

She could tell that Jeremy was quite intrigued by some of her statements, although she considered her conversation as well-thought out confusion, at times, and felt that the uncertainty within herself didn't always translate into acceptable logical dialogue. These were very valid questions and concerns that an adopted child would have since part of their life was missing and although thoughts didn't always present themselves for her in coherent orderly fashion, Amanda was pleased that she could talk to Jeremy so easily. She wasn't able to do this with her parents.

"Have you ever talked to your mom and dad about these feelings and concerns that you have?"

Amanda felt her body jerk back in disbelief. It almost seemed that Jeremy had heard her thinking process and she knew that slight discomfort had entered her body. Her thoughts, that she had kept secret from her family for years, were obvious to Jeremy. How did he know? Did he realize her panic and worry about offending her mom and dad?

"No, I've never said anything and I wouldn't. I have to appreciate what they did for me. They gave me a good life. I never even talk about my thoughts of my birth mom, because it might hurt them."

"I think they would understand. It seems perfectly normal for you to have thoughts and questions about your birth mom and dad."

"Maybe, but I wouldn't want to hurt them in any way. They've been wonderful to me."

"I know they have, but they are your parents for better or for worse. They wouldn't expect you to feel wonderful all the time. Do you ever get mad or angry? I was just thinking that I don't think I've ever seen you get mad. I have seen you just a little bit irritated a few times, but do you ever get mad?"

"I do inside but I don't usually show it. I try to handle it internally."

"Have I ever made you mad?"

"No, I don't think so. But you are a rather consistent

person and I can only remember a few times that you even irritated me, but we discussed them remember?"

"Yeah, I do remember. And I find that you are such an easy going gal. And that's good but when something is hurtful you have to be able to get mad, handle it and let it go. Can you do that?"

"If it's important to me I can. I don't think I've ever seen you mad more than once either." Amanda saw Jeremy nod in agreement.

"Yeah, that's probably true. Anger doesn't seem to solve a difficulty for me. I usually try to find a logical solution. But there are times when anger does overtake me,"

"We're probably not too different then." Jeremy thought he saw Amanda pleased at the similarity.

"Have you ever gone back to the orphanage to try to find out some information that you would like to know? In these modern days they might give you more data than they would have a while back."

"My parents would have to know and they would probably be hurt or mad."

"I don't think so Amanda. I think they'd totally understand. I know I would understand. Just wanting some information about your beginnings, that would be so normal."

"Really? You really think so?"

"Yeah, I'll bet they are still waiting for the day you mention it. It's only logical. Look, you've got a good relationship with your parents. You love them and they love you; I know they would understand. At least think about it. It could help."

"Maybe I will."

Amanda did a lot of personal thinking after that conversation and it wasn't just about going back to the orphanage. She realized a lot of things that were bothering her and the many questions fighting for the front position in her mind. She couldn't talk to her parents, although she would have liked to. She would have liked to talk to Bryan too, but she wouldn't. With the positive changes in Jonathon's personality in the last few years, she would have liked to talk to him possibly most of all since he had overcome his rage. He had even hinted about talking to her, but she couldn't talk to him either. She termed her inner feelings "quiet anger" because no one else ever knew they were there. It kept her depressed as the dark shadows were usually there even as she woke up. She fought them of most of the day and never ever let the world know what was going on inside her. Now she wanted to talk to someone, but she didn't know who.

To be honest, a few years ago she had tried and secretly went to see two different therapists. They didn't even begin to understand her. She needed to find a professional who was familiar with the problems of adopted children.

Knock. Knock.

Back to the present, Jeremy was here to take her to her birthday celebration. Today, she was hoping to have a few minutes to talk to Jonathon, privately.

Amanda's birthday party was one to be remembered. All of the family was present, plus Jeremy which completed her inner circle at this time. Looking around the room she thought, "I'm happy at this moment. Life is good."

"Jeremy, you're in engineering too. I am too and so is Jonathon," began Dave Peterson. "Bryan goes in a few directions but he may end up with us too. What kind of engineering work do you do?

And so it went for quite a while. Looking around the room from her favorite seat on the brown couch in the family room, Amanda remembered vividly the first time she had accidentally let her father see her cry. Smiling in remembrance she knew that was the first moment she had made a small stepping stone in her life. Yet she never opened up any more after that day. She was very careful never again to let her feelings be known. Today she realized that was not the best course of action but at the time it seemed to be her only road to follow.

"How everything going?" asked Jonathon as Amanda finally found him alone. "How does twenty-five feel?"

"It feels good to me and I'm glad we're all together. Your little Michael seems to be such a happy three-year-old. Is he always happy like that?"

"Well, not always of course, little children do have their difficult times. But I am trying to encourage him to get his feelings out. You know, like the other day he fell down and hurt his arm and he really cried. We thought at first it might even be broken but soon found out it wasn't. Thank God. But he just kept crying and then I thought that I would try what I learned on him. Validate his feelings. So instead of saying that everything was all right and that he should stop crying, I just held him and told him that when he fell on his arm that it must have really hurt and crying was part of that. I told him that I knew when you fall down that it hurts. And he just kept looking at me with tears coming down his face. It still hurt but he stopped crying and his eyes showed me he was happy I understood."

"Oh I see. I know what you mean. We adults do that when we tell children that everything is alright and they will be okay but we don't let them know that we understand that it does hurt at the moment. Later it will be okay, but right now it hurts. Is that what you mean?"

"Exactly. And that is true of adults too. When something has really hurt us like a death in the family or a sickness or a thousand other things that can happen, we need to acknowledge that a hurt is happening and just be there physically for a person. Later on pain will subside and we all handle what we have to, but right now, at this moment, we must validate the pain."

"Yes, I see what you mean. You sure have learned a lot working with those troubled kids. You know Jonathon, I always wondered why and how you got started with those kids."

"First, I must say, that I was always glad how you and Bryan turned out, in spite of me. But maybe you remember Lindsey Holloway, that friend of mine from college. I was friends with her father Bill. He was an adopted child and told me that he was a troubled kid and got the help he needed so, as an adult, he decided to return the favor. Later on after my problems got better I contacted Bill and I sometimes work with him. I learn so much Amanda; it's hard to explain."

"I always wondered how you discovered about the attachment disorder? How did you find out about it?"

"That too was Lindsey's father. I happened to be visiting the weekend that he was going to meet his birth mother. He was so nervous. A grown man of fifty-two years old and in sweats and nervous tension about meeting his birth mother for the first time. Oh Gees, Amanda, I didn't mean to be insensitive seeing that you're adopted, I'm so sorry."

"Oh no, no. That's okay. Maybe I can learn from what you found out."

"Okay, well, that night Bill opened up and told me his entire story about being adopted at five years old and I thought he would have been a happy little kid, just like you were when you first came to live with us, but he said he was just the opposite. He was angry and full of rage and meanness, just like me. He sounded just like I acted but I didn't make any connection at the time because I wasn't adopted."

"He was an angry child too?"

"Yep, then he talked about this attachment disorder but said that you didn't have to be adopted in order to have it. Remember I was in the hospital as a little kid, well that is probably where it started with me. I know we talked about it a little. But I didn't even make the connection in my mind until Bill said that after some separations due to illness or divorce and a lot of other reasons, that some children living with their birth parents can run into these same problems too."

Amanda got very, very quiet. She had developed some trust and respect for Jonathon in the last few years. If she hadn't, she would have thought that he might be trying to tell her to check out this disorder; it might help her. Amanda swallowed hard a few times but listened intently as her interest peaked.

"Yeah, you had several separations when you were little and in the hospital. Very interesting."

"Exactly. I felt abandoned and scared and became distrustful, especially of mom. Remember how mean I used to be with mom. This disorder isn't something you choose, it is something that happens to you."

"How did Bill do with his birth mother?" asked Amanda as it had a special interest for her.

"His meeting went very well. It seems she was a seventeen-year-old who was pregnant and had no family. His father loved his mother and planned to marry her but he was killed in a car accident before it happened. She couldn't care for the baby alone. After trying to do so for about six months, she gave him up for adoption. He was told that he'd gone to several orphanages and was almost five years old when he was finally adopted. He had frightened away other adoption possibilities with his rage and inappropriate behavior. But the last family was ready to take him, anger and all and they made it through everything. He really is a wonderful man and he does wonderful work with troubled kids."

"And he got you started?"

"Yeah but only after I went to some good RAD therapists and got the help I needed. I had never told Bill my story because I was too ashamed but later, I took a chance. Bill said something to me once, '"We are so much harder on ourselves than anybody else would ever be."' Isn't that a true statement.?"

"Wow —"

"Heh are you two gonna stay in here all night or are you going to give the rest of us the pleasure of your company?" That was Janice trying to get everyone together to light the candles on the birthday cake.

"Okay, okay we're coming."

After the candles were lit and a few people teasingly hinted that Amanda's wish for her twenty-fifth year would be to find the man of her dreams, everyone looked over at Jeremy. Janice and Dave wanted Amanda to settle down especially now that Jonathon was married to Amy with a nice little boy, and Bryan was engaged to Kathy and was soon to be married. But Amanda surprised everyone by telling her wish. She said she never believed it had to be a secret anyway.

"I have made it to a quarter of a century thanks to mom and dad. I've been happy and fulfilled thanks to my parents and my brothers and the rest of our family. My new friend Jeremy, well, we'll see about the future later. But I have another more pressing wish," she said as she raised her glass. "Here's to me finding out what I want to attach to."

And with that, she looked directly at Jonathon and smiled. No words were spoken but they both knew and acknowledged the hidden message by their eye contact. Jonathon and Amanda both knew that she had many roads yet to travel.

Amanda found a RAD expert within five miles of her apartment. She shared with Jeremy what she needed to do and had his total support. In fact, he was proud of her and also admitted he just might benefit from some of her lessons. Amanda found Jennifer Freeland after searching for months and through several word of mouth references. She was an attractive lady in her mid-fifties and surprisingly enough, she had been adopted. She had been working with adopted children for almost thirty years and luckily she was well versed on both sides of the picture. She could truly understand the feelings of the adopted because she had been there. She almost always had an instant rapport with her clients.

Amanda's first few sessions were mostly talking about background necessities and helping Jennifer get all the facts about the experiences she had. Some experiences were known but others were simply a guess, due to her background. By the third session Amanda was feeling very comfortable and able to acknowledge to herself that she had found someone that was a confidante and who truly understood her feelings. This was a little bit of heaven for her since she had kept everything to herself for so long.

While in the waiting room before her fourth session, she happened on an article explaining the importance of acknowledging losing a parent when you were adopted. Usually, the article said, if the comment was made, "I lost my mom when I was very young." an empathetic stranger might say, "I'm so sorry for you. It's so difficult to lose a parent." But if that same stranger was told, "I was adopted," the response is usually "Really, that's wonderful. How nice for you." The article continued on to say that in adoption, we need to affirm that in order to be adopted a child has to have lost a mother and father and although she may be lucky to have wonderful, loving adoptive parents, this blessing followed an enormous loss. The following are two facts that adoptive parents need to accept in order to allow their child the validation that they need.

1. The child has two mothers and two fathers. (Even if the birth parents are deceased, they must be acknowledged as having existed.)

2. The child has a history and comes with a lot of baggage. Some will be positive and some will be negative.

When Amanda asked Jennifer about the article, she found that she was very familiar with the ideas it presented and the discussion began.

"Did you ever talk to your mom and dad about your birth parents?"

"No, not really. There was one time when I needed a baby picture of myself for a class project and I asked my mom why she didn't get any pictures. But I think that was probably the only time."

"Weren't you ever curious or didn't you care?"

Amanda sat for a few minutes pondering on that question. This was opening up a very private area of herself that had been closed for a very long time. It wasn't that it was only painful, exactly, but it was also fearsome.

"I was very curious all of my life. I would have loved to talk to my mother and father but I was so afraid that my parents would get mad at me or else they would be very hurt. Maybe they would think that I didn't love them or that I didn't appreciate what they had done for me. It was kind of mixed feelings but it stopped me from ever talking to them about my birth parents."

Tears welled up in Amanda's eyes at these memories. Many nights she had cried herself to sleep wondering and guessing about the other side of her life. She knew that she would never know some details and that always troubled her.

"Why did you think your parents would get mad at you? Did they ever tell you not to talk about your birth mom or dad?"

"Oh no, they were very kind to me; I guess that was my interpretation. At the beginning I thought that if I made them mad they might send me back. So I tried to do everything to please them. I wondered if the orphanage would even take me back if the Petersons didn't want me because if I was returned, it would probably be because I had been a bad girl. That was probably my most fearful times."

"That's a lot of fear for a little girl to face alone. I can see why you cried yourself to sleep at night. Did you ever learn to trust them? Did you ever feel comfortable and wanted by them later on?"

"I sort of trusted them but only if I was a "good girl," you know. I felt if I displeased them, I might not be on solid ground. They were always nice to me so I can't blame them for my discomfort. And then we had Jonathon, my older brother, who had developed attachment disorder but no one found out what it was for years."

Jonathon's story was already in the record. But the effect of his treatment of her did not make the situation easier. It was so noted.

"Do you blame Jonathon for the way he acted?"

"I certainly did at the time and I hated him for being so mean to me. I tried everything I could think of to please him and nothing worked."

The frustration from the early years brought out the little girl in Amanda and even her voice changed for a moment. She was reliving the experience to such a high degree that her feelings and actions were that of a three or four year old.

"I was very angry at him for many years but not anymore and he apologized and wrote me a beautiful letter asking for my forgiveness."

"How about your anger Amanda? Tell me about your 'quiet anger', as you call it."

Amanda tried to get some words out, but they wouldn't come. After searching her mind for several moments, she began, albeit hesitantly.

"It is very difficult to admit to someone out loud that although I seemed like such a nice little girl, always pleasing to everybody, that I had a tremendous amount of anger, hate and rage inside, not only for my mom and dad and my family but also for the outside world. I didn't trust anyone, sometimes not even me."

Amanda paused for several moments, but had more to

say.

"I remember once when I was about five or six, I held in my anger for so long that I had reached the end of my endurance, so when it got too much for me I would dig my fingernails into the palms of my hands. There were times my palms would actually bleed but I didn't feel the pain at the time. The only pain I felt was the anger inside. I hurt so much at times that I wondered why I didn't burst."

Jennifer added, "And when the obvious pain wasn't brought to the surface, it remained inside of you and you became depressed and unhappy. In the midst of all this, you probably still tried to show a happy face to the world, right?"

"Oh yes, that is pretty much the way it was."

"Did you ever wonder why your birth mom gave you away Amanda? Has that thought crossed your mind?"

Amanda had difficulty talking about the difficult times in her early years and she knew her therapist was aware. After all, she had been there. Opening up to the tough, raw pain that had settled into the cells of your body required courage unknown to those inexperienced ones. Amanda realized that opening up her painful memories was merely a stepping stone. She was happy Jennifer decided to share her story and let her refocus for a time.

"You know Amanda, I was adopted before the age of one. No one ever thought that I would remember or even needed to know anything about the adoption, so for years I thought I was born into my adoptive family. But sometime around ten years old, I overheard a conversation, which usually happens sometime or other in this type of situation, and I had a very difficult time adjusting to the fact that I was adopted. I was a lot like you after that. I kept everything inside of me and let my family think that my adoption was just fine with me and I was so appreciative and felt lucky to be adopted into a nice family. I wouldn't dare let anyone know my negative inside thoughts and I had lots of them."

"Did you ever wonder why your birth mom gave you away?"

"Oh yes, almost every night. I used to think that I must have been a very bad baby because no one would give away a good baby, right?"

Amanda smiled in recognition. Of course she had had the same thought so many times.

"I used to wonder what I could have possibly done so bad before the age of one to be given away." Amanda and Jennifer kept total eye contact during this time.

"Did you ever find out why you were given away?" asked Amanda.

"No, I didn't. I was one child that came to the orphanage without much of a history. All the information on my birth certificate turned out to be phony so I've never had a place to start. Sometime later I'll tell you about it but right now I want you to know that I had so much anger in those years after I found out about my adoption status that it took me into my late twenties before I decided I couldn't live with the inside anger anymore. It was always on mind and it was ruining my relationships and my chance at life, so I had to find a way to heal."

After these last comments, Amanda noticed that Jennifer just stopped her story. She got up and poured them more coffee and then she sat down and waited. Amanda knew it was now her turn. She needed to gather the courage to continue. It took well over ten minutes, yet neither of them felt uncomfortable.

Amanda slowly began. "Um, I'm trying to get my thoughts together but they just won't fit into any pattern, so I'll just begin. This is really very hard, but I'm sure you already know that. I've always kept my anger hidden inside of me. When I was little my anger was just below the surface and harder to control, although I always managed to control it. But in later years, I used to bury my anger and sometimes I could even pretend that it didn't exist. To be honest with myself, I knew it was there depressing me and creating what I called dark shadows inside. Most of the time these shadows were already there in the morning when I woke up, so I had to push through the shadows and through the depression before I even started my day. It was very hard."

Amanda stopped for a few moments since her painful memories had already pushed two or three tears past her eyelids and down her cheeks. Brushing them away, she continued. "I remember so many nights crying into my pillow. I wanted to know who I was and where I came from. My new brother Jonathon said that I didn't belong with them. I know now that he had his problems, but those comments hurt so much at the time. And besides that, I still didn't know anything about myself. Why did my mom give me away? Oh yes, that was a question I desperately wanted answered. Who was my father? Did I have any brothers and sisters? Did I look like my mother? What were my grandparents like? Did anyone else in my family like to draw? Oh God, Jennifer it never stops. Years ago, I was just a little girl asking these questions, but now I'm older and I'm still asking these same questions that have no answers."

"Have you ever searched for answers? You know if you were able to get at least some answers, you may like them but then again, you may not like them. Of course, it could help but you have to be prepared that the answers may not be the ones you want to hear."

"I think now that knowing about where I came from

would be so much better than not knowing and always guessing. I worry so much about having children some day. My boyfriend Jeremy and I are quite serious and are thinking of becoming engaged soon. I have recently told him that I was adopted and he is fine with it and very supportive of me. In fact, he suggested therapy to help me sort of some of my feelings."

"The fact that he understands must help. But starting today, we are going to go through some exercises that will help you in dealing with those inner feelings and pain that have caused you anger for so many years. It's time to let it go, don't you think?"

"Is that really possible? To get rid of all that pain and anger and questions that keep running over and over again through my mind? Is that really possible?"

"In time you and you alone can put everything in a comfortable area that you can live with. Will you get all of your answers? Probably not. Will you get rid of all your anger? Probably not. But you can put your life in perspective and alleviate most of your pain. Everyone lives with some painful memories, not just us adopted children. And you can understand and use it to your benefit and live a comfortable and happy life. That I know you can do, because I've done it."

With that discussion concluded, the therapy sessions began in earnest and tough exercises followed. Some sessions pulled up forgotten memories that had been hidden deeply and buried carefully because of the intense pain. There were always tears and frustrations and by the end of the next several sessions, Amanda felt totally worn out emotionally and very tired physically. People would have been surprised seeing some of the behavior that came from Amanda. Jennifer wasn't surprised. She knew her "quiet anger" as Amanda termed it, wasn't really that quiet at all.

One time when Amanda came into Jennifer's office, she was surprised to see a lady there with a one and a half year old baby. The lady was a friend of her therapist's who had volunteered her baby for a few minutes to help Jennifer make a point. As the lady went out of the office, she gave Amanda her little baby girl to hold for a few minutes.

"Now I want you to bring little Ruth over here by the large mirror, okay Amanda?"

Not knowing what to expect, Amanda approached the mirror and saw herself standing there holding a very sweet little baby who kept trying to fall asleep but her inquisitive nature kept her aware of her environment. She had a contented look on her face and just kept looking around and blinking in childlike curiosity.

"Hold little Ruth up right in front of the mirror and look at her, will you?"

Amanda did as she was told wondering what this was all about, and not yet having any clue as to what was happening. Then Jennifer asked a very tough question.

"Now Amanda, take a good look at this little baby. She's very dependent on the adult who must carry her and feed her and love her and just generally do everything for her, right? What she is doing is beginning to understand and interpret the world around her."

"Yes, that's right. She is a very sweet, normal little baby."

"Can you tell me, Amanda, what this little child could possibly do to be a very bad, bad baby? A baby that acted so badly that her mother would have to give her away? Tell me, what could she possibly do that would be that bad?"

Amanda was dumbstruck. She had nothing to say. She

just kept staring in the mirror at this innocent little baby, wondering and wondering. The face of the baby was awesome in its innocence and no words came from Amanda.

Then Jennifer took the baby from her. Amanda watched Jennifer as she cuddled her and played with it for a moment and talked to her like any mother would do. She was forced to see this little baby on another woman's lap to realize further that she was just an innocent baby, not necessarily good or bad, just an innocent new soul in this world trying to figure out what life was all about. Amanda realized the truth. This baby couldn't be bad; she just was.

Within that moment, a torrent of tears started falling from Amanda's face as she realized that most of her life she had thought that she must have been a very bad baby and that was why her mother gave her away. She didn't know until now that it was a common belief among adopted children. That was one of the reasons that she felt she had to be good all the time. Yet looking at this wonderful, dependent baby, she finally knew in a very quick second that being given away really wasn't her fault. It wasn't her fault at all.

"I couldn't have been a bad baby like I always thought. Thank you Jennifer. I finally get it. I couldn't have been that bad."

"I'd love to take credit for this experiment but it was done to me in therapy years ago and it helped me to realize that a little baby couldn't possibly do anything to warrant abandonment. You see Amanda, that was the way I found out that I wasn't a bad baby either."

This had been a turning point in her sessions with Jennifer. In a way, they were all turning points but this one gave her a place of reference inside that she could relate to. She had been given up for adoption for some reason but it wasn't because she had been a bad baby. She remembered so many nights of crying and sobbing when she tried to relive her baby years pretending that she had been a perfect baby. Now she knew she had been as good as any other baby. She could begin her intense scrutiny of herself at another location because she had been as good a baby as any other, and knowing that helped a lot.

Lately she had asked Jeremy to drive her home since she usually needed to sleep for a while after her sessions. She noticed that her anger had not dissipated much, nor was it expected to—it was much too soon. But when she thought of her birth mom she was more curious about her life instead of being frustrated, fearful and disappointed. Her usual anger wasn't there. *"Am I still mad and angry that life had dealt what she thought was a bad hand? Yes, that had not changed. But she was thinking of other things now in a more intellectual and less emotional manner."*

"Wake up honey, you're home."

"Gosh, I must have slept all the way home. Sorry."

After relaxing in her apartment for a few minutes, Amanda realized that Jeremy had something on his mind.

"Is something wrong Jeremy? You seem distracted."

"I was just thinking that sometime in the near future we'll have to talk about a wedding date and all the other stuff, but right now I think we need to talk about a few other things."

"What other things?"

Well, I see some improvements in you lately. You seem more contented and calmer somehow. But I know this is a slow process so I think we should wait about our plans until you can enjoy everything. It won't be that much longer but it will give you time to work on the important things in your life right now, okay?"

"Okay, I appreciate that. My mind has been so stretched by concentrating on what I have to do in the sessions and after, and then planning, or trying to plan things for our wedding that my head seems too full sometimes."

"I know, I know. We'll take one thing at a time and this comes first, okay?"

"Yeah, that's good. I know that I don't seem as enthused as I should be about the plans, but I just can't seem to concentrate on everything right now. I love you dearly and want to be in seventh heaven, as I should be, but ..."

"You've got too much on your mind right now. Let's get further along with your therapy and then we can both enjoy the wedding plans and the wedding."

"I guess I'm lucky that you're so understanding. These sessions just get me thinking about so many things that I've tried to hide away inside of me. I've had a good life and I'm engaged and happy but I feel so much is still missing. I wish I didn't feel that way but I do."

Now that Jeremy and Amanda were engaged Amanda appreciated his understanding so much more. His sharing of the sessions were encouraging her along her path she needed to travel. But there was one area she couldn't discuss with him. There was a void that was still there and although the dark shadows had lessened they still were around too. It was hard to explain but inside the dark shadows moved around a bit. When they were in the background and to the left side, Amanda was more in control and her days were pretty smooth. Lately, in her happiness they remained in this position and didn't move forward and to the right side or to the center where they caused most of their severe problems.

But they still remained and this was quite frustrating to Amanda. She could talk to Jennifer and she understood but Amanda was afraid that Jeremy would think she was a little off center. So Amanda hid her problem from Jeremy and sometimes even from Jennifer.

In a recent session, Amanda knew that Jennifer wanted her to confront more hidden feelings and bring them out in the open. Amanda realized that she did lock away ideas that she didn't want to deal with and believed that she had progressed sufficiently to lighten up on herself.

"Amanda, you have progressed nicely and can be very proud of yourself. Some of our sessions have been tough. But I need to ask, are you where you want to be yet?"

"What do you mean?" asked Amanda, feeling anxious of the answer.

"Some adoptees want to confront their past. They'd like to go back to their roots and see what they can find. Personally, I tried but didn't have any leads to follow. How do you feel about it?"

Amanda knew how felt. She had felt the same way for many years. Her desires were always to find out whatever she could—then maybe she would feel satisfied. But then there was another hurdle that was too high to overcome. She said, "I've always wondered and I must admit that I'd like to find out whatever I could. But I don't think I want to do it now."

"Why not now? What's stopping you?"

"I'm not sure. I just don't think I'm ready. It's kind of like a mystery in my life. I know the orphanage where I was adopted from, so I'm sure that I probably could find out something. But do I want to do that or not?"

"Okay, maybe you're just not ready. That's a possibility. Or maybe it's something else. What do you think?"

"There are a couple of things on my mind, but I want to think of them a little bit more."

"The decision is up to you. You're the only one who will ever know if you really want to find out about your past. There's no right or wrong here. I, personally, would have liked to know something about my birth parents. But there was no place to start. But that is me. I may have been happy with what I found out and I may have been a little bit sad. Or I may have been devastated. So you have to be ready. Anyway, you'll know. I think you've come a long way since we've begun talking. What do you think?"

"Oh yes, so many things are more settled in my mind. And I don't feel weird that someone gave me away. I know that's probably a strange word to use but it's a throwback from my childhood. Whenever I thought that my birth mom just gave me away, I had a weird feeling inside that depressed me. I don't think that way anymore. I feel okay about myself because I believe there was probably a good reason. I think that maybe I wouldn't like finding out there wasn't a very good reason. And like you just said, it's a real possibility."

"But you know Amanda, we've been talking about these tough issues and you haven't even cried. If I'm guessing correctly, you haven't been close to tears at all today. Do you recognize how far you've come?

"Yeah and that's what I meant earlier. I still have many of the same questions and no answers but I can look at them more logically now. I can spend time looking for answers and solutions without getting my emotions in the way. That's a very good thing."

"Yes, that is a good thing."

"I know, but there's one more thing. I do have another something that I recognize about myself and I must solve it before I make my decision about searching or not. It does give me a lot of anxiety and I'm sure that's why I can't make a decision right now. I don't want to talk about it yet. But the best part is I tell myself, 'That's okay, Amanda. You don't have to decide today, and you're still an okay person. I don't want to disappoint you, Jennifer, but one of the last shadows inside can bring me to tears."

"Heavens, Amanda, you're not alone. Everyone has some shadows that are hard to face and some never face them. And that's not just us adoptees either. All people have rough times in their lives that are difficult to face. It's called being human."

Amanda smiled at that comment. "It does make me feel more equal, you know?"

"I know and there are times we all need a good feeling like that."

As more time passed, Amanda felt good about her sessions with Jennifer. She had put many things in proper perspective in her life and some of the lifelong shadows had lessened. It had taken time but it was time that inched her ahead to a better future. Occasionally Jeremy brought up his ideas about confronting her past. He felt it was possibly a good idea, but relinquished the decision to her. Lately, he had understood that she had a self-created barrier. Amanda had realized it too but denied it to herself.

Just talking about the subject made Amanda extremely nervous. She didn't know how she could face it. In discussing it again with Jeremy, he agreed. In fact, he urged her on. "You've got to face it honey. You might even find out a lot of those answers you need. But even if you don't find out anything at all, you won't always be wondering what else you could have done. It's your decision but I think it's a good idea."

Amanda knew Jeremy was right. Her nervousness always brought her close to tears. But she knew Jeremy was right. She knew Jennifer was right.

"Yes, I understand and I know you and Jennifer are both right but that would mean…"

With that Amanda started crying and sobbing and just couldn't stop. Even with Jeremy holding her and trying to console her, she knew the time had come when she was being pushed to do something she promised herself she would never do. And surprisingly enough, Amanda was the one doing the pushing. After a few minutes she managed to stop sobbing.

"Jeremy said, "We both know what panics you, don't we? I'd like you to put your fears into words now so you can hear yourself say them."

Amanda pulled away abruptly from him at this point. She was very angry but not necessarily at Jeremy. She knew he loved her and wanted to help but he didn't understand. He could never understand how she felt inside. Jennifer knew the feeling and then she remembered that Jennifer had faced the fear and that helped her to conquer it. Maybe facing the fear would help her to settle down inside and then she could focus on the important things in her life now. Would it work that way for her? Would the end really justify what she had to do?

"I know when you pulled away from me you were mad. Even approaching the subject makes you mad. Tell me what is so upsetting to you. I know I can't feel what you are feeling, but I love you and want to help you get through this."

"Give me a moment, will you? I want to say this out loud but it is so hard. But I've got to say it and I want to say it now."

Amanda got up from her chair and began pacing back and forth across the room. She was almost stomping her feet and was definitely talking to herself out loud. The person walking heavily across the floor was an adult woman physically but the emotions and fears bottled up were those of a little child. She talked in a somewhat coded language that Jeremy couldn't understand. She was in her own world and for a few moments not even aware that anyone else was in the room. As she heard herself talking much louder than usual, she realized how angry she was and felt that she was talking to some inner force. Then, in a sudden moment she stopped moving. She just stood there and started yelling, mostly at herself. "I can't do this. It's too much to ask of myself. This is very painful. It hurts. It hurts a lot. I can't do it. I just want to disappear. But I can't fail myself. I must do it. Life is so hard. Why does it have to be this hard?" For a long few moments she stood there, talking to herself as if she was the only person in the world who existed. Then, she started moving again and this time she started stomping again. She was angry. She had only anger and pain on her plate at this moment and this pattern lasted for a few more minutes before Amanda came back to reality and finally spoke.

"I just can't do it." Amanda screamed the words loudly and it shocked Jeremy.

"I can't hurt them that way. They will hate me. I can't do it and I won't do it."

"You won't do what Amanda?"

220

"I'm not telling my wonderful adoptive parents who have been so good to me that I want to search for my birth mom and dad."

After Amanda said those words, she stopped stomping. She actually stopped walking and just stood there in the middle of the room as if she were in another world. And for a few moments, she was somewhere else. Finally, she started crying again. This time the sobs came from very deep inside her. She knew that she probably frightened Jeremy with these type of sobs but he again reached out to Amanda and she let him hold her and it felt good to be held as she let all the tears flow. Tears had been almost unknown to Amanda in the past, except in the privacy of her own room, but they were becoming much more common in the present. She cried for a very long time as they both sat silently lost in their own individual thoughts.

"Wow, that was really hard," said Amanda. "I feel rather ashamed."

"Why?"

"The statement probably doesn't sound like a big deal."

"It is to you."

"Yes, I know and I know, and I must confront my past. It's the only way. But how will I ever tell mom and dad?"

"Do you really think they will be so surprised that you want to find out something about your past? Especially now?"

"I know they will be nice about it. But I hate to hurt them that way."

"Why are you so sure they will be mad or hurt. I don't think they will, not at all."

"But you didn't live with them. They were so happy to have a little girl who was happy to be there."

"And you always showed your appreciation for all they did for you. You are thinking from a little girl's emotions who thinks if she doesn't act perfect she will be sent back to the orphanage."

"Yes, I always tried to be perfect. But I still believe this will hurt them."

"But searching for something in your past so you can get the missing links of your life together would be normal for any adopted child. Maybe they have been waiting for you to talk about it because I'm sure they figured someday you would want to search."

"Do you really think so?" said Amanda, amazed at the thought, "Could that be possible? I don't want to hurt them, ever, but I'm so twisted inside because I know I have to do this. Oh, what a mess."

Amanda put her head in her hands for a few moments. Why couldn't her life be simple? Why couldn't she have been born to the Petersons? Jeremy gave her a few minutes before he started again.

"You've gained a lot of strength in your life. You are so much stronger now than when I first met you. But everyone has problems to overcome. You can choose not to face this and stay the way you are or you can face this situation and grow to your best potential. But don't forget to give your parents some credit. I personally would be very shocked if they didn't realize you needed to search for answers and I know they won't take it personally."

Taking a deep breath Amanda said, "You really think they might not be too upset and think I really didn't love them but was just pretending?"

"I don't think they will be upset at all."

Amanda thought about it for a few moments. She always knew this moment would come. The question was whether she had the courage to move forward now or would she stay forever stuck in her past. The answer was really very simple. She had to move forward.

"Will you come with me?"

"Of course I will."

"Okay, I'll let them know that I need to talk to them. They will think it's about the wedding so I'll tell them ahead of time that it is not about the wedding, right? It's only fair."

"And you always have to be fair" Jeremy said as he winked at her. She knew he was proud of her and truly, she was proud of herself. She was at long last climbing this final hill, mostly by herself and keeping her feet secure.

Amanda put a call to Jennifer and let her know what she was doing. Jennifer was very pleased and also calmed her about the idea of facing her parents. The next Saturday night found Amanda and Jeremy at her parents' house for dinner. Amanda saw everyone at the table looking at her, and found herself fidgeting. When she tried to say something, it was as if she'd been walking in a hot desert for several hours—her mouth was so dry. She took a sip of water and began. "I really don't know how to begin, so give me a moment." Amanda knew she was making the situation worse by prolonging it and fortunately, her courage finally caught up to her and she just put out the first carefully thought-out sentence quickly. "You know that Jeremy and I are starting to plan our wedding and someday we hope to have children. I've decided that it would be to our benefit if I could find out something about my past."

Amanda had thought out these words very thoroughly.

Putting everything in the context of the wedding and future children gave her a reason to check out her past for possible medical and psychological reasons and it seemed the easiest way to present her case. And there was some validity to what she said. Part of her felt that she took the coward's way out, but another part of her was pleased that she'd at least managed to speak.

"Okay, that makes good sense." Amanda saw her mom look at her as if she was waiting for more to come.

"I hope that you are not upset that I will need to see if I can find my birth mother or my birth father. You must know how much I love you and appreciate both of you but it's something I need to do."

Both Amanda and Jeremy were surprised that she got that last sentence out without breaking down and crying. But Amanda seemed to be in full control. She was looking back from her mother and father to see any signs of displeasure but found none. Finally, she just asked the question.

"Do either of you have a problem with this?"

"No, of course not honey. I guess I thought you would have done it years ago. I know I would have been so curious about my beginnings, It's only normal." Her mom was the one that Amanda thought would have the most difficult time with this and she seemed to be in total agreement and not surprised at all.

"Well that's good. I don't want to hurt either one of you. You are both so important to me."

"Why would that hurt us honey? asked Janice.

"I thought maybe you would think I didn't love you. But I do you know."

Finally Amanda felt the tears begin forming in her eyes. Yet she had come this far tonight and talked about something that had frightened her for years. Bringing up one of the ghosts that was buried inside her seemed to ease some tension, but it also gave her a feeling of self-respect since she had faced this inner demon known only to herself over the years.

Janice walked over and put her arms around Amanda as only a mother can do. The comforting feeling was just what she needed at the moment. Then as she looked over at her dad and noticed the same look on his face that she had seen so many times before. He never said a word but Amanda knew that her dad, more than anyone else in the room, was in tune with her inner feelings.

Finally Dave spoke. "Tell me Amanda, how many months or years have you worried yourself about this? I'm sure quite a while. We used to bring up the subject of your mom, occasionally, but you always turned away. I knew you just feared talking to us about your past and I also knew that this day would probably come sooner or later. I'm so glad it's now. You can face what's necessary and be ready when you become a parent."

Amanda was really crying now. It seemed that lately whenever she tried hard to keep control over her emotions, the tears had plans of their own. They were happy tears that had been buried for too many years and everyone understood.

Her father's final comment said it all.

"Jeremy, I hope you're ready for the female tears. But seriously, Amanda, Janice and I worried every once in a while because you didn't seem to want to face your past and that wouldn't be good. And you, Amanda, worrying about hurting us. You have been such a good daughter, really the best. We thank your birth mother for giving you to us."

Well, that did it. Amanda gave her father a big hug. It was wonderful when people understood. She didn't know if her past would have some frightening events to face, but she knew she had a very powerful team to stand with her.

Amanda made her decision a few weeks later. The admirable part was that she made her decision alone, although there was support all around her if she needed it. For once in her life she was ready to stand alone and she suddenly felt strong. To say that Amanda was proud of herself was too small a declaration. It was one of those feelings that you know in your heart will be remembered because you are finally powerful enough to following through on your chosen action alone.

Once the decision was made, she let her family, therapist and Jeremy know. Everyone assumed that they would be the one asked to go with her. Her mom was sure it would be her as was her dad. Jeremy, of course, was positive he would be chosen. To everyone's surprise, Amanda wanted to face her past alone. Amanda's newfound   strength gave everyone more surprises.

"I know I'll be anxious to share with you when I get home but I want and need to do this alone."

Jeremy's body language was telling Amanda a different story from his words. He wasn't sure Amanda could handle this alone. "Are you sure? If you need me to come I won't have any problem taking time off work. If you need me later I could fly down to be with you?"

Amanda looked at Jeremy like she was seeing him in a different light. She knew he loved her and was proud of her but she wondered if secretly he liked her dependence on him. How would he handle the fact that she was becoming an equal to him emotionally and psychologically? Soon she would enjoy his opinions while depending more on her own logic. How would Jeremy handle that? With her twenty-seventh birthday approaching quickly, Amanda was happy she was on the road to healing. The world was taking on a more wondrous meaning to her now and she loved the newness the sudden light presented. She was facing the monsters of her past and anyone who felt that they had to help her didn't realize that this was a road that must be traveled solo. Jennifer was the only one who could truly understand, which was why a coded language between them was satisfying. Some things could not be explained in words; they could only be experienced.

Now the time had arrived. Tomorrow Amanda was leaving for Prescott, Arizona alone to face her past. She decided she wasn't so much afraid and nervous anymore but just extremely excited with so much anticipation toward facing the unknown. With her new strength whirling inside of her where it belonged, she could now face the good or bad with equal acceptance.

CHAPTER VIII

Amanda ultimately arrived for her second appointment with Mrs. Benson at the orphanage about 10:30 AM. The backed-up traffic from the accident was incredibly slow to clear, and although control of the situation was out of her hands, her patience had been put to the ultimate test. Parking her car in the visitor's lot brought on the nervousness that she had so well kept under control until now. The steering wheel was damp from the sweat of her hands, yet that was understandable and acceptable as her feelings and emotions were well within the realm of normality. Anyone would be nervous in a situation like this, she thought, and some might exhibit a slight panic. So, instead of jumping out of the car and rushing to the door, Amanda took control of the muscles of her body and forced herself into a calmer demeanor and took great satisfaction that she was now able to do this without too much effort. She didn't think she had become vain about her control, but she was quite proud of herself. Vanity could tempt her a little if it wished to do so, but several years of very hard work had gotten her to this point. Now, she could face her past and she could do it on her own power. Forcing herself to walk slowly to the door, Amanda delighted in the fact that she was pleased with herself at this moment in time.

Stephanie Mallik met her at the door. She had spoken to her at great length yesterday with understanding and compassion, which apparently lingered on into today. Was it only yesterday that she had visited the orphanage? Somehow it seemed like a long time ago.

"Welcome back, Amanda. I'm happy you made it back today. That accident has disrupted many businesses in our area. Come in, come in, this October air is beginning to get a bit chilly." Stephanie managed a big smile which Amanda was beginning to expect from her.

"Thanks. Yes, winter is definitely coming but it's a beautiful day, despite the cooler temperature."

"Come, let's go into my office. I've sent for Mrs. Benson as soon as I saw your jeep pull up. She will be here very quickly. I wonder if you will remember her."

"I've tried to get a picture of her in my mind and I really can't. It's only an impression or a feeling," Amanda answered with a slight touch of disappointment.

"You were so very young when you were here. Not many people have clear memories of that time in their lives."

"I'm hoping Mrs. Benson will remember some of the things I don't. Knowing anything at all would be a pleasure for me. It would be something I can put in my scrapbook and fill in some of the blanks in my early life." Amanda still managed to create a lump in her throat as she thought of her past. Yet, along with the excitement that presently consumed her, she felt satisfaction that only anticipation could bring her.

"Yes, of course, I understand," said Stephanie as she nodded in agreement.

Just about this time the door opened to Mrs. Mallik's office and in walked a woman of at least sixty years old. She smiled easily and quickly and gave the impression that she was happy with life and most who crossed her path would have to notice it. Although dressed in a type of uniform, she looked neat and well tailored and self-pride was definitely a part of her overall impression. She immediately walked over to Amanda and gave her a big hug. It was a comfortable moment and since the women were about the same height, they patted each other on the back as people often do during such a moment.

"Oh Amanda, Amanda. It is simply great seeing you as an adult woman. What a pretty gal you've become and if I can judge character, you seem to be a happy gal too.

"Yes, I've been fortunate and had a good life with a very nice family."

"I can tell because your face is telling your story. What are you doing now?"

"I graduated from college with a degree in art and I'm working for a publishing company. I do illustrations for book covers and sometimes I do portraits on the side."

"Yes, yes that would make sense. Even as a little one here you liked to draw. I mean, I know kids all like to draw and color, but your pictures were particularly good for a child of two or three. I know you were about three years old when you left us but you could draw rather well. We all saw the talent back then. I've saved a few things of yours and I'll get them for you later. I'm sure you'd like to have them now."

"You save some stuff of mine? Yes, I would love that." Amanda suddenly felt lighter inside as excitement entered her body.

"I always save things in the children's files for them. If they come back with an interest, then I give it to them. Usually it makes them happy to find some personal belongings from their past."

At this time, Mrs. Mallik announced that she would leave the two women alone and they could use her office as long as they wished. A pot of coffee was brought in with some sweet rolls and as the door closed behind the director, a sudden silence casts its shadow and they remained quiet for a few moments. Amanda spoke first.

"Mrs. Benson ..."

"Please call me Vicki."

Amanda smiled as she continued, realizing that she wasn't three years old any longer and could talk to Mrs. Benson as an adult.

"Vicki, I came here hoping to find out something about my mom and dad. I have never known if there was any information about them or their families. Also, any details that you can tell me about when I first came to the orphanage that would help fill in some blanks of my years before I was three years old would be great. What kind of a child I was or anything at all that you can tell me. I think you are the only one left now who was employed here when I first came."

"Yes that's true. All of the others have moved on or died quite some time ago. I'll tell you whatever I can and let's start with your mom. I did meet her, but only one time, well, actually twice but on the same day. I can tell you that you do have somewhat of a resemblance; at least I remember the hair color is about the same and I know that she was petite, like the two of us. I always write notes in my file and I wrote she was about 5"2" with dark blonde hair. She was very quiet and extremely upset. I don't know anything about her family; she didn't talk about them. I've never heard anything about your father, except that he died in a traffic accident. Sorry about that. I've rechecked my notes in your file before you came today and they say very little about family. I can say that it was a hard choice for her to give you up. I'm not sure if that is helpful and what you want to hear. I really don't know much of the facts, but at that time, I had worked here more than five years. You get to sense a lot of things in that time."

"So you actually met my birth mom and did, in fact, see her yourself."

"Yes I did Amanda and I'm not one to put sweetness on a story regardless of the truth. You will get the truth from me as I know it."

"That's what I want, please. Even if you don't remember anything at all, that is what I would want you to tell me. Please don't make up something nice. I want to fill in memories of my early life, but they have to be true memories. It would be better for my mind to remain blank, if need be, than to add lies even if they were made with the best intentions. Do we understand each other?"

"Exactly. I would never lie to any of my children. But I needed to know for sure what you wanted to know. Although I've never told lies to my children, there are some who need the blow softened somewhat, if you know what I mean?"

"Yes, I do understand, but please don't do that. I should tell you that during the last few years, I've finally started to grow up with the help of therapy." Since Mrs. Benson showed a curious and surprised look on her face, Amanda offered, "I had what they called attachment disorder, are you familiar with it?"

"Actually, I'm quite familiar with it. So many of our orphaned children get it and other foster children also have a tendency toward that disorder. Their little lives get so disrupted and baffling to them that their lose their ability to trust and love. It is a tough problem to overcome."

"Yes it is and I thought, working here, you would know

about it. I hid anger from my family for years and just kept it all inside while I put on a pleasing appearance for the world to see. I was so afraid that if my adoptive parents saw my anger inside that they would send me back and then I thought that maybe you wouldn't take me back because I had been a bad girl. So all that anger and fear stayed inside for years and I functioned as well as I could outwardly, but my self-confidence and trust in life and in myself suffered greatly."

"So you were a child that carried everything on the inside. Some do that and others let their anger and rage take over their lives on the outside and are usually labeled as troublemakers."

"Yeah, so I've found out." Amanda realized that Vicki was totally familiar with attachment disorder problems. It was nice to know that she could be of some help to the children living at this orphanage.

"In the last few years I've done a lot of hard work in therapy," Amanda continued, "and finally I'm feeling much better about myself and my life and where I'm heading. I just got engaged to a nice guy I've known for more than two years. And he's an architect."

"Well, that certainly seems like a good match. You two have a lot in common."

"Yes, we do and he has supported me so much during my therapy which also helped in getting rid of my fears of the past. I've been worried about having children because I don't know much about my background. I don't even have any baby pictures of me and I hate that."

"I'll take a look in all the files I have here. It wouldn't be a little baby, but I might have one of when you first came so that would be just a little over one."

"Oh, that would be great. I'd appreciate that. Also, is

there anything in my background that I should know like medical, psychological etc?"

"Okay, I'm sure I can help you there a little. I'll be getting all those files shortly."

"I know that you might not have any information but I had to be able to tell myself that I tried. Jeremy, my fiancé, and I thought if there was any information about me like that, it would be valuable to know."

"I certainly will tell you all that I can. It does seem that you are quite in balance to handle anything. Are you here alone?"

"Yes, and that was my choice. This was something I wanted to do alone."

Amanda had a moment of fright. Did Vicki remember something that she didn't think she could handle alone? She didn't look concerned, but why did she ask? Holding a steady smile, Amanda knew Vicki recognized strength in her and that made her happy. She had certainly come a long way from the frightened little one year old that had come here many years ago.

"Let me get all my files and then I'll have my notes at my fingertips. I'll be back in a few moments."

With that said, Vicki left the room and although Amanda was anxious, she took those few moments to get all of her emotions under control as she realized now was the time to get as many questions answered as possible and later would be the time to let her feelings rule for a while, if that had to be the case.

"Where do you want to start?" Vicki returned carrying several folders in her arms, which pleased Amanda considerably.

"First, I'd like to know anything that you can remember. Even if it doesn't seem important, it would be important to me. Can we start with my mother since I know now that no father information is available?"

"Actually, it wasn't quite like that in reality. But let me start at the beginning. Your mother's first name was Annie, at least that is what she told me; it's in my notes here. She was very young, maybe twenty, and she said that her husband had been killed in a work-related traffic accident. I have no way of verifying anything because occasionally people do tell us a lot of stories. But I do know that she was having a very rough time leaving you here. She came back twice within the course of two hours and asked if she could spend a little private time with you. Of course, we gave it to her. I was here on her last visit and she picked you up and gave you a big hug and a kiss. She did tell me that you didn't relate very well to men. She said that her husband had been killed when you were a little over six months old and that you did relate well to him. She said she had tried to make a life for both of you but couldn't do it on her own. She had no relatives. Let's see, what else. Oh yeah, and this may be important. In the last few months before she gave you away, she was almost homeless and had to live in some pretty shabby places. Welfare could only help up to a certain point. Anyway she did mention that there were a few, what she termed "male characters" around and a few times she found some of them around you and you were crying and didn't stop crying even after she picked you up. She doesn't think any of them had time to harm you sexually or physically, but she worried more and more that it could happen. She knew that you began to get scared whenever a male figure came around. That was when she realized that she had to give you up and hope you would get a better life with a nice family. She has one message here, if you want to hear it."

"She left me a message for me?" said Amanda with tears coming down her face, "oh, yes, I want to hear it."

"It is a nice message, but they can be dramatic so I need to be sure you want to hear it. She said, and I quote, 'Tell her that I love her and always will. Make sure she understands that I didn't give her up because I didn't want her, but only because I was so afraid something bad would happen to her and I couldn't take care of her all by myself. Make sure she knows that, okay? Tell her I'll always love her, wherever I am.' Tears were rolling down her cheeks as she quickly handed you to me. When she turned to leave the last time, she hesitated again at the door as if she were going to come back again, but then after a long pause, she walked out the door and that was it."

Amanda sat quietly for a few moments as if she was trying to relive the scene with Vicki. She knew now that her birth mom really did love her and didn't want to give her up. Amanda herself felt more tears well up inside her eyes.

Amanda almost apologized for all the tears, adding "Thank you for remembering that. That was a long time ago."

"Tears are very much okay and understandable. I probably wouldn't remember so much but I have my some notes here. I try to do that for all of my children. Also, she I wrote that she seemed so sincere. She didn't talk a lot, she didn't say it wasn't her fault or make excuses and she wasn't a showoff. I wrote in my notes that I had a good feeling about her. She wasn't very tall, like I said, kind of like you and me. I'm sorry I don't remember any more details except what I've written down. My impression here was a sincere young woman who was in an impossible situation and wanted to do the best for her child. I know she didn't give you away easily. Of that, I am sure."

With this Amanda let the tears go and there were quite a few of them. What a great thing to know. Her birth mom did want her. She didn't give her up easily. That was a statement and a memory that she would cherish. That was something that she could tell her family and later her children. She could tell her daughter someday that she had another grandmother, who unfortunately had a tough life but who loved them and was wishing them well every day, wherever she was. And another thought occurred to her for the very first time. She didn't know if her mother was alive or dead. And she knew that she would probably never know about her or her deceased father, but she could wish them well and wish them blessings every day wherever they were. Those new memories were now finding their position inside her, adding some contentment and satisfaction. To some it might have been such a little thing, but to Amanda it added links to a long forgotten past.

"Oh I'm sorry, Vicki, but these are happy tears."

"But I can't tell you anymore than that," added Vicki cautiously. "We don't know her story. I'm not even sure if her name was Annie. I do know that she had been to the Welfare Office and had talked to some social workers and they gave her permission to bring you here personally. I had known someone was coming with a one-year-old baby girl for almost a week. They had the paperwork; your mom didn't have anything like that with her. She just had you. Also, the last name didn't check out from the hospital. It seldom does. But she did mention there wasn't any family."

"You have told me so much. Any little detail is a treasure to me. Even that is something to tell my kids about their grandmother, don't you see?"

Amanda watched Vicki's satisfaction as having a chance to provide her with information that completed some of the open areas of her young life. It seemed both of them felt contented.

"Finish your coffee and I'm going to get another folder I

forgot to bring. I think you'll love seeing some artwork you created as a child."

Silent tears brought relief to Amanda as she sat there alone in the room. At last she knew something. True, it wasn't very much but it was something real and to her that made it important. She'd always wondered if she had been a bad baby and possibly that was why her mother gave her away. She'd discovered in therapy that she couldn't have been a bad baby, but she'd always wondered why her mother hadn't wanted her. But now she knew that her mom did want her and she wanted her very much. She knew now that her mom had a hard time giving her up. No one else could possibly understand how important that was for her to know. Not her adoptive family, not Jeremy and probably not even Bryan. They would all try to understand but they could never know. Jennifer could understand and she would share her delight with the information. It was a difficult feeling to explain but all of the others would be genuinely excited for her and they would attempt to know how she felt. But they couldn't. Many people could empathize and sympathize, but in this important part of her life, only another adopted person like her therapist Jennifer, could share her feelings. She alone would know how it felt deep inside where it counted. And when Jennifer said, "I know how you feel, Amanda," Amanda knew that she really did know. Knowing someone like Jennifer was like having a savior in her life.

When Vicki returned with her folder, she took out picture after picture that Amanda had created as a little girl. And true to her word, the pictures confirmed a talent for art beyond a two or three year old level. Some pictures utilized very dark colors and Amanda thought her therapist would understand them better than she did. However, she planned to keep these pictures to herself for a while. As she felt the paper and ran it through her fingers, she loved the thought that she was holding something that had been hers as a little child. That just fed something inside that needed to be filled up. Satisfaction was becoming more and more common to her now and she was finding herself more in a state of relaxation than she would have ever thought possible in this situation.

After another hour of rummaging through pictures and paraphernalia that had been left behind, they were both ready to call it a day. Except for taking a picture on her wall, her parents had chosen to leave this stuff behind, except for one or two drawings, since they felt too many reminders of her past would delay her adjustment into her new life. But being an artist by trade, these pictures drawn by her as a little child were priceless to her. Putting all of her belongings into a box, Amanda was preparing to leave when Vicki unknowingly let out a bombshell that she wasn't even aware of.

"You know when I first saw you Amanda, I almost walked in and said, "How's my little Sarah?"

Hearing that comment, Amanda actually dropped her purse on the floor as she slowly turned to let Vicki see the totally shocked look on her face. With all of the treasures she had accumulated today, she had forgotten to ask about her memory of the name Sarah.

"What did you just say?" asked Amanda.

"Oh, I'm sorry, I didn't mean to startle you Amanda. It's just that we used to call you Sarah, you seemed to like it. Hope I haven't upset you?"

"Oh no," said Amanda, trying quickly to put her thoughts in gear and make some resemblance of sense to Vicki. "You used to call me Sarah?"

"Well, yes, I'm sure you don't remember…"

"Please let me tell you. I do remember. I remember it

very well. Oh maybe I don't remember consciously being called Sarah here at the orphanage at three years old, but let me tell you what I do remember."

Amanda was totally trembling now. She had never connected the name Sarah directly with the orphanage exactly; she just knew she thought it was her name, yet it seems possibly that this was when it first began.

"When I was first adopted, my parents told me that I wanted to be called Sarah. They explained to me that my name was Amanda but I wouldn't hear of it. I threw tantrums and cried and was very upset because they wouldn't call me Sarah. I'm not sure I remember that but I do remember them telling me about it. But the name Sarah stayed with me and even though I didn't fight it after a while, I've had a memory inside all of my life that my name should be Sarah. If you know something, please tell me."

At this point, Amanda saw tears beginning in Vicki's eyes. She put up the palm of her right hand to Amanda asking silently to give her a moment. Both women sat down again and after a long pause, Vicki continued.

"Please forgive all of us for that. No harm was meant. It's just that when you first came here, you were one and a half years old. You were just about the saddest child I'd ever seen. We tried everything to love you and help you. You cried a lot for the first few weeks and kids, especially little ones like you usually cry for a few days but then they slowly begin to adjust to the new people taking care of them. But you didn't. After almost three weeks you did stop crying though and you did eat a little better. But you didn't play with anyone. You just sat there by yourself looking very sad. We would put you in the playroom with the other children but you wouldn't play. You sat by yourself off in a distant corner watching the other children play but you wouldn't join them. You had the saddest and most desolate look on your face. Honestly Amanda, that is why I remembered you so well. Mr. Lyman, the director of the orphanage at that time even tried to help you, but like your mom said, you were afraid of men and cried whenever he came near you. All of the caregivers took turns trying to connect with you and make you laugh and play, but no one could get through to you."

Amanda sat there in stone silence. Vicki seemed quite upset as she started to relive the story.

"After you had been here more than three weeks, we had another little girl come to live here by the name of Kisha Pitfield. She was a little ten-year old gal with a lot of maturity and she was a sweetheart. Her story was very, very sad, and I need to tell you. Her mother and father both drank and her father was also a drug addict. Mostly she went from one grandparent to another and they were good people. Then Kisha's parents got killed. Her father got into a fight about a drug deal and someone shot him. Her mother died soon after. There was a big fight over who would get Kisha because both sets of grandparents wanted her. They immediately began fighting for custody in court. Time moved on and foster homes didn't work so they brought her here and she was with us for almost two years before an arrangement was finally worked out between the grandparents. She was a very brave little girl and she had intelligence way beyond her years. I've often wondered what she'd experienced in her younger years, but she never talked about it."

At first Amanda listened intently to this intriguing story about another child living at the orphanage but then she wondered what the connection was to her. Then Vicki started to tie the ends together.

"I know you must be wondering why I brought up Kisha'a story. You must wonder what her story has to do with you. Actually, it has a very big connection. And it is

241

strange that I never thought of it until I almost called you Sarah. Well, it was a very long time ago, but let me continue. Like I said before, you were a very sad little baby and no one could get through to you. At least, not until Kisha came. She took an interest in you from the beginning. I know she was attracted to you as a type of challenge at first. Later, I think you helped take her mind off of her own problems. Be that as it may, she started coming with me for playtime after school to sit with you. Sometimes I left the two of you alone and then she did some interesting things that I saw through the window. She always talked to you, constantly. Now, I know at 1-1/2 years old you don't talk a lot in total sentences but you do know a lot of words and phrases. Yet, you, Amanda, had said nothing from the first day you came here, but that didn't stop Kisha. She kept talking to you just as if you'd answered her. I remember after about a week, I was off to the side of the door and neither one of you could see me and I simply listened. I wanted to know what she had to say to you every day."

Vicki stopped for a moment or two. She went to get more coffee and poured a fresh cup for Amanda. Amanda noticed that she was so totally involved in her story that she never shifted gears at all, kept the same serious look on her face, despite the interruption.

"Well, she did talk about her schoolwork and everything that was going on in her life. And on and on she just kept talking and talking. Sometimes she brushed your hair and she always hugged you, when she first entered the room and before she left."

"She spent a lot of time with me. Did I ever respond to her?"

"Yes, that is what I'm getting to. This is what happened. One day, and this was about three weeks after Kisha came to us, so that makes it almost a month and a half since you'd been here in this state of silence and depression. Anyway, that was the day I heard Kisha telling you the story of how she hated to move from where she was living with her mom and her dad. She liked her school and she liked the teachers and sometimes Kisha cried for her friends. We never found out for sure, but I don't think she had any brothers or sisters. Anyway, there was a little neighbor girl, who went to a different school, but was a very special friend of Kisha. She talked about her a lot and cried because she missed her very much. Apparently those two little girls told each other everything and that helped them get through tough times in their lives."

As Vicki took a sip of coffee and a breather for a moment, Amanda was trying to picture these things in her mind. Of course it was too long ago and no thoughts came back to her, but she pretended they did. She anxiously waited for Vicki to continue.

"Now this is the important part for you Amanda. This particular day I heard Kisha say how much she loved you and she was always going to be your friend while you were here. She wanted you to know that you could count on her. Remember, this was after three weeks of her talking and hugging you with no reaction. In the meantime, the director had given orders to us caregivers that we take turns every day to try and connect with you. But you know, sometimes children can have a connection with each other that adults can never understand or emulate. Kisha held your face in her hands and told you that she also loved her other friend who had now gone out of her life, but she decided she was going to call you Sarah, which was her friend's name. It would be a secret between the two of you, although I know of a few other kids that found out about it, and so did I. So for the next few days she started calling you Sarah and you began to smile at her. It was so strange to experience. And then you wanted to play with her. Your appetite got better and you even began playing with the other kids when Kisha was in school during the day. Most of the very little kids played Kisha's game and called you Sarah during playtime. For some reason, you responded to that name and you would smile and even giggle, most especially with Kisha. It was as if the two of you had something going on that couldn't be put into words, only felt."

"Wow, so this Kisha really made a difference with me?"

"Oh yes, you had a connection with her or she connected with you and you became much happier. I remember discussing this situation with the director and he was so happy that you were laughing and playing and eating good that he said to let Kisha call you Sarah or anything else because you were finally becoming better adjusted. And that is how it started and that is how it continued for almost a year and a half. I called you "My little Sarah" too."

"And I apparently never lost that name in my mind. I know that I don't remember the story consciously, gosh I was under three years old, but the name of Sarah must have triggered some happy memories for me and I wanted to be called Sarah. Well, that makes sense now."

"Many times we all called you Amanda too, even Kisha did. She said that she didn't want you to forget your real name. But it was like a game the two of you played and kids play games all the time. We didn't think any harm would come of it and it sure helped you adjust. I'm sorry we didn't tell your parents about this. That would have helped all of you understand. But we didn't realize."

"I'm sure that I'd have done the same thing," Amanda remarked "to get a child out of their depression and it worked. I'm just happy to know why I always thought my name truly was Sarah. That makes so much sense to me now and I know that my mom and dad will appreciate this story."

Amanda was still a little weepy at discovering some answers to her questions about her past. Although she was disappointed to realize that she wouldn't ever get information on her mom or dad or their families, nonetheless she was surprised at how much she was learning about herself.

"What ever happened to Kisha? Did she ever keep in touch with you?"

"That is a great story on its own. You stayed about a year and a half. During that time 'her feuding grandparents,' as I called them, couldn't agree on anything. By this time Kisha was eleven years old and I considered her to be quite bright. She knew that the grandparents had lost their only child, on both sides, her mom and dad, and she knew they all loved her. Shortly after you left, she asked for a meeting with everyone, including the social workers and a judge because she had worked out a plan."

"Really? What did she come up with? I can't even imagine."

"Neither could I at the time, but she had it all worked out in her mind. Not all of the details, of course, but a lot of the main ideas. The meeting was held in our parlor room and at the time of arrival, the grandparents wouldn't talk to each other. By the time the meeting was over, they were all congenial again and ready to cooperate with each other. It was quite amazing. This is what Kisha did. First, she told them how much she loved all of them and she told them she loved her parents too. She knew her parents had the disease of drinking and drugs and it was sad that they didn't get healed and had to die young. But that was in the past and now we were in the present. She reminded them of her eighth birthday party when everyone came and had fun, and she asked them what happened to their friendship, because she didn't understand. She knew they all loved her and wanted her and she told them she appreciated that. But she reminded them that she loved all of them and this was what she'd wanted to do. She wanted to go back to the same school as before. She'd lost her parents and she didn't want to lose all of her friends. She felt that she had been away from them too long time already."

Amanda simply relaxed in her chair and let out a big sigh. This gave Vicki a moment to take a breath too.

"I see what you mean by maturity. How did a little girl her age begin to think of all this?"

"I think she was speaking from the heart and she told me that she asked God to help her to say the right thing. What she wanted, as a final result, was to see all of her grandparents all the time. After all, they all lived in Prescott so there shouldn't be any problem. She wanted to finish her middle school where her friends lived, which was in a certain school district. But she always wanted to go to this other high school which was in another school district that the other grandparents lived in. And most important she wanted to be able to go back and forth all the time. She wanted everyone to be friends, not enemies, and since they used to be friends, she didn't understand why they couldn't be friends again."

"Wow. That is quite a speech. I am amazed."

"Honestly, Amanda, if you had been there and seen this little eleven year old girl simply take over the floor and put all of us in our place in a respectful and considerate way, well, it was something I will never forget. And she finished by saying something about the fact that since her parents were in heaven, they were probably healed now and looking down on all this. Would we want them to see us feuding and mean and nasty to each other, or, would we want to make them proud of us? I want my parents to be proud of me, I know that was her final statement."

Both were very silent for a moment as Amanda reflected on the scene and Vicki shook her head in remembrance.

"There was hardly a dry eye in the place, including the men. One little girl had dissipated all that anger. My, my, it was really something to see."

"I can imagine," continued Amanda "and I think I was lucky to have someone like her caring and taking an interest in me. I think that the name of Sarah will be extra special to me from now on."

"Oh my gosh. Wait a minute. I'm sure that I still have a few pictures of some of the kids at that time. And I know I took some pictures that included you and Kisha. Give me a few minutes and I'll retrieve them. I'm anxious to know if you could pick out Kisha."

With that said, Amanda watched Vicki hurry away with excitement at remembering some photos and she sat there thinking over the impressive story that she had just heard and wondered why life turns out the way it does. She started wondering why her life and Kisha's life paths had crossed each other. Most times in the present, Amanda no longer believed in coincidences and although she wasn't sure yet that she believed in something called karma that Jeremy sometimes talked about, she presently felt that life happened about the way it was supposed to.

Vicki was back very quickly with yet another file. This time her face glowed as she remembered something Amanda had said earlier.

"When you talked about having earlier pictures of yourself, I wasn't thinking. I have about three pictures here of you shortly after you came. I know you were not a newborn baby, but I'll bet you'll like to have them. Now,

I'm going to show you this one picture first and I'll tell you why later."

With that statement Vicki handed Amanda a picture of a group of about twelve girls. They were all sizes, ages, shapes and colors, but all were female. It took only a moment when Amanda let out an involuntary gasp and pointed to a little girl.

"That has to be Kisha. I just know it's her."

"And you are right. How in the word did you know? I purposely showed you this picture first because I think it is the only one where Kisha is not right next to you, either holding you or having her arm around you. She was always with you. But this one picture has you and her at opposite ends of the group so I thought you wouldn't know."

"And of course, this must be me," said Amanda as she gazed intently at the picture of a one and a half year old with a very sullen look on her face.

"Yes that's how you always were, very sad. But as you see in the other pictures you are smiling a lot. That's after you and Kisha became friends. "I'm surprised you picked out Kisha so quickly."

"I don't know exactly how I knew, but I just knew." Amanda was reluctant to explain herself at first, but then she continued.

"I want to tell you something else. This picture answers a very confusing question for me. Besides always wondering why I thought my real name was Sarah, there was something else that has always bothered me. It wasn't anything tangible exactly but working in art, many different textures are utilized and I kept searching for something, a certain feeling, and I didn't know what I was even looking for. I didn't even know until I saw the picture of Kisha."

She saw Vicki look back quickly at the picture and by the confused look on her face, one knew Vicki wondered what she had missed. A picture of Kisha had told her all that. What was going on?

"What are you talking about? You lost me at the last corner."

"Well," laughed Amanda, "there are two other African American gals in the picture. But Kisha is the only one who has a rough texture to her hair. Look at the picture again. See what I mean. She has pretty hair but it's curly and has the texture of many blacks, which is slightly rougher than mine for instance. None of the White girls or even the Asian girl would have that type of hair. I know now that I remembered, not consciously of course, that when Kisha would hug me her hair would have to rub against my face and there was a certain feeling of her face and hair against my cheek. It must have been what I experienced over and over again and therefore I remembered. I've always been searching for a certain texture or feeling of something but never knew how to express it. I think I've found it."

"Well, Amanda, that could be. She certainly did hug you all the time. It was so wonderful to see the rapport that developed between the two of you. It also was very helpful to me and the other caregivers. When I saw Kisha, I knew you were close by or if I saw you somewhere I knew Kisha was not far away."

They both laughed and sat there in their satisfaction for a while.

"Does Kisha every keep in touch?"

"Yes, she does and she would love to see you. She's thirty-four years old now, married with I believe two little girls. She did very well, went to college and she did keep the peace between both sets of grandparents. I know that for a fact because I was invited to her wedding eight years ago and everyone was there all sitting at the same table and laughing and having a good time. I went over and talked with them and they admitted their friendship had grown and how proud they were of Kisha. She is a social worker, you know. That is part of the reason we see her occasionally. At least twice a year she comes and takes some of the children to her home for the weekend because she knows how important it is to them."

"I guess she always had a big heart. She is quite a gal."

"I was here two years ago when she came. And I remember that she asked about you?"

"Really, she did. She asked about me?"

"Yes, she has asked about you a few times. She said that you were so special to her. She kind of mentioned that the two of you helped each other. At that time we hadn't heard from you, but now she'd be happy to hear that you are doing so good."

"I'd love to talk to her. Would that be possible?"

"Oh my, yes. I know that she 'd love to talk to you. And come to think of it, she spent more time with you and got closer to you than anyone else. She could probably tell you some things that no one else would know. Let me get you her phone number."

"I'm so excited. I want to talk to her very much."

"Do you want to call her now?"

"Yes, I would and I'd love to see her. I'm leaving tomorrow but who knows?"

Vicki gave Amanda some privacy and as the phone began ringing, a certain excitement became evident inside of her with each ring. Finally, a calm yet friendly voice answered. It would have been hard to tell who was more excited, Kisha or Amanda, but here were two little girls, some twenty plus years later, whose life paths were crossing again. Given the circumstances of her visit and having to leave for home tomorrow, Kisha insisted that she must come over and visit right now. It didn't take much to convince Amanda, and after getting directions to her home, she was ready to leave. She was walking slowly toward the door trying to etch the hallways and the entire area into her memory. This wonderful caregiver, who had taken such good care of her, was a special memory of its own. Amanda was still emotional and as she opened the outside door to say her "goodbyes" and "thank yous", to Vicki, she needed to say more.

"In some ways I feel that you are part of my family too. You are such a caring person and reliving my young years with you today I know you enjoyed it too and were excited right along with me. I could feel it. I would like to keep in touch with you, if that's okay. It is something I need to do but I also want to do. And I wanted to ask you, "Would you consider coming to my wedding? It isn't until next year but it would mean so much to me."

"I'd love to see you get happily married and the way it sounds, I might bring Kisha with me, right?"

"Well, I'm certainly going to ask her and I think we will always have a friendship. Maybe my life didn't start out the best but looking back at some of the people I've met because of my abandonment, it evens out the game, if you know what I mean."

"I do understand and I'm pleased that I was a part of it. You be careful driving now. I love you Amanda or

Sarah…whatever you prefer."

They both laughed and Amanda then slowly walked down the pathway to her car. She couldn't resist turning back one more time and looking at the building. It now held such warm feelings for her and only yesterday when she first walked up here she felt scared and hesitant. Looking up at the blue sky with the white clouds she loved, she felt a kinship that glowed inside of her.

Twenty minutes later she was pulling into Kisha's driveway. She found her home easily, nestled in a moderate yet comfortable neighborhood with each home having its individual charm. She was just beginning to feel a little nervous as to what she was going to say, when the door suddenly opened and out came a very lovely young woman, slightly taller than she was with shiny black hair tied back in a pony tail. Her slight build gave her a willowy appearance and her bright excited smile flashed across her face, while her agility took her to Amanda's car quickly. She hadn't yet opened the car door and Kisha was already there. She immediately gave her a warm hug, put her arms around her and led her up the path to her front door.

Amanda entered a lovely, very well kept home with tasteful furniture and décor while still emitting an atmosphere of friendliness and comfort. This certainly was Kisha, inside and out. Sitting on a comfortable sofa with coffee nearby Kisha began first.

"I've got the advantage on you Amanda. I was ten years old and I remember you. You were too little to remember me. You certainly have grown into a beautiful girl."

"Thanks and look at you. You are quite lovely Kisha and I'll bet you would be surprised to know that I picked you out of a picture earlier today.

"No kidding. But I think there were only three or four Black girls there at that time."

"But I didn't remember if you were Black, White or Asian. I was only three years old."

Both laughed and that broke the ice, if any needed to be broken.

"I understand you have two little girls."

"Yes I do, Tisha is seven now, hard to believe and Misha is five. I know it sounds like I've kept their names like mine. But actually, Tisha was my mom's name and Misha, well, I just liked the name.

"Where are they now? I'd love to meet them."

"As soon as you called I asked my neighbor if she would sit with them. She helps me out a lot and since she has no children of her own, she enjoys my girls. They are really nice little girls, but I wanted to be able to sit and talk with you. We have so much to talk about and it would be rough with them around. First, they would have to show you all their toys and Tisha would have to exhibit all of her homework. Anyway, before you leave I'll bring them home, but tell me what finally brought you back here. How old are you now, about twenty-five."

"No, I'm almost twenty-seven."

"Oh yeah, that's right. You were almost three when you left."

"I spent a lot of time talking to Vicki today. She told me so much of the missing pieces of my past. It has always bothered me a lot, and of course, I was the kind of kid that kept everything inside."

"Did you have a nice life? I've thought about you so often. I remember the people that came to adopt you. They seemed very excited to get you."

"And they have been wonderful; I was lucky. But first, I really want to thank you for spending time with me when I first came to the orphanage. Vicki said that you were the one that got me laughing and eating again. It seemed that you help me a lot."

"Amanda, you are so welcome. But you know what; you really helped me too. Did Vicki tell you what happened to me?"

"She told me about your parents getting killed in a car crash and about what she referred to as your …"

"Feuding grandparents, right?" At this reminder, she saw Kisha put her head back on the couch and laugh quite loudly. You could see the memories crossing her face and causing a slight strain across her forehead, but it passed quickly and was replaced by another expression that agreed it was okay to laugh about it now.

"Yeah that is what she called them. "The Feuding Grandparents," confirmed Amanda.

"And that was exactly what they were. Here I was a ten year old girl who had lost both parents and they were fighting and so mad at each other that I ended up in foster homes and in that orphanage because no one could agree on what should happen to me. Eh Gaads!"

"But Vicki told me the story of how you worked it out and called a meeting with the judge and the social worker and both sets of grandparents. You were really something at eleven years old."

"Well, maybe it sounds better when you are retelling the

story now. It didn't seem so good then. I was very depressed and cried a lot. I knew my parents had problems with drugs and alcohol, but they loved me. I knew that for sure. They were just sick and they didn't get any help. When they died I hurt so much inside and all the grandparents would do is fight about me. I knew they were hurting too but I used to think that was when everyone should help each other, not fight. I needed them to help me."

"That must have been a tough time for you. You were such a little girl."

"Yeah and I felt so alone Amanda, that there were times I thought I was going crazy with them fighting for so long and my mom and dad gone. I could feel the dark shadows taking over my body."

"I know about dark shadows too, Kisha. I still experience them sometimes."

"I do only once in a while now," said Kisha. "Probably everyone does one way or another because no one's life is perfect. But then after a try at a foster home, they took me to the orphanage until they could decide what to do with me. And there you were. I remember the first time I saw you. They had you sitting up in this little swing thing and they had put a pink bow in your hair. But you jut sat there and didn't swing. You were the saddest little baby I'd ever seen in my whole life. I remember even now that I took one look at your face and thought to myself, 'that's exactly how I feel inside.' Then I asked Miss Vicki about you and they told me you had been there for over three weeks and you didn't smile or talk or play or anything. You didn't react to any of the other caregivers either. The first time that I walked up to you I noticed that you had very blue eyes and that your eyebrows reminded me of someone and that was my little friend Sarah who lived next door to me. She had been my best friend forever. And to me, you reminded me of Sarah so I later started calling you by that name. Did Vicki tell you about that?"

"She did tell me that you called me Sarah."

Then Amanda proceeded to tell Kisha how she always thought her real name was Sarah. At first, Kisha just sat there in disbelief and expressionless. She didn't know how to react at all, and so she didn't say anything.

"Oh Kisha. It's okay. No one meant any harm; I know that. I can almost see the humor in it. At least you got me laughing and eating and playing and that was very good. No one else could do it at the time."

"I'm so sorry though for the extra grief. To me, it was only a game and I called you Amanda too."

"I know. Vicki told me that you didn't want me to forget my real name. It's okay."

"I guess you never know," said Kisha. "But then you were so young. I can see what probably happened. You associated feeling better and laughing with the name Sarah. Does that make sense?"

"It sure does and that is the exact thought that I had when Vicki first told me."

"How interesting? I am a social worker now you know."

"Yes, and anyone would be lucky to get you."

"Thanks, but I want to get back to you and me back then. Maybe you were a challenge to me or maybe you were something to help me keep my mind off my own problems, I think probably both, but I really wanted to help you. You see, I can remember a lot of things back then and you probably can't, you were so little. But after you started to laugh and play, then you were just like any other baby, except you didn't like men. The director used to get upset because you wouldn't relate to him. Whenever he needed to see you, they would ask me to bring you and then you were okay. But that only lasted for a few months. Later, you even let him pick you up and kept smiling. We had fun and played games and you always waited for me to get out of school every day so we could play. It meant a lot to me too. I know I felt a lot of love for you Amanda."

"Maybe you can call me Sarah."

And then they both laughed and saw the comical side of the situation. They needed to stop and laugh for a few minutes because the memories were still somewhat painful for both. Although Kisha had handled the situation between her grandparents very well, it seemed obvious to Amanda that she kept a lot of feelings inside too.

"You know Kisha, when I was about seven my parents got me a dog. I really wanted to call her Sarah but I didn't want to stir up problems again."

"Oh my God," said Kisha giggling openly like a little child. "They probably were happy you were now accepting your name and then you call your dog Sarah. That seems hilarious now, but probably not then."

"Yeah, I didn't even tell them, but I thought I'd better leave that one alone. They thought I had accepted the name of Amanda, and I let them believe that. Inside, I always thought my real name was Sarah but I didn't want to make them mad so I never said anything again. And I called my dog Muffin. She was a great little dog, a Shih-Tzu, and I told her everything that I couldn't tell my family. She died about six years ago and it's still hard. She was my best friend for a long, long time. She helped me a lot because I was so unsure of myself and always tried to please everyone."

"What happened to me was tough, Amanda, but I was ten years old and at least I had known my parents. I knew they were on drugs and alcohol but to me that was a sickness and they never got help. But they really loved me and I knew that. On the other hand, you were given up for adoption. Being a social worker, I know how much that affects children. And when you get adopted, especially by a nice family, everyone thinks that is so great, and it is, but it doesn't mean that the terrifying memories are gone."

"When I was driving here today," Amanda remembered, "I knew that we'd connect because we had such a strong bond from years ago and something like that doesn't ever go away. But I also felt that you would understand some of my feelings because you lost your mom and dad too. I was lucky to have a therapist who was adopted and she was really the first person I ever spoke to that understood. To me, it's like when you get adopted everyone thinks you are so lucky, and you are lucky if you get a good family. But, in order to be adopted, it means that you lost something too. For instance, I'm sure when your parents got killed in that accident everyone around you felt bad for your loss. And they should, after all, you lost both of your parents. But with me, no one ever acknowledged that I lost my mom and dad too. I don't even know who my dad was and very little about my mom. But I also lost a mom and dad and the only thing people talked about was how lucky I was to be adopted. Do you know what I mean?"

"Wow, I see what you mean. These thoughts have crossed my mind in my work but never to this degree. It is so good for me to know how you feel."

"They both sat quietly with their own thoughts for a while and then Kisha continued. "What would have helped Amanda?"

"In my case, it was probably mostly my fault. Well, not

my fault really, but I had this thought that I had to be a perfect child or they would send me back to the orphanage."

"Amanda, were you diagnosed with attachment disorder?"

"Yes, yes I was. Of course you would know about it."

"Sure and now it is beginning to make sense to me. Of course it wasn't your fault. But you didn't want to talk and ask questions about your birth mom because your new parents wouldn't like it, or so you thought. You sound like you were the covert personality, right? You kept everything inside."

"Yes and sometimes, I'm not even sure what I thought in those days. But inside, I think that if someone had mentioned, even one time, that they were glad that I was here but that it was sad that I had lost my birth mom and dad, it would have helped a lot. I would have realized that my feelings weren't wrong, you know."

Amanda was offered more coffee so they both wandered into the kitchen together and kept right on talking and reminiscing and they made a fresh pot. As fate would have it, Kisha told her that her husband was working a late shift tonight, which was unusual, and wouldn't be home until much later. It seemed as if someone or something had cleared both of their schedules to give them the time they needed to make this important connection.

"What type of work do you do?"

"I'm an illustrator for a book company. I do book covers and also some portraits on the side."

"Of course, that would make sense. You did draw very well for a little one. Everyone talked about that."

"Vicki had some of my drawings from back then. It was so exciting to see what I drew as a little girl. You know something else I wanted to mention, other than the fact that I thought my name was Sarah, there was something else that I was always searching for which I found an answer for today. This is hard to explain, but let me try. I work with textures and fabrics and paints, but you know Kisha, I was always searching for a certain feeling that I remembered unconsciously but I could never find it. I was always feeling things like cloth, wood, any textures, to see if I could trigger my memory, but I never did. Then when Vicki showed me the group picture and asked me to pick you out, I was shocked and knew immediately what I had been searching for."

Well, I'm certainly intrigued. Don't keep me in suspense. What is it?"

"The picture I saw had about twelve girls in it. You and I were at opposite ends, so it wasn't that you were right next to me. I think there were three African Americans, one Asian, one maybe Spanish and all the rest were White. But you were the only Black with curlier black hair with a rougher texture, you know. Now I didn't consciously remember this but it was like a fleeting thought in my mind because Vicki told me that you used to hug me a lot. And then I knew that the texture or feeling must have been the feel of your hair on my face when you hugged me."

She saw Kisha sit there in amazement. Amanda knew, as she was searching through all of the memories in her mind when she was less than three that Kisha understood how any detail of even a slight memory was a treasure to her.

"It really helps to tie up some of these loose ends, doesn't it?"

"Yeah, probably some of these little memories wouldn't

mean anything to anyone else but I'm still trying to fill in the blanks of the first three years of my life. I wish I could have an authentic memory or two but of course I can't."

"You know what, I just thought of something that might help. Back then, I had about three little moles right by my right ear and you may have felt my hair but you also must have felt those moles. They always irritated me because they were a good size and I finally had them removed. But they were quite prominent back then."

Amanda just sat back and smiled as she chocked back some tears. Both Kisha and Amanda had their teary moments during this reunion and anyone walking in on them wouldn't have believed the wonderful and unforgettable happiness they were creating for each other.

"You wouldn't think that talking about your moles from childhood would be so important, would you?" said Amanda as they both let out a rip-roaring laugh at that one.

"What is more important," continued Amanda " is that you told me about the moles because you understood the importance of what I was trying to remember. I know we are very close to feeling each other's experiences. It is quite awesome when you think about it."

"Just having you sitting here in my home and sharing some coffee and memories or gees, just us being together again is unbelievable luck in my book. We must forever keep in touch. What is distance with airplanes and emails, right?"

"Absolutely, and another thing I forgot to mention in all my excitement of talking about the past, is a new event in my present life. I just got engaged."

With that Kisha jumped up and gave Amanda a big hug and started with the usual questions.

"I met him in college and believe it or not, he's an architect. He is truly a nice person, very sensitive to me and urged me to get some therapy to clear up some of the old memories that were bothering me. Oh, his name is Jeremy Sloane. We haven't set a wedding date yet, but it will be sometime next year and I'd love to invite you. Would you maybe think of coming?"

"Amanda, I would love to come, for goodness sake. For all we shared in our young lives, I think of you as family, always have."

"I don't have a sister, only two brothers, so we can be sisters from now on. In fact, the way you helped me when I was at the orphanage is what families do for each other. It makes you wonder what the word family means, doesn't it? It really isn't being born in the same family, it is all about caring and loving each other."

"Yes I think so Amanda; what a lovely thought. Family is whom you love and take care of. I like that thought."

"I've also invited Vicki to the wedding and she says she will come too."

"Well, I'll be there. I've often wondered about you because you were so shy and alone when I first met you and so I wondered how your life would end up. What type of personality will 'My Little Sarah' have." Kisha winked with the last comment.

"I think I've finally grown up a lot. I was slow maturing because I was always afraid of what other people would say and well, you know. But now, I'm happy to stand on my own two feet. It feels good. My mom and dad and my fiancé all wanted to come with me, singularly or together. They all felt I shouldn't come alone, except for my dad. He knew I could now handle this situation. Yet for once in my life, I knew I had the strength and although I appreciated their love and caring for me, I knew that I would rather come alone. Even Jeremy has seen a change in me and he has to get used to it too."

"He will. But you have to be who you are first. You have come a long way through the darkness. I know attachment disorder is very tough. I didn't have it totally because I was older but I was close during that time at the orphanage. I didn't trust anyone anymore; I was mad at my mom and dad because they killed themselves, even though I knew they had a sickness. But then my 'feuding grand-parents' left me no one to bond with until I met you. Isn't it funny how life turns out? I've missed you over the years and really never thought I'd see you again. But now I have a sister in my life and this time she won't go away."

"I'm so grateful for you too. There are times that we must look beyond the present since very good opportunities can happen from what appears to be difficulties. And you are one of the best of them. I love you, Kisha."

"Oh my gosh, I almost forgot. I have something for you that I've kept for years. Remember my feuding grandparents, well, both of them always tried to give me special presents that would please me. One of the things I loved in those days was perfume so they used to get me my favorite in little bottles. It was called Taboo and I used to love it. At one time I think I had five little bottles. And I always put some on you and me so we would smell alike and you used to always be smelling my neck and behind my ears. I meant to give you a bottle when you left but I forgot. I've kept it all these years."

With that Kisha hurried and was back in a moment with the bottle of perfume. It was a sweet little present. Also, Amanda thought that might be the smell she was always searching for.

With the hour getting later, Amanda had to leave because her plane was departing early in the morning. Kisha brought in her two little girls, so beautiful in their resemblance to their mom that they took your breath away. A family portrait confirmed that Kisha had done very well. Amanda asked for a picture of the family and then allowed Kisha to take her picture. Memories were not only for the past but also for the present and the future.

On the drive back to the motel, Amanda realized that her life had been such a puzzle but now the pieces were slowly starting to fit together, She knew that probably the puzzle wouldn't be totally finished with all the pieces fitting in, but other people didn't know everything either. For now, she was quite satisfied and happy with the information and pictures that were new treasures for her to cherish. She felt like a different person in some way because, in some ways, she was brand new. New memories had been added to her repertoire alongside others that were already there. And the strange part was that for all the hours spent with Vicki and then Kisha, there had been no dark shadows. Wasn't that amazing? So these dark shadows that had depressed her so often in her earlier years and even in the present were definitely connected with her hidden young life and once new memories were being added, the lightness and happiness that should have been there were slowly finding their way back.

After she reached her motel, she picked up the phone and the first person she called, surprisingly, was her mom. Since she had been talking about her birth mom for two days, calling her adoptive mom seemed like the logical move.

"Hi Mom, it's Amanda."

"Hi sweetie. Are you okay?"

"I'm just great, mom. I just wanted you to know how much I love you and dad and Bryan and Jonathon." Then she laughed at herself for a moment. "Sorry, mom. I'm so excited and just babbling like a child. I think it's because I've been talking about my childhood all day. And mom, I just can't wait to share. This was the best idea for me. Thanks for caring about me and thanks so much for understanding what I had to do."

"You sound so happy that your excitement is coming right through the phone."

"I'm coming home tomorrow morning, as planned."

"Jeremy has been so nervous, waiting for you to call. I think you've got a great guy there."

"Yes, I think so too. But making this trip alone was the right choice. I couldn't have done it any other way. Would you mind calling Jeremy and telling him when to pick me up at the airport? Never mind, I'll give him a quick call or he'll be hurt. I'm back at the motel now and I've got to pack and get some sleep. You know, mom, finding out about your childhood is very tiring."

Amanda laughed to her herself and left her mom on the other end of the line wondering what could have happened to get her so enthused about everything.

After her shower was over and the bags were packed, Amanda went to the motel restaurant for dinner. She had a glass of Piesporter white wine with her steak and laughed at those who thought only red wine went with meat. She was comfortable eating alone in a nice restaurant tonight replacing the nervousness of the past. She really was a new woman and was happy to have the time tonight to sort out some of her feelings before facing her entire family and Jeremy. He had made it clear that he thought Amanda going it alone was not the best choice. But it was. She had depended on her own feelings and thoughts and they were right for her. Going through everything she had today with Jeremy sitting there would never have worked. He couldn't understand and she knew he would have tried. Some things had to be done alone and she was learning more and more to trust her own judgment. She certainly hoped that Jeremy would like the new Amanda. In fact, she was counting on it.